PRAISE FOR

Full Mortality
A Nikki Latrelle Racing Mystery

"Nikki is one of the most appealing fictional characters I've ever met. You are rooting for her every inch of the way. The descriptions of backstretch life are enchanting."
— Lucy Acton, Editor of *Mid-Atlantic Thoroughbred*

"I thoroughly enjoyed Full Mortality — the pages fly by, the characters are vivid, and Hill captures life on the backstretch perfectly."
— Charlsie Cantey, racing analyst
for ESPN, ABC, CBS and NBC.

"If you like the work of Dick Francis or Sue Grafton, you will like Sasscer Hill. With a true insider's knowledge of horse racing, Hill brings us Nikki Latrelle, a young jockey placed in harm's way who finds the courage to fight the odds and the heart to race for her dreams."
— Mike Battaglia, NBC racing analyst and TV host,
veteran track announcer, and "morning line"
odds maker for the Kentucky Derby.

Full Mortality

A Nikki Latrelle Racing Mystery

Sasscer Hill

WILDSIDE PRESS

This book is for the two people who had
the greatest influence on my life:

Rhoda Christmas Bowling,
the Maryland horse breeder and racing columnist
who taught me how to ride.

Alfred H. Smith, Sr.,
breeder of 1966 Eclipse Award Winning steeplechase Champion
Tuscalee, and the man who took a fatherless sixteen-year-old
under his wing and gave her a steeplechase horse to ride.

FULL MORTALITY
A Nikki Latrelle Racing Mystery

Published by
Wildside Press LLC
9710 Traville Gateway Dr. #234
Rockville, MD 20850
www.wildsidebooks.com

1

Chasing the dream, I tapped the thin whip on the mare's left shoulder. She switched leads and opened up down the stretch. Wind blew her mane into my face.

The dirt track ahead was empty, and I could hear the field battling for second place behind us. The first murmur of the grandstand roar teased my ears. I could almost smell the mare's determination.

Then the vision fragmented, dissolving as my eyes slid open.

The bedside clock read 12:45 A.M. My twisted sheets suggested a whirlwind had whipped through the bed, leaving my jaw tight and strained. Sleep remained a longshot. I pulled on some jeans, shrugged into a T-shirt, grabbed the Toyota's keys, then paused in midstride.

A framed photo stood on my dresser. Me, Nikki Latrelle, aboard a muscular Thoroughbred, my face lit with a laser-bright smile. My first win. I saluted the picture and said, "Make it happen tomorrow."

The beautiful mare of my dream, Gilded Cage, was my ticket. Incredible that I'd be viewing the racetrack between her classy ears the next day. Her regular jockey had broken a collarbone eight hours earlier, and I'd captured the ride. I didn't like the circumstances behind this miracle, but wild horses couldn't drag me from a chance like this.

I worked as a daily exercise rider for Gilded Cage's trainer, Jim Ravinsky. When the mare's jockey fell in the ninth, Ravinsky talked the owner into putting me up on the big horse in the $200,000 Venus Stakes race.

I grabbed an elastic band and stuffed my dark hair into a ponytail. I needed to see Gilded Cage, the mare we all called "Gildy." Wanted to feel her proud confidence, let my fingertips vibrate with her magical energy. Maybe then I could settle down and sleep.

Outside my apartment the August night enveloped my skin like warm molasses. Somewhere in the tree canopy overhead, a cicada reached a crescendo, paused, and began again. The dream had left me thirsty, and after deciding on a detour for a diet soda at the 7-Eleven, I climbed into my blue Toyota and cranked the engine. Late-night treats were okay as long as I didn't slide over racing weight.

Inside the shop, a thin-faced guy with a gold earring stared as I walked in. He leaned against the counter, giving me a long appraising look that settled on my chest.

Oops. I'd pulled on the thin white cotton T-shirt, forgetting to wear a bra. Exasperated, I clutched my purse to my chest, marched to the soda dispenser, and pushed the Diet Coke lever.

A candy stand lay in wait between me and the cashier. My resolve crumpled. Hershey's, cheap but effective. Besides, Gildy was the favorite and carried top weight in the race tomorrow. I grabbed a chocolate-with-almonds and paid the woman behind the counter.

The guy with the golden earring moved closer. As I left, he said, "Beautiful evening, really sweet."

The unwanted attention stirred up the past. I double-timed it out to my car, drove down Route 198 to Brock Road, and entered Laurel Park's backstretch after flashing ID at the startled security guard. Nobody hung around this late. Only the horses sleeping in the dark stables laid out like dominoes along the paved road. Dirt paths intersected the pavement and disappeared in the darkness toward the vast, mile-oval track. At night, the race course remained invisible, but I could sense its expanse.

Closer to Ravinsky's barn, cooler air spilled through the car's window. A reminder of coming winter and the frigid northwest winds that cracked my skin in the predawn cold. I shivered, then braked suddenly. A light glimmered halfway down Ravinsky's barn aisle. No one should be there. A finger of fear touched me. *The horses.*

I left the car and hurried across the wet grass into the shedrow, the rich scents of hay, manure, and sweet feed saturating the night air. Nearing the stall spilling light into the darkness, my senses heightened. Gildy's stall.

A man's silhouette emerged from the glow, then froze. I paused.

"Who —" I demanded.

He ran straight at me. Before I could get out of his way, he knocked me down hard. Air whooshed from my lungs.

Rolling over, I sucked in a gasping breath, then climbed to my hands and knees. His back vanished into the darkness.

"You son of a bitch!" I gasped. What had he done?

Scrambling to my feet I jerked open the door to Gildy's stall. The mare was down, not moving.

I sank to my knees and placed my cheek next to her nostril. No warm breath, nothing. I pressed my ear to the fur on her rib cage. No heartbeat, only silence.

"Gildy, *no.*"

With a half sob, I ran to Jim's office. My key unlocked the door. With fingers fumbling, I punched the phone number for security. Five long rings before they picked up. Voice stammering, I told them what had happened.

They came running. I met them at Gildy's stall.

They stared at the mare and called the police.

An Anne Arundel County officer with close-cropped hair had me sit in his cruiser while he filled out a report. The scent of stale cigarettes clung to the upholstery.

"Can you give me a better description of the person who knocked you down?"

"He came at me so fast." *How could Gildy be dead?*

"Was he heavy? Tall?"

Who would do such a thing? "Average, average. You're making me feel inadequate here."

The officer shifted in his seat, his leather holster squeaking, keys and cuffs jangling. He smiled for the first time. "I've had worse descriptions."

His radio crackled; he paused, listened, then chose to ignore it. "Got to tell you, a dead horse, even one as valuable as you say this one is, won't be a high priority. I'll check with track security tomorrow evening and see what the vet's necropsy reveals." He handed me a card. "If you think of anything else, call me."

I slid from the car and watched the taillights on his cruiser disappear. One of the track security guys, Fred something, lingered outside Gildy's stall. He walked over.

"Tough break. Wasn't you riding her in the Venus tomorrow?"

I nodded.

"Listen," he said, "Ronny's gonna be back with some crew and the truck. You might wanna leave before they put the winch on and drag her out."

My lips twisted. "I don't want to see that."

My legs shook going back to the car. Another shattered dream, and not just for me. I still had to call Jim.

At six the next morning, Ravinsky's shedrow seemed strangely quiet. Usually a barn overflows with noise, color, and motion. Bits jingle, hooves clatter, and chestnut, bay, and dappled gray coats gleam in the sunlight. The grooms and hotwalkers gossip and joke while consuming quarts of coffee and boxes of doughnuts. They wash the bright-colored leg-bandages and saddle-towels as steam from the hot water rises in the air. Laundry hangs in strips of color along the shedrow to dry in the morning sun.

Today the picture played in black-and-white, the sound muted.

Two grooms stopped their quiet talk when they saw me. I nodded at them and headed toward the office. Jim sat at his desk sipping a 7-Eleven coffee. I'd gotten used to his taciturn manner, but today a gloom enveloped him that stopped me in the doorway. The usual clutter of vet bills, *Racing Forms*, and bloodstock magazines littered his desk. A bottle of liniment, some halters, and a stopwatch sat one one of the metal office chairs. The other chair was occupied by a fat orange tabby cat, currently comatose.

"I know how much Gildy meant to you," I said.

He stared at his Styrofoam cup. Behind him, confined by glass and picture frames, a row of horses, members of the racing Hall of Fame, gazed at me from the past: Secretariat, John Henry, Citation, Man o' War, and the lone female, Gallorette. A chestnut mare. Jim always said Gildy reminded him of this classic racehorse from the 1940s who somehow beat the leading male horse, Stymie. Beat him three times.

Jim crushed his cup, tossed it into the trash. "She might a been the best horse I ever trained."

He was tall and thin. Today his shoulders appeared stooped, his eyes hollowed. Bushy brows, sprinkled liberally with gray, were easily the most expressive feature on his face. Rogue hairs strayed up his forehead, and there'd been times I'd swear they were waving at me. The light filtering through the dusty office window revealed features shadowed and drawn tight with pain.

"You said you saw the bastard?"

"I don't even know if it was a man or a woman." I slid the snoring cat over and slumped into the remaining chair-half. A sharp tangy scent from the liniment bottle drifted in the air. "Have you heard if the vet found —"

"Necropsy results might come in this afternoon. We've got other horses to get out." He nodded toward the door, pushed his bent frame from the metal chair behind the desk, and went out. He'd finished talking.

A few minutes later I rode out onto the track with Kenny Grimes for the morning's first set. Kenny was small, wiry, and sat his horse with easy skill and confidence. He'd had a jockey's license and ridden races for a while, but had found the game too rough. Now he just rode as an exercise rider in the mornings.

"Don't do it," he'd told me when I first planned to get a jock's license. "Those boys will cut you off and box you in. You get a live mount, they'll gang up on you. Being a girl won't cut you any breaks."

I'd ignored him and, though people said I had magic hands and a reckless courage on horseback, I'd had a tough time. After the first jock's room brawl, I'd bought some steel-toed boots and used them on a particularly obstructive, testosterone-laden rider, earning some respect and maneuvering room. But I wanted to rise above that. Winning on Gildy would have boosted my career.

I snapped back to the business at hand as we approached the half-mile pole. Kenny and I sat lower in our saddles, our hands and heels getting real busy asking our mounts for speed. A stiff breeze whipped at us from the infield, carrying an earthy scent that lingered on the nearby, freshly watered turf course.

The rhythm of the Thoroughbred's gallop usually lifts my spirits with a high only surpassed by racing. Today, as we rounded the turn and accelerated down the stretch, I felt a heaviness. No joy, only regret. And beneath that, anger.

My jaw tightened. I white-knuckled the reins, telegraphing rage to the colt beneath me who bolted forward in sweeping strides. I wanted to know who'd killed Gildy. I wanted to get the bastard.

2

Kicking my feet from the stirrups, I slid to the ground and stroked the gray filly, my last horse of the morning. Bourbon Bonnet's coat was damp, warm and rich with that heady, intoxicating horse smell. I hefted my leather saddle onto a rack, grabbed a sponge, smeared it with saddle soap and started rubbing. A stable groom, Ramon, led the horse away.

A peal of laughter erupted from Ravinsky's office a few yards down the shedrow. Louis Fein, one of Jim's younger, flashier racehorse owners, appeared in the aisle. "Call me if he gets in, Jim. That's a race I don't want to miss."

Jim gave his predictable monosyllabic response as a stunning woman stepped out of his office. Tall, with a knockout figure and large brown eyes. Wavy blond hair cascaded to her shoulders. Her skin was golden olive, her age, thirty-something.

I stared like I would at an exceptional Thoroughbred. Bright energy emanated from this woman. Her expression held humor and curiosity.

"Nikki," Louis said, "meet Carla Ruben." He sounded like he'd just won the lottery.

I put the sponge down, wiped my hands on my jeans, and moved toward them. Carla wore tight pants, snazzy western boots, a stretchy white top, and silver-and-blue earrings.

She grabbed my hand, "I'm so impressed by what you do. I love horses, but they really scare me. You like being a jockey? Do you get scared?"

"Here we go," Louis said. "Carla, give Nikki a chance to breathe." He gave a grin and a palms-up shrug. "This is how she is, something catches her fancy, there's no stopping her. Hell, there's never any stopping her."

Carla smiled. "Like you'd want me any other way." She gave a little tug on my hand. "Take me for a tour of the barn?"

"Sure."

Louis slid on a pair of designer sunglasses. They went with his baggy black pants and leather jacket. In *August*? He'd always been too much of a hot dog for me, but Carla struck me as cool. Something real flowed beneath her surface. I would've made book on it . . .

"Keep her out of trouble, Nikki," Louis said. "She doesn't know jack about horses."

I nodded and turned to Carla, wondering what to show her with Gildy gone. Heading past the empty stall, my feet dragged.

Carla's face tilted. "Someone's missing?"

"You'll probably hear about it. Jim lost his best horse last night." I told her the story.

"You saw the guy?"

"I wish I could kill the fucker." Instant regret for the "F"-word. Louis was an important owner, and I didn't even know this woman.

"Don't worry," she said, "I hear worse language every day of the week."

"What do you do, anyway?"

"Sell meat."

My involuntary double take made her laugh.

"For a wholesaler in Baltimore. I sell to restaurants, hotels. Most of my clients are men. Plenty of four-letter-words." She looked me up and down, her brown eyes appraising. I felt like a Purdue chicken.

"You get tired of being a jockey, you might think about going into sales. Lot of money, especially for a gal with your looks."

That surprised me. Sometimes I thought I looked kind of cute, but nothing to get sweaty about. I took a breath. "I don't think so."

"Oh, no question. Lose the ponytail. Get something short and spiky, set off those blue eyes. Lipstick. You've got a great mouth."

As we moved along a set of bared teeth and pinned ears stretched toward us. I yanked Carla's arm. "Watch it!"

"Damn. I could feel his breath. Doesn't he like spandex?"

She made me smile, but then Dr. Dawson stepped around the corner and disappeared into Ravinsky's office. "That's the vet doing the Necropsy on Gildy. I ran down the aisle with Carla right behind me.

"Nothing," the vet was saying to Jim when I arrived out of breath. "No traceable toxins in the blood. Has the appearance of a heart attack."

"But someone was in her stall." My voice sounded strained. "I *saw* them."

"I heard about that," said Dawson. "But if someone messed with the mare, he sure didn't leave a clue."

"Isn't there something that'll kill and not leave a trace?"

Dawson gave me a sharp look, like maybe I shouldn't ask that question. But he thought a moment. "Give a horse a jug of calcium and the heart would overload, lock up. There's a number of ways." He glanced at Jim, then at me. "What were you doing here last night anyway?"

The accusatory tone surprised me. "Why are you asking me that?"

"Security will, maybe the cops, too. You might want to have a good answer."

My stomach tightened. What was this? Don't grill *me* about Gildy.

Jim's lips were pursed, his left forefinger tapping against them. What with Louis standing right there, he probably didn't want any more talk about this trouble. The track grapevine grew thick, and gossip could strangle.

"Didn't you want me to show Dr. Dawson that bay colt's leg?" I said.

Jim nodded and began making goodbye noises to Louis and Carla.

I marched to the colt's stall with Dr. Dawson in tow. No more conversation about Gildy's death. I showed him the colt's tendon, let him talk about cold-hosing, poultice and leg wraps, and when he finished I vamoosed on out of there.

Beyond the barn, Louis and the divinely blond Carla headed for Louis's convertible. Carla waved at me.

"Hey, Latrelle," Jim called from his office. I went inside. He'd moved to his desk, still covered with charts, and *Racing Forms*, with the new addition of paper cups and an empty doughnut box. A hoof pick and some bandages littered the floor near his feet. The cap he always wore covered his graying hair but failed to hide the kindness in his eyes. "Got a race for you at Shepherds Town."

I hadn't ridden a race for days and needed the extra cash. Rent was due, and an old fear of existing without money shadowed me, especially when times got rough. "Sure, I'll take anything you've got."

Jim gave me the details and I stepped into the aisle to find Kenny studying the departure of Louis and Carla in the silver Jaguar convertible. Kenny handed me a Dunkin' Donuts coffee. "That blonde is hot. Louis is one lucky dude."

"Too much woman for Louis," I said. "She deals in meat." I loved Kenny's startled expression. "Get too close she might grind you up and spit you out."

"God, I wish she would."

I got quiet. My hand holding the paper cup was dirty, the nails broken, the skin rough. This didn't usually bother me. I pulled the band from my ponytail, and felt my hair hang in sweaty, helmet-head clumps.

"You want to watch the Venus Stakes with me this afternoon?" Kenny asked. Then he remembered. "Sorry."

"It's okay." But I'd visualized gliding Gildy to the wire, far in front, so many times it seemed almost real. Only reality now was an image of her chestnut body spread motionless on the straw.

I did a mental head shake and felt the creepy sensation of someone staring. I turned my head, panning the barn directly opposite, but saw no one. Wait, there, leaning on the painted railing of the barn catty-cornered to Jim's. Black hair with dark eyes, and they were on me. Prominent cheekbones. His body echoed his face, thin and hard. I felt uneasy. The assessment wasn't that of a man checking out a woman; it appeared more cold, calculating.

I turned back to Kenny. "Who's that guy over there?"

"Where?"

My hand rose, finger pointing. "Right . . ." But he was gone, leaving the little hairs on the back of my neck standing straight up.

3

Damn it, I was going to be late. I pushed the accelerator, willing the road to reel in faster beneath me, determined to make up time lost in a Washington Beltway backup. The dash clock said I had 15 minutes before check-in time at the jock's room. My horse had a real shot to win, but if I was late, I'd lose the ride. And the $40 jockey fee. The race came by default, as the regular rider's ego was too inflated to follow Ravinsky's horse to a second-rate track like Shepherds Town. No such illusions here.

Not so long ago, before Jim took me under his wing, I'd been a runaway in Baltimore. I still shoved away memories of stealing packaged snacks from gas stations and quick-stop food shops, of sleeping in stalls where my only comfort had been the warmth of the horses. I'd worked hard to boost my life up the ladder, and I'd never slide back, not ever.

The aging Toyota shuddered and balked at my insistent pressure on the pedal. I eased back on the gas, crossing the Potomac River bridge. Far below white water surged over gray protruding rocks, and a lone kayaker struggled against the torrent. I crossed a second bridge over the Shenendoah River and climbed the steep hill past Harpers Ferry, West Virginia. Maybe I'd make it. I didn't want to let Ravinsky down. A good guy, he hadn't wasted time commiserating about me losing the stakes race on Gildy. Instead he'd found me this ride at Shepherds Town.

The grandstand loomed ahead. Rubber burned as the Toyota slid to a stop in an illegal parking spot near the building. I ran in, flashed my badge at the ticket-seller, and flew up the steep, narrow steps to the jock's room.

A round-faced man, a wad of chewing tobacco tucked in his cheek, sat behind a desk in a cramped foyer. "You Latrelle?"

"That's me. Did I make it?"

"Just. Sign here."

I did, then entered the room beyond. A TV monitor sat high on one wall, a race rerun playing in black-and-white. Orange plastic chairs littered the floor beneath, and two guys in racing britches and undershirts played pool in one corner. Vending machines and a battered row of lockers lined one wall. The smell of sweat, steam, and laundry detergent hung in the air.

A short, ferret-faced man, dressed only in white breeches and dirty socks, crumpled the racing charts he'd been reading.

"I see the little piece from Maryland's here."

I worked to keep my lip from curling. Dennis O'Brien. I'd run into him before and was careful to ignore him now.

"Don't plan on stealing the feature race today. Might be unhealthy," he said.

He fancied himself a tough guy, but the way his small eyes nestled up against the bridge of his nose, I'd always thought of him as a meany-weeny. I walked past him, but he grabbed my arm, his fingers hard.

"We don't like when outsiders come up here to take our money."

His breath reeked of onions, and I tried to back away. "Dennis, I wanna make a living like everybody else. Give me a break. Let go of my arm."

My voice might have grown a little shrill. I thought about stomping my boot on his foot, but another rider pushed between us.

Unlike Dennis, Will Marshall's green eyes reflected some intelligence. He wore his thick hair cropped short. "I don't like it when they come in from out-of-town on the favorite, either, but leave her alone, for Christ's sake, before you get yourself in more trouble."

I jerked away from them, rubbing my arm, and found a seat in a far corner. I laid down my canvas tote, picked up an abandoned program and turned to my race, the Sunday feature race with a purse of $10,000. Impressive for Shepherds Town. The winning jockey's share would be $600. Reading on, my breath sucked in. A jockey change since yesterday's *Daily Racing Form*. Dennis O'Brien named on Vengeance, with post position number one, in my race. Damn. He spelled nothing but trouble. He didn't like women, had no regard for racing rules or ethics.

The tinny loudspeaker crackled, then rattled the first call for my race. I found the silks man, grabbed the owner's racing colors and slipped into a curtained cubicle to change. They didn't have a whole lot of amenities for women. I shrugged into the shiny fabric, my fingers hurrying to fasten the velcro down the front. The colors were hot-yellow and electric-orange, not exactly flattering to my pale skin and freckles. With the orange against my dark hair, I looked like a psychedelic Halloween cat. I pulled the helmet on, making sure the gaudy cover stayed snug.

My stomach tightened with nerves as I headed for the paddock, so I did my mental mantra. *Just another race, like dozens before, no big deal.* Jim waited for me in Flame Thrower's saddling stall, and I hoped the smile I flashed him held the confidence I didn't feel. Iron rails encircled the Shepherds Town dugout paddock. Above, bettors crowded against the barrier, examining the horses parading below, hoping to pick a winner.

Flame Thrower had drawn post position six in the field of nine, and with those yellow-and-orange blinkers blaring from his face, I picked him right out. The colors didn't do much for him, either. He was a small bay gelding who habitually displayed speed early in the race. My job was to make sure enough gas remained for the finish.

I knew he had a tough scrappiness and had won over a hundred grand at the Maryland tracks. But five years of racing developed sore hind-quarters that Ravinsky couldn't cure. Though he was an experienced trainer and a good horseman, Jim could only do so much when a horse had that many miles on his legs.

I watched the bay walk around the paddock. I galloped him every morning and knew him well. Today his movement appeared fluid.

The saddling stalls lined one wall of the paddock. I stepped into number six and joined Jim where he stood with Bob Davis, the horse's owner. Davis appeared to be over 50 and way too fond of the dinner table. He pumped my hand and wished me luck. Sweat trickled down his wide cheeks and left his fingers slick.

"Do you think he's got a good chance in this race?" Davis asked.

"I appreciate the ride, Mr. Davis. He'll probably toy with those other horses," I answered. *Well maybe.* Davis turned to admire Flame, and I swiped my hand on my breeches to remove his sweat. . . .

The paddock judge called for riders to mount, and Jim gave me a quick leg-up onto Flame Thrower. He touched my ankle. "You know what to do, Nik."

Flame's groom, a tall, thin black guy named Ron, led us around the paddock once, then into the tunnel leading to the track. Outside the sun flamed hot, and a heavyset pony girl named Kathy rode alongside us on her dun horse. She waited while Ron pulled a strap through Flame's bridle.

This West Virginia girl was something. Even squished under a hel-met, Kathy's teased blond hair attained the obligatory "big-hair" look, and her bright orange lipstick complemented the Davis silks. She leaned over, grabbed the strap and broke the two horses into a jog, beginning our warm-up.

The late-day heat cooked my helmet, while a stiff breeze from the backstretch blew the track flags and scuttled discarded paper cups and plastic wrappers along the concrete. We'd just eased into a gallop when Dennis sped by on Vengeance. He steered his horse in close, causing Flame to pin his ears and fight Kathy's hold.

"Idiot," I said.

"Yeah, Dennis the jockey menace," said Kathy.

We snickered, Flame Thrower calmed down, and I got a chance to study the rest of the field. Not much talent appeared in the race, and a little thrill sped through me. I could win this thing.

I lined up with the other horses waiting at the starting gate. O'Brien, with the one hole, went in first. The next four horses loaded right up, and a man from the gate crew took Flame Thrower into number six, then climbed onto the side platform and steadied the bay's head. Someone shut the bar behind us, and Flame Thrower thrust his nose against the exit door, staring straight ahead, waiting.

"You game old thing," I whispered, patting his dark neck.

The last horse loaded, and the announcer cried, "They're all in line."

I moved forward on Flame's neck, anticipating the shock of his rocket start. The bell rang, the doors crashed open, but the gate assistant held onto Flame's bridle for maybe two-fifths of a second.

Stunned, I started to yell, but he released Flame, who burst into action, a good two lengths behind the rest of the field. No choice but to use his early speed and pick up stragglers down the backstretch.

Flame's acceleration carried us to midpack, past Dennis, definitely startled to see us roll by. Now we lay third. I saw room and angled my horse toward the rail, and then, hating to use him up, I "sat chilly," reins long, my body and hands quiet, almost motionless. I let him run at his own pace as we raced toward the first turn.

Nearing the tight curve I sensed Dennis asking his horse for more speed, and Vengeance responded by bulleting from behind until his nose drew even with Flame's. They lay outside us now, and Dennis pulled Vengeance onto Flame, forcing the smaller horse dangerously close to the rail, where he took a bad step in the softer dirt before steadying himself.

"Stop it, you son of a bitch!" I screamed.

Dennis grinned at me idiotically, until I shook my whip at his face.

He yelled, "Bitch," and cut me across my right cheek with his crop.

Tears from the stinging pain flooded the inside of my goggles, blurring my vision. Rocketing into the turn, the centrifugal force peeled Vengeance away, and Flame moved off the rail and found good footing again.

Screw this.

I flicked my whip forward where Flame could see it. I didn't need to hit him, just show him, he was that game. His stride extended. The eighth pole flashed by in a blur of green-and-white stripes.

"Go, baby!" I screamed.

We were ahead by two lengths, closing in on the wire, when Flame took another bad step. He stumbled and went down, engulfing me with the panicked dread of falling through space. A flash of white. The rail appeared to flip upside down. Hard, sharp thuds as I hit the track and bounced. I curled up, making myself a smaller target. I could hear Flame beside me, struggling to get up.

The ground shook. Dirt peppered my body as the field overtook us. Jockeys screamed, frantic to stay clear. Flame became a protective barrier until another horse slammed into him. Close to my face, his legs churned in a blur as he fought to climb over Flame.

Something smashed my head. An explosion of noise, lights, then nothing.

4

Light pierced my lids. I turned my head away, then stilled as pain stabbed my skull. I cracked one eye open. Floating freckles and curly red hair. A voice.

"Hey, she's coming around."

I remained quiet, getting my bearings, while noting the scent of iodine and rubbing alcohol.

"How you doing?" Cool fingers on my wrist. Probably reading my pulse. "Can you tell me your name?"

I realized I was in the emergency alcove in the track security office, a place jockeys hope to avoid. I thanked my lucky stars I hadn't woken up in Jefferson County Hospital . . . or worse.

The face beneath the red hair belonged to a guy. He peered at me. "What's your name?" he repeated.

"Nikki Latrelle."

I studied the pattern of his freckles, trying to stay focused, while I stumbled through his neurological show-and-tell quiz. Suddenly the track rail flashed by, white and unyielding. The screaming of jockeys, the fear.

"Did we fall? What happened?" I asked

"You got a bonk on your head," the freckled guy said. His head turned toward the far side of the small, cinder-block room.

Jim Ravinsky sat in a gray metal chair against the cream-colored wall. I squinted at him, confused and disoriented, then the memory surfaced.

"Is Flame Thrower all right?"

A long breath escaped him. "We had to put him down, Nikki."

My resolve crumpled, and I couldn't stop the tears. A tissue box sat beside my cot on a metal cabinet. Jim appeared, grabbed one, and pushed it into my hand. I swiped at my eyes with the tissue and struggled for control. "He took a bad step. That Dennis O'Brien pushed us into the rail. I felt it. I should have pulled up. Why didn't I pull up?"

"Stop it, Nikki. You don't know that. Don't beat yourself."

"But Dennis . . ."

"Let it go, Nik. People like that, sooner or later they get what they give." Jim's calm gray eyes rested on me.

I grabbed some air, and a thought crept into my head. "Mr. Davis. Is he upset?"

"Nah, not him. Horse was insured for $30,000. He figures he made out."

I looked away. A big-hearted horse gives his life for the guy, and Davis figures *he made out?*

"For some people it's just business," Jim said. "And if at the end of the day they show a profit, they're happy. They don't get attached to the horses and maybe they're better off that way."

I stared at him. For Jim, who didn't have much to say on a good day, this was a mouthful. His eyes were hollowed, and he put his hand on the metal cabinet as if for support. Guilt over Flame's death probably rode him harder than it did me.

Two horses dead in less than two weeks. A question flickered in my head. I turned to Jim way too fast and stopped, my head jolted by mesmerizing pain. I waited a few beats and the ache receded. "Did Gildy carry insurance?"

"I don't know if Mrs. Garner had a policy."

"How could I find out?"

"Ask." The sudden creases around Jim's eyes and mouth signaled his impatience. "Why do you want to know?"

"What you said about Mr. Davis not caring because of the money. They snuff people for 20 bucks, killing a horse would be nothing."

"Mrs. Garner? You gotta be kidding."

"She could've had it done." I'd gotten the bit in my teeth and couldn't slow down.

"Not Martha Garner, no way. Her horses are her children."

With great care I moved my legs over the edge of the cot and waited to see what happened. I figured I'd probably live. "Have you heard anything from Security about Gildy? Anyone see something that night?"

"Maybe you should worry about getting home and into bed, Nikki." Exhaustion shadowed Jim's face.

I felt kind of bad, the way I'd asked about Martha Garner pulling an insurance scam. "I know Martha loved Gildy. How's she doing?"

"Upset. Said on the phone she didn't want to come to the track." Jim rubbed at one of his brows, leaving a few hairs pointing my way. "Maybe you oughta take a few days off."

"No way. How many rides will I lose if word gets out I need time off?" I'd nailed that one and Jim didn't argue. Superstitions haunted many owners and trainers. They'd bolt at the first sign of trouble.

"Gotta get back to Laurel, Nik." Jim went back to the chair and retrieved his cap. His movements seemed slow and uncertain.

I kept quiet, restraining the urge to ask more questions. The insurance. Who would gain from Gildy's death — or my loss on Flame? Was it a betting scam? Had someone paid the gate guy who'd delayed Flame's start? And Dennis O'Brien . . .

The cream wall began to dance and circle before me. I put my elbows on my knees, my face in my hands. The head pain blossomed, overruling curiosity, making me think I should take Jim's advice.

Ron drove my car back to Laurel Park. From there I nabbed a ride home with a jockey who lived in my apartment complex off Route197. The wooden structures where we lived appeared well-made at first glance. My place was on the second floor. An outside staircase with suspect wooden railing led to my door. This close the building looked seedy, stained with mold, the siding warped and peeling away. I'd fought back, lining the landing with terra cotta pots overflowing with cheap-thrill petunias and gaudy pansies.

Inside I got as far as the couch. Slippers, my Heinz-57, part-Persian cat, appeared at my feet. He sat and opened his mouth in a silent meow. I lay down, carefully placing my head on a pillow. The couch, like the rest of my yard-sale furniture, hid beneath blue-and-white batik slipcovers. A bronze statue of a horse — my only home-decorating splurge — stood on the floor at the edge of a straw rug. I loved books, and a collection of favorites stuffed a battered IKEA cabinet. Those books, with the help of a dictionary, had taught me a lot.

Slippers stretched and rubbed against the couch, his tail a plume. He inspected me for a moment, then levitated himself onto my stomach and rumbled into full purr.

The ringing phone woke me. I let the machine take Jim's call.

"Nikki. I'm entering Bourbon Bonnet in a claimer, going a mile and a sixteenth. Wanna put you on, if you're up to it. Let me know."

A mediocre horse, running in a mediocre race, but I'd take the ride. Just hoped my luck improved, and the *horse's* luck.

Louis Fein owned this one, and a couple of promising two-year-olds almost ready for their first starts. Sometimes I worried. Louis seemed flighty, and Jim was so terse, with little ability to sweet-talk clients. Some owners needed pampering. Jim didn't dish that out and had probably lost good horses because of it.

A few days, several nightmares, and a half-bottle of Ibuprofen later, I walked into the Laurel paddock wearing Louis's black-and-silver silks. Bourbon Bonnet looked dull, but she'd been known to produce a late kick. I hoped she would, as I rode her onto the track, a pony escort hardly necessary. Bourbon tended to be quiet and lazy. I booted her into a gallop, chirping and shaking the reins, trying to wake her up. I let the other horses and red-coated outriders move ahead on the backside. Away from the spectators, I whacked her once with my whip. Her head came up and she grabbed the bit.

"Good girl. Don't go back to sleep." And *don't fall.*

Push back the fear, the images of Flame buckling, the white rail upside down, flying past my head. I focused on the immediate present, throwing up mental battlements against panic. Think about Bourbon drawing the number one post position, dwell on the old track saying, "First one in, last one out." Bourbon was a prime candidate, likely to fall asleep in the gate while waiting for the remaining eight-horse field to load.

Sure enough, when the bell rang and the pack erupted from the gate, seven horses blasted away from me. Their hindquarters churned, muscles bulging as they sprayed hard, stinging dirt into my face. The pounding of aluminum-shod hooves was loud and rhythmic. Their bodies pumped air, adrenalin, and blood, producing a hot horse smell that flew back to me.

There was no point asking Bourbon for speed. She'd run her early, plodding pace, tucked just behind the gang ahead. I sat chilly through the first turn and midway down the backstretch I went for the whip, but my hand froze. Would she take a bad step? So much safer not to push. And what . . . retire? *I don't think so.*

I cracked her twice, she lengthened her stride, and we passed three horses on the inside going into the last turn. At the top of the lane my filly ran fourth, and I got into her again with the whip, hoping to evoke that late run. She kicked in suddenly, passed the number three horse and drove for the wire. The lead horse faltered and bore out, her stride losing the rhythm of speed. We swept by, leaving one horse still to catch. Here comes the wire. We flashed under in second place. It was over. I'd made it. My legs felt shaky and tears of relief stung my eyes.

My 10 percent of the place money gave me $240, not bad for less than two minutes work. A Venus Stakes place on Gildy would have paid $4,000.

The Mexican groom, Ramon, waited for me, his gold earring bright in the afternoon sun. I slid off and handed the reins over.

"Hey Nikki, great ride." Carla Ruben, long legs supple beneath a short white skirt, stood next to Louis. They were out in the deep sand of the track, Louis in shiny tasseled loafers and Carla in turquoise sandals.

Louis wore the satisfied owner's grin. "Way to go, Nikki. After the way she broke, I don't know how you got her up for the place."

Carla darted a glance my way. "Louis and I are going back to the box. Join us?"

"Why don't you?" Louis said. "I'll buy you a drink."

"Sure, thanks." I went to the jock's room, showered, and changed into street clothes, relieved I'd brought the black slacks and clean polo shirt.

Inside the Laurel grandstand Carla and Louis were sitting in a box near a glass wall that sealed away the late summer humidity. Outside, the immense mile track stretched in the distance, a vista shimmering in heat. In the infield geese swam in a miniature lake. Carla, wearing silver and turquoise jewelry, looked cool and beautiful. Somehow her sandals remained spotless. Louis patted a seat for me next to her.

Bright laughter from the next box turned my head. A well-dressed, polished woman, maybe 60-something, sat close to a younger man who spoke in her ear. Her salon-perfect makeup and hair complemented her blue eyes, but were no competition for the diamonds that flashed from her fingers. The man touched her wrist and murmured something. She flushed and laughed again.

Carla leaned over to me, her voice low. "Who's that guy?"

"No idea."

"He's hot. You should meet him."

I hadn't asked to meet anyone and opened my mouth to protest.

Louis's face lit with recognition. "Clay Reed. I can't believe it."

Introductions circled around. The woman, Janet LeGrange, said she was a friend of Clay's uncle. Yeah, right.

"Janet, are you an owner or just a fan?"

It seemed Carla liked to dig. The woman's name sounded familiar. I thought Bill Burke, the trainer in the barn behind Jim's, might be her trainer.

"Janet has a great little horse running later this afternoon," said Clay. "You guys might want to put a couple of dollars on."

Carla turned to him. "And what about you, Clay?"

"I enjoy racing and dabble a little in the industry."

"He's so modest," said Janet. "Clayton's really in the loop, buys and sells, consults, knows *everybody*. He's really helped me, and such a dear to keep me company since my loss."

Janet gushed, obviously quite taken with Clay. But he was a handsome one. Streaked blond hair, blue eyes, great bones and the pronounced curve in his nose kept him out of "pretty boy" territory. His eyes roamed over Carla and me. He surprised me when his gaze made a final landing on me.

"You rode in the last race." His stare made me nervous.

"Nikki's wonderful," said Carla. "She rode Louis's horse and almost won."

"Almost isn't the same thing as winning," I said. Did I have to sound so sharp?

"No, it's not," Clay said. "You strike me as someone who likes to win . . . . I am." His eyes on me again, speculative, almost too familiar. My blood rushed.

"Since you two have so much in common, maybe we should all go out sometime." Carla put a hand on Louis's arm. "Do you think Clay's a candidate for the limbo stick at Coca Mocha?"

This moved way too fast for me. Clay wasn't interested in going out. Why did Carla have to play match-maker? What would I *wear*?

Janet seemed to rear up in her seat. "Clayton's quite busy most of the time," she said, her smile thinning.

I glanced at Carla's program. It listed Burke as Janet's trainer, though I'd never seen her around his barn. She probably didn't want to dust up her diamonds.

Louis chose to ignore Janet's outburst. "What do you say, Clay? Been a while since we've partied."

Janet studied a perfectly manicured fingernail, scowling as if the pink polish had become offensive.

Then Clay surprised me, saying he'd like to go. He'd call Louis.

Well, that's an easy out. He just won't call. But he was so good-looking, his voice sexy, his gaze a caress. *Easy,* Nikki. I took a mental breath, then stole a surreptitious glance at Clay while he spoke to Louis. I sensed something then, under the surface, a depth unclear and disquieting. Like the dark man who had stared at me from the catty-cornered barn, Clay disturbed me.

5

Almost Labor Day. The color of the morning light more mellow, the air less hazy, the thermometer a few degrees kinder. Kenny Grimes, hustling after an extra buck, rushed past me carrying his saddle, no doubt off to another trainer's barn to catch a couple more rides before the track closed at 10. He called over his shoulder, "Some guys in Jim's office want to talk to you."

"Who?"

But Kenny scurried away, not answering.

I stepped into the office. Two men stood near Jim's desk. One I recognized as the track security guard from the night Gildy died. I'd learned his full name since then, Fred Rockston, maybe 35, short, but wiry and thick with muscle. The other I'd never seen before. He looked about40, with receding dark hair and sharp, bird-like eyes that peered at me from behind black glasses.

"This is Miss Latrelle," said Jim.

"Peter Beamfelter." He didn't offer to shake my hand, just dipped his head. "I'd like to ask you some questions about the racehorse, Gilded Cage." His voice intimidated, and his manner felt aggressive as he moved closer.

"Why?"

His mouth tightened. "You're the one found her."

This guy irritated me. Maybe I should scream, "I did it," and grovel at his feet. Instead I said, "Who are you, and why do you need to know?" Maybe I'd said that too loud.

Jim eased between us. "Take it slow, Nikki. This guy's an insurance investigator."

My interest perked up. "So there was an insurance policy, with Martha Garner the beneficiary? How much was Gildy insured for?"

Beamfelter pointed his beaky nose at me. "You're not in a position to be asking questions, Miss Latrelle. That's my job. Why'd you just happen to be here so late the night the mare died? Care to answer that now? Or would you prefer to be subpoenaed, answer in court? I don't give a crap, lady, it's up to you."

"Oooh, tough guy," I said, then realized the foolishness of aggravating him. No need to make it harder on myself. Dr. Dawson had asked the same question. Did these people really consider me a suspect?

Jim tapped his lip, avoiding eye contact. I sank into a metal chair. "I had the ride on Gidled Cage in the Venus Stakes. It was a break for me. No way would I hurt her. I saw the guy run from her stall. Why don't you ask me about him?"

Jim turned to Beamfelter. "She didn't kill that horse. I'd bet my stable on it."

"Let's hope you don't have to."

Jim made an exasperated sound, but Beamfelter never softened during my verbal walkthrough of that night. He took notes and asked a few more questions, his beady eyes sharp and unsettling. Like the Anne Arundel County cop, he gave me his card. I tried one last time to pry out some information about the policy and got nowhere.

I waited for him to leave, then turned to Jim. "Would I put you in a bad spot if I called Martha Garner and talked to her about the insurance?"

"Go ahead. Guy's a prick, trying to point a finger at you."

"Yeah, that's what I thought." Using Beamfelter's card and Jim's Rolodex, I jotted down Martha's number and went outside. A cloud scudded away from the sun, releasing a burst of sunlight, and Carla stepped around the corner, her hair iridescent gold. She spotted me and hurried over.

"Great, I caught you. Louis called Clay yesterday. It's all set. Saturday night we go to Coca Mocha, so get your dancing shoes." Today she modeled the shrink-wrapped look, with a stretchy silver top and zebra-print shorts.

My God. What would she wear to a dance club? Wait, there wasn't going to be a dance club and I started to say so, but Carla's enthusiasm and jingling silver bracelets drowned me out.

"I read in the *Post* that you won a $21,000 race yesterday. I follow the racing section now. What do you get for your share?"

Probably, I should ask about her take on a side of beef, but she disarmed me so completely. "Ten percent, of sixty ercent of the purse."

"So you got $1,260 for, like, two minutes work?"

Mental double take at the speed of calculation. "What are you, computer brain?" My mouth forgot to stop. "And do you always look so good?"

Carla raised a brow, then a seriousness settled over her. "A piece of a piece is my game, too. Think I'd survive without knowing how many chicken breasts or tenderloins I have to sell to each account every week? As for looks, there's a lot of us sales reps out there, but these restaurant and hotel guys are suckers for eye-candy. Can I help it?"

We both grinned. Maybe at the absurd power of the hand that wields the lipstick case.

"But about Saturday night," I said. "Have to be at work by six Sunday morning. Probably, it'd be too much."

Jim suddenly materialized next to me. "I'll give you Sunday morning off. You could use some fun."

This was a conspiracy and maybe not a good one. Clay hadn't called *me*. I didn't really know these people and . . .

"Nikki, you look like a recalcitrant filly," Jim said. "Go on, enjoy yourself."

Carla gave me the once over. "People get lollied up for Coca Mocha."

"That could be a problem," I said. "Maybe insurmountable."

"You just won money. We'll go shopping."

I threw Jim a desperate look. There were medical bills, the rent. "I probably don't have the time . . ."

"Don't you get a day off?"

"She gets Thursdays off," said Jim. He turned and disappeared into his office.

"We're going to have so much fun," said Carla.

Probably this is how racehorses feel when led into the starting gate — doors locked behind, no way out but forward.

That evening I punched Martha Garner's number into my phone, picturing the older woman while I waited for the line to connect. Stout and short, she favored nylon wind-suits, pink or some other pastel variation usually her color of choice. For a 60-eight-year-old, she sure did get around, her gray head and thick, pink glasses appearing at the barn at ungodly hours of the morning and in all kinds of weather. Her smoky voice rasped in my ear, and we did the how-are-you stuff, then talked about Gildy. Martha, a sharp old bird, paused for a beat, probably wondering if a reason lay behind my call.

"Please don't take this the wrong way," I said, "but did you insure Gildy?"

"Everyone's asking me this. That insurance investigator person, Beakfeather. Now you. Do you people think I killed my own horse?"

"No, Martha, they think I did."

"You!" She sounded incredulous. "Hold on a minute."

I heard the flicking sound of a lighter, then that breathy sound as Martha sucked smoke through a filter, a hacking cough following right behind. I wondered how she managed to hang out at Jim's barn like she did, with his no-lighting-anything-in-the-shedrow rule.

Martha's voice came back. "That investigator bugging you, too?"

"Yeah."

"Suspicious little shit, isn't he? I'll tell you what I told him. I had a full mortality policy with Eastern Seaboard Insurance for $150,000. That's what she was appraised at. And now, it's like pulling teeth to get the money. Almost wish you hadn't seen that guy coming out of her stall. All I get is 'suspicious circumstances, ongoing investigation.'"

"Hate to be ignorant, but what is a full mortality policy?"

"When you insure only for death, not for illness, injury, or loss of use. That kind of additional coverage costs as much as the horse."

"Oh."

"Honey, I don't want to talk about this anymore. The whole thing makes me sick. That mare gave me a reason to get up in the morning."

I closed my eyes, pretty much knowing how she felt. After we disconnected I figured I'd drawn a blank. Martha seemed unlikely in the role of animal killer, and with her listed as beneficiary, who else could gain? If someone had wanted to remove Gildy from the race, a bucket of water offered just before she ran or any number of drugs would have sufficed. I found investigating frustrating. If it were up to me to figure this thing out, I'd be in trouble.

6

By 10:30 the track merry-go-round slowed down. Most horses were back in their stalls, leg bandages on, hay nets filled, water buckets brimming. Feed and hay trucks finished their deliveries and blacksmith and vet vans rumbled away, finally clearing the pavement.

Earlier I'd been forced to park over by the catty-cornered barn, and now as I lugged my saddle back to my Toytota, a row of hanging pots caught my attention. They decorated the barn's low cinderblock wall, overflowing with yellow mums, price tags still in evidence. The flowers hadn't been there earlier. Maybe a new outfit had moved in. The grape vine murmured horses in that small section had recently tested positive for illegal drugs. Chances were the trainer had been forced to move on. The guy hadn't seemed like the flower type anyway.

The drug rumor didn't surprise me, since I'd always thought of this as the dark barn, most of it run by a trainer named Arthur Clements, a creep who cut corners with feed, hay, and help. His shedrow carried a heavy, pervasive smell of dust, mold, and stalls only partially cleaned. His help looked like they slept in those sour stalls, and foul language and hostile attitudes abounded.

A hacking cough sounded as I stashed my saddle in the Toyota. Clements stood on the pavement outside the catty-cornered barn, clearing his throat, his hand clutching a bottle of nasal spray. I cringed as the noise crescendoed, ending in the inevitable splat as Clements' gunk hit the pavement. Yuk, why did anyone find it okay to spit in public? Average in height, his most memorable features were a weak chin, thin lips, and colorless, watery eyes. He reminded me of a photo negative.

I wouldn't expect a guy like this to enjoy success like he did. He even had some stakes horses in his barn. Go figure. And somehow he prospered from unclear connections with track management and certain Maryland bigwigs.

Standing with Jim one time, an unsavory-looking Clements' groom had led a pitifully thin horse by. The animal had walked with the crablike steps of an impending breakdown.

"Clements is so cheap," I'd blurted. "Why is he so well-accepted? I'd rule him off."

"Clements knows where the bodies are buried, Nikki."

"What do you mean?"

"Clements ever gets dirt on you, you're screwed."

Jim had refused to say more, but I'd heard stories.

Now the man tilted his head back and dripped solution from another plastic bottle into his eyes. He straightened and his glance moved through me and settled on a horse moving down his shedrow, led by a Latino guy with greasy hair and spider tattoos. Clements said something I couldn't hear, and the groom laughed.

I'd seen this pretty chestnut filly earlier that morning. A tall, strong-boned horse, she'd hadn't traveled the track surface well, her stride short and choppy like she hurt somewhere. If she needed heal time, she wouldn't get it from Clements.

None of my business, but something drew me to the filly and I eased over to get a better look. Something about her looked familiar, but I couldn't put my finger on it. Clements disappeared into his office, and the groom led the chestnut toward a stall. She balked, backing away from the dark entrance. The groom cursed and jerked the chain encircling her velvet nose, so she reared. Who wouldn't? Then the guy whipped out a crop and struck her on the head.

"Stop it, you jerk!" Anger boiled over in my stomach.

"Fuck you, bitch." He whacked the horse like he was just getting started.

The filly rose again, struck the groom's shoulder, and twisted away, pulling the lead with her. Instead of the wild, frenzied gallop I'd expected, she jogged toward me, her metal shoes clattering on the pavement. The groom had collapsed against the barn wall, and was busy rubbing his shoulder, no longer interested in me or the filly. A breeze came up, swinging the potted mums near her head. She snorted and shied closer. I grabbed her shank.

Might as well have grabbed a rocket. *Oh boy.* I tried to go with her as she blasted back toward the chrysanthemums. She brought herself up short, as if deciding where to go next, and I locked my elbows into my sides and rocked back on my heels. Grounded, I managed to pull her around me in a circle when she started up again. I cooed soft nonsense and asked her nicely, through the shank, to slow down.

Those furry ears pricked and dipped toward me and her frantic jig slowed to a walk. Someone in Clements' barn had left a stable hose trickling and water pooled near my feet. The chestnut filly's hooves splashed and sprayed me with drops of moisture as she drew closer.

"Good girl, you pretty thing, let's get a look at you." Keeping my hand low and slow I touched her shoulder, and she stopped, turning her head to me. A white star with a jagged blaze darting below, like a lightening bolt, decorated her finely made face. Two small white anklets circled her front feet just above the hooves. I stepped in closer, scratched her neck, and read the brass nameplate on her halter . . . "Helen's Dream." The shank fell from my hands. I stood rooted.

"You okay?" A man had stepped in close and scooped up the shank. "This is some red devil you've got a hold of. She hurt you?"

"No. It's the name, Helen . . ." I stopped, realizing I made no sense, at least not to this guy. I focused on him, recognizing the man who'd stared at me from this barn the day after Gildy's death. Up close, his sharp face made me think of a gunslinger. He exuded the kind of self-confidence that brings coolness under pressure. His brown eyes on me were sharp, yet shuttered, covering a hidden agenda.

Another of Clements' grooms ran up, thanked me for catching the horse, and took the shank. The filly accepted this man, allowing him to coax her into her stall. But just before, I'd swear she turned her head back and stared, like she needed to get a line on me. Just my imagination, stirred by the name on the halter. The gunslinger finished a half-heard sentence.

". . . a way with horses." He knew I hadn't been listening. "I said, 'You have quite a way with horses.' I call her the she-devil down the shedrow. She's gonna hurt someone bad."

"She's injured," I said.

The man nodded slowly, then put out his hand: "Jack Farino."

We did a brief shake. His hand slid firmly into mine, solid and sexual.

"Nikki Latrelle." Even as the words came out, I moved a small step back. This guy alarmed me.

His expression softened. He became chatty, said he'd come down from Belmont with a string of horses that weren't quite good enough for New York. "They should be more competitive down here, probably do well, as long as they don't get sideswiped by any of the trouble I keep hearing about."

"What trouble?"

His eyes locked on like I was a target, his voice hardened. "Something bad's going on around here. Wasn't it your barn had a horse killed?"

My head came up. I felt cornered — and mad. "Why is that your business?"

"Just heard rumors, that's all. You don't have to get all defensive."

"Look, Mr. Farino. When that mare died, nobody, except maybe the owner, had more to lose than I did. Anyway, I wish you all the luck in Maryland, but I gotta go. Nice meeting you."

I left him standing there, got in my car, and drove away. Something about him I didn't trust. Funny how he'd shown up in Laurel right when Gildy died. Yet I liked the way he'd stepped in to help. God, that name: *Helen's Dream*. My mother. . . . Helen Latrelle. My mental shields weren't up and pain blindsided me.

I pulled the car into a gravel lot where horse trailers parked, sheltering in the shadow of a blue-and-silver four-horse rig. Damn, I didn't want any emotional storms, but the memories gathered big and black, like thunderheads. My mother standing in the narrow kitchen inside the Baltimore rowhouse. She'd had so many dreams for me. Dreams tarnished by my father's early death, smashed by her misguided choice of a second husband. And finally, dreams that died with her. An accident on an icy street, an express bus speeding too fast. Helen, my mother, suddenly gone, leaving me with no protection.

My ragged breath jerked me back to the present. My hands covered my face, and sobs racked me. Get a grip. I really needed people asking why I hung out in the Laurel parking lot weeping. Then I felt the old unreasoning fury at being abandoned. I rammed the car into gear and left the racetrack.

7

Martha Garner finally appeared early Wednesday morning. The sight of her forlorn figure hanging outside Gildy's empty stall stopped me cold. Her clothes were drab shades of gray that added a dismal aura to the petite, elderly woman. Startling not to see her in her usual pink or lavender nylon jog-suit, the colors she'd habitually worn when Gildy would prance into the winner's circle carrying a beaming jockey decked out in Martha's lavender-and-fuchsia racing silks. Now she swiped ineffectually at the tears that spotted her lined cheeks.

"I miss her too, Martha."

"Oh, Nikki. Hold these." Martha pulled her thick, pink-framed glasses from her face, thrust them at me, dug a tissue from her pocket and dabbed her eyes.

"That insurance investigator, Beakfeather? He won't return my calls. First he accuses half of the county of murdering Gildy, and now, with them not finding criminal evidence, he doesn't want to talk about my payment." Martha's cigarette cough took center stage for a moment, and then she fidgeted with her glasses, settling them on her nose.

I knew Martha's husband, a successful developer, had left a substantial inheritance. Gildy had been the last of a string of quality racehorses Martha inherited after Ed Garner's heart attack.

"I hope you won't give up on the horses, Martha."

"Everybody says that. Even this nice agent I met, Clay Reed. He thinks I should get back in the saddle, so to speak. And of course Jim thinks I should buy one —"

"Clay Reed?" I asked. Boy, he sure got around these older widows.

"Yes, polite young agent, a real charmer."

"That's the one."

"You should put your hook in him, see if you can reel him in." A familiar spunk had returned to Martha's voice and a smile worked the corners of her lips

"Not looking for a man," I said. Was that true? "But if you want a horse, Jim knows how to pick 'em."

"We're supposed to look at a couple of two-year-olds, so I said I'd come by." Martha's expression darkened. Probably Gildy's death haunting her again. "I don't think I'm ready," she said slowly. Then she touched my arm and headed for Jim's office.

I tacked up my next horse, a gray colt, joined Kenny Grimes on a bay filly and we all headed for the dirt path leading to the track.

"What's old-lady Garner up to?" he asked, nodding in the direction of Martha and Jim, rolling by on the paved road in Jim's truck.

"Jim's trying to get her another horse."

"Hope he hurries up — we got two more empty stalls this morning."

"What?"

"Mr. Crockett fired Jim last night. Sent his two colts over to Arthur Clements."

"Clements?" I almost shrieked. "He'll ruin them." Like Helen's Dream. "Why did Crockett do that?"

"Something about too many things going wrong for Ravinsky, and he likes Clements' win percentage."

I shook my head in disbelief. "Clements runs a slaughterhouse the way he goes through horses. He gets wins, but he breaks horses down doing it, and then throws 'em out like trash. I thought Crockett was smarter than that."

"It's business, Nikki."

Some business. Suddenly my hands were full of my colt who'd spooked at a rooster perched on the rim of a nearby trash barrel.

"Damn chickens," Kenny said, as his filly stared bugeyed at the bird, then plunged sideways. "Why does anybody want a chicken?"

The rooster puffed himself up and flapped his red wings, causing my colt to bolt forward and a few swear words to escape my lips. I stood high in the stirrups, and after reining him in, felt the laughter bubbling up inside me. The rooster crowed, the early morning sun warmed my back,and Kenny broke into a verse of "Camptown Races." I loved this world.

But when we rode into the barn it hit me. We'd lost Gildy, Flame Thrower, and now the two colts. If Jim lost any more horses, he'd have to cut our salaries. After dismounting, I sank onto a bale of straw. With those colts gone, I'd have even fewer race rides in the upcoming weeks. I hoped Martha found a horse, but a moment later she emerged from Jim's office, looking weary,and disheartened. I left my straw bale and moved toward her. "Good thing I'm not ready for a new horse. Jim didn't like those two-year-olds."

"What's wrong with them?"

"Jim said one looked crooked as crap, and the other's top line's all screwy."

I could picture Jim exasperated by a horse with misaligned leg bones, and another lacking the pleasing proportions in the head-to-tail line denoting a potential runner. Some trainers would have a client buy any horse, just so they could charge their owner the day rate. But Jim suffered from honesty.

When I'd finished for the day I stuck my head into his office, trying to gauge his mood. He sat at his desk, shaggy eyebrows drawn in concentration, writing entries in a log book.

"He ain't never going to believe all this stuff." Jim refused to look up and continued muttering to himself about the costs of getting a horse to the starting gate.

Maybe this wasn't the best time. He hated book work, but had to charge the day rate, then bill out separately for blacksmith fees, medicines, special equipment, and even procedures as exotic as acupuncture. I pulled a wooden chair over, scraping its legs on the floor.

Jim's head came up and he glared at me. "You want to explain this bill to Mr. Why-is-it-so-expensive Peterson?"

"Not really. Just talk about cutting-edge technology, how his horses should get the same stuff the other trainers use."

Jim's glare eased into a slow smile. "That'll work."

"Jim, what's with this new guy in Clements' barn — Jack Farino?"

"Came down from New York?"

"Yeah. Him."

Jim's unruly brows climbed in question. "What's your interest?"

"He asked me about Gildy, made me nervous. And why would anybody want to move into Clements' barn?"

Jim's smile disappeared with the mention of Clements and his shoulders sagged. "People are gonna talk, Nikki, and probably that barn space got allocated by the stall manager. Far as I know, Farino's just another trainer hoping for better luck in Maryland."

Probably smarter not to ask, but I couldn't ignore the problem. "Kenny told me about Crockett taking his colts from you. I can't believe he did that."

Jim's head turned away and he held up his hand, refusing to discuss it. Jim avoided subjects that might pierce his shell and draw blood. Maybe I followed his example too closely. He stabbed his log book with the pencil. "Anything else?"

I stood up and stepped near the door. "Yeah, you know anything about a horse Clements has, called Helen's Dream?"

"Nope." Jim glared again. A quick exit might be wise.

*　　*　　*

I went looking for my buddy with the unlikely name Lorna Doone. She galloped horses for a trainer who had an office computer and online racing and pedigree accounts. I jogged over there and found her in the trainer's office with a bag of doughnuts. Her frizzy red hair haloed her face, and a gold ring pierced one auburn brow. A tattoo of Pegasus engraved her left forearm. She might have been short and a bit round, but no one would mistake her for a shortbread cookie. Why would parents name their kid after a Nabisco product?

I'd met Lorna about a year earlier. Jim had sent me to the track near the 10 A.M. closing time to exercise the stable "pony." Always a treat to take out an older, sensible track pony like Mack that has a big old western bit in his mouth, knows he can't run off with you and rarely wants to.

Lorna had been out there on a two-year-old colt. Trainers send these unseasoned, often volatile youngsters out late when the track is less crowded and most of the speedy breezing's finished. I'd jogged Mack about a mile, stopped him and dropped the reins, his signal to just stand and watch a bit. Mack loved to loiter about, feeling superior as he watched the shameful antics of some of the uneducated two-year-olds.

A big colt blew past us, eyes wild and fearful, a broken rein dangling uselessly from his bit. A girl clung to his mane, her face tight with panic.

"Yah," I'd yelled at Mack, gathering the reins. Being a track pony, he knew what to do and took off in hot pursuit. In his day he'd been a useful sprinter, and with his quick acceleration we drew alongside the colt in no time. I grabbed the dangling rein, then stood in my stirrups, leaning back slightly to get leverage on both horses' bits. We'd rocked and careened a little, but eventually I'd pulled the horses down to a jig.

"Wonder Dude, you saved my life," the girl said after struggling for her breath. Lorna'd been a loyal buddy ever since.

Now she grinned up from her chair and held out the bag of doughnuts. I peeked inside. Fresh, fragrant, and chocolate-covered. Oh boy.

"Can I pull the past performances on a horse?" I asked, taking a bite of doughnut.

The way her brow ring rose up I could tell she was curious, so I told her about Helen's Dream.

"This sounds like a karma thing," she said, licking chocolate from her fingers and firing up the computer. The filly's life history materialized on the monitor, and we got busy tracing Helen's story in *Daily Racing Form* charts listing information like breeding, racing dates, speed figures, and order of finish.

"Dude, this filly's bred like a queen." Lorna's finger pointed to the sire, Dream Boat Special. "Like, he's a Kentucky Derby winner. And look here, your Dream's dam earned over three hundred grand. Whoa dudarina, the dam's name is "Helen's Last Wish"

I got blind-sided again, emotion welling up.

"Nikki, baby dude, you crying?" Lorna's voice quivered with concern. "You want more chocolate?"

I shook my head and fingered away tears. Lorna stared at me, curious. "I was thinking about Gildy," I lied. No, we weren't going to ponder my mother's dying wish. Not going there with Lorna. Instead, I pointed to the monitor, hoping to distract.

"Look how they treated her," I said. Helen's first trainer had run her three times in five weeks, maybe too much for a two-year-old. She'd had a second, a third, and gotten her first win. Nine days later, she was entered in a stakes race. At Belmont.

"Ignorant trainer," Lorna said, indignant. "Why not just shoot her?"

We stared at the page. In the stake the filly led most of the way around, then died in the stretch. After that, a long layoff.

"Bet she cracked a cannon bone," I said.

"Pulled a suspensory ligament," Lorna offered. "Some of these guys'll cut off their own foot to make an extra buck."

We shook our heads, thinking about greed and stupidity. Fortunately, many trainers lived for their horses, lavishing them with the best feed, conditioning and love.

Helen's next start listed a new owner and a cheaper purse. We read comments like "unruly at the gate" and "fractious at the start." Her story went downhill through the claiming ranks, where one trainer after another bought her, then ran her back for a cheaper price. Finally she hit bottom, claimed by Clements.

8

Carla's black Mercedes sped over the Potomac River on the I-95 bridge, while Cheryl Crow sang "My Favorite Mistake" on the radio. We'd left the capital city's marble testimonials to our forefathers behind in a haze of heat and pollution. Ahead lay the air-conditioned shopping-extravaganza of the Pentagon City Mall. I'd never been there, but I'd heard about Nordstrom's, our apparent destination.

Carla eased back the volume and pointed her Gucci sunglasses at me. "Nikki, I'm curious about something."

When wasn't she?

"You've never talked about a family or how you got into horses."

I paused, glancing outside. To the right, the Pentagon stood in a huge parking lot, encircled by looping highways. I stared at the spot where terrorists had crashed a plane, and took a breath. Life was so short. I'd locked up my past, letting it fester. Maybe it was time to crack a window.

"I grew up in inner-city Baltimore," I said. "In one of those narrow rowhouses."

"And?"

I sighed and the words tumbled out, an unhappy list. "My father died when I was two. Heart attack. No brothers or sisters, just my mom. She worked for this prissy girl's school as a cook. Got me a job working in the school's stable for free riding lessons when I was 10." I paused. A jet flew behind us, declining steeply for its landing at Reagan National Airport. I could feel my spirits going down with it. "She remarried this . . . person, and then she . . ."

"What?" Apprehension laced Carla's voice.

"She died when I was 13."

"I'm so sorry." Carla chewed her bottom lip between perfect white teeth. "I didn't mean to push . . ."

"A traffic accident." We didn't need the details.

"Sounds pretty rough, Nikki."

"You don't know the half of it." We could both hear the anger in my voice.

Wisely, Carla let it go, zooming up a ramp into the mall's parking garage. We focused on happier things, like shopping.

*   *   *

Carla powered into Nordstrom's like she owned the place, and I followed in her wake, sniffing the perfume-saturated air. Glitzy makeup counters swarmed the entrance, while fashionably dressed women with painted faces lay-in-wait behind elegant displays of cosmetics and products touting high-tech ingredients, all of it Greek to me.

"I could move into this place," Carla said, bee-lining for the Christian Dior counter.

She grabbed a lipstick and peered at the color. She wore a stretchy black suit, with silver buttons. A silver clip fastened French braids at the nape of her neck.

A 99-cent Goody band corralled my ponytail, and from there I slid downhill. Wait, my sneakers were clean.

Two saleswomen purred over Carla, while a suspiciously perfect redhead insisted on spraying the blonde with sample perfume. Graciously, Carla extended her wrist. I didn't mind being invisible; this was entertainment.

Carla purchased more products than I could figure out how to use in a year, then slowly turned her gaze to me. "Can you do a make over for my friend?"

"Certainly," the two saleswomen replied at once, staring at me. At least they didn't shudder. They frowned, scrutinized, conferred, and pulled lipsticks, brushes, bottles of foundation, mascara wands, eyeliners, blusher, and powder puffs. They stuck me on a stool and went to work.

Later we rested in the Nordstrom's coffee bar, inhaling buttered scones and sipping mocha latte. I'd stopped at every mirror along the way, amazed at my dramatic eyes and the illusion of perfect skin. Were those my lips? Surrounded by shopping bags, my head spun from a glut of purchases that included a red dress, a black evening bag, a pushup bra, and three shades of lipstick. Outwardly shocked by the indulgence, somewhere deep inside a thrill sped through me.

Carla finished her coffee and gave a feline stretch. "So now you're beautiful, which is no surprise to me. But we need to do something about your hair."

Mentally I resisted. Cinderella gets dragged to the ball kicking and screaming. "Most people think my hair is pretty," I said, folding my arms against my stomach.

"Your hair's lovely, the style needs help. Wait! I've got the answer."

Her eyes took on an alarming gleam. "Felix Alfonso. He'll transform your hair." She inspected her Rolex. "It's just 2 o'clock. I'll call now, see if he has a cancellation."

"I don't think so," I said, feeling a sudden sympathy for the race-horse's fear of those large, electric clippers.

But Carla had already whipped out her cell phone and connected the call. The salon must be on speed dial. The conversation raced to a rapid finish and Carla disconnected. "You're in. Let's go."

I sat in Felix's pink-and-chrome chair gazing at my reflection in the mir-ror. Most of my ponytail lay in heaps on the black-and-pink tiled floor. My eyes looked huge, my hair — okay, I'll admit it. My hair looked fantastic. Carla knew style. Short and spiky with tendrils at the neck, an amazing improvement.

Alfonso tweaked a spike more upright, admiring his work. "Darling, you look divine. But you simply *must* use my product." He held up the can of Spike! that displayed a picture of an effeminate bulldog wearing a pink metal-studded collar.

"Yeah, sure," I said. "I'll get some on the way out."

Carla, appearing way too pleased with herself, examined the can. "My treat. This way I know you'll have it."

"Sweetheart," Alfonso said, shooting a glance at Carla "Make sure she *uses* it." He looked sternly at me. "It doesn't work sitting on your shelf." Then, as if he couldn't help himself, he stroked my hair: "I'm an artist!"

Skinny and dressed in black, I might have taken him seriously, ex-cept for the pink shoes. I paid my bill, a major ouch, and we headed out. Collapsing into Carla's Mercedes, we made tracks for Laurel.

Armor-clad in Spike! and new makeup, perhaps I appeared invin-cible. Whatever the reason, Carla decided to dig some more. "So you wanna tell me about it?"

"What?"

"Tell me to shut up if you want, but maybe you should talk about what happened, when your mom died." Carla's expression grew tenta-tive. "I mean, if you want to."

Her body held the tension of someone creeping through a mine field. Would you do that for somebody you didn't like? I exhaled some air.

"I was an orphan, left with a pedophile." There, I'd said it and hadn't experienced a mental breakdown.

Carla watched the road. "I'm listening."

"Stanley, my stepfather, one sick dude. He was after me even before Mom died. I'd probably have run anyway." I spoke to the dashboard.

"Maybe two weeks after she died . . . I'd been locking my bedroom door at night, sleeping with my clothes on. Then he tried to break in. I went out the window and down the fire escape. That was it."

"So he never . . ."

"I said that was it!" My voice shook, my hands curled into fists.

"Right." Carla paid close attention to her driving for a few beats. But curiosity rode her hard. "You've been on your own since? How'd you ever avoid social services?"

I sagged into the leather upholstery. "I climbed the goddamn chain-link fence at Pimlico." I remembered the cold barbed-wire at the top, how it drew blood. "I spent the night, balled up in the corner of a stall, hoping I wouldn't get trampled."

"Why Pimlico?"

"My mother loved the race track, she used to take me there. She was crazy about horses and she liked to bet. The first time I went, I fell in love with those horses. They seemed almost supernatural, so beautiful and proud. They gave me a whole other world."

Carla slowed the Roadster, and pulled onto Route197 from the Baltimore Washington Parkway. "So you slept in a stall?"

I sighed, my body slowly relaxing. "I lied about my age, begged this trainer for work, walked hots."

"Hots?"

"You've seen the people leading Louis's horses around after they've galloped or raced?"

"Right. But where did you live?"

"This groom, he knew I slept in stalls, got me some ID, told me to apply for a groom's license and backstretch housing. It worked."

"Jeeez. Weren't you scared? I couldn't have done that."

"Beat living with Stanley. Kind of like running away to the circus. Everyone sort of looked after me."

Carla appeared dubious. "I think your spinning a rose on this picture."

Maybe I was, and I still overreacted when guys, like the one in the 7-Eleven, leered at me, but I felt safe now. No one could abandon me, and nothing would ever equal the terror of the night I ran from Stanley.

9

I rolled into Laurel Park at dawn the next morning, cut my engine, and headed for Jim's barn. A light drizzle cooled the air, and a potpourri of molasses, liniment, and neat's-foot oil hung heavy in the damp air. I ran my fingers through my newly shorn hair and stepped into the shedrow.

Kenny Grimes barreled around the corner and stopped abruptly. "Hey Latrelle," he said, sounding puzzled. "You look different. You look . . . good."

"Was that supposed to be a compliment? Never mind," I said, waving my hand. "Have you seen today's schedule?"

He had, and we tacked up the horses for our first set. I took out Bourbon Bonnet for her first strong gallop since she'd raced. Jim gave the horses three or four days off after a race, then maybe a couple of easy gallop days before sharpening them up. I pushed her into a two-minute-lick, Kenny right alongside on a bay colt entered to run in four days. I had a pretty good clock in my head and could tell by Bourbon's rhythm and speed we moved at about 15 seconds to the furlong. There's eight furlongs to a mile, so at this rate a mile took two minutes, giving it the name two-minute lick. We zipped counterclockwise around the track, staying near the inside rail. Slower-moving horses went the other or "wrong" way. They mostly jogged or walked near the outside rail.

There's a little lake in the infield at Laurel, and that morning Canada geese swam on its surface and pushed beaks into the damp ground near the water's edge. A pair of the birds flew in, low, over our heads, five or six goslings flapping and honking in their wake. They splashed down on the lake, wings folding, tail feathers wiggling. A set of three horses, hugging the rail, abruptly blocked my view of the geese. The trio blasted by in a high-speed work, probably going in 12s, way faster than our 15 seconds to the furlong. The sound of their breathing and the cadence of their hooves played my favorite music.

When we'd done our mile, we walked the horses back to the barn. I finished untacking Bourbon Bonnet, and Juan, one of the Mexican grooms, led her away while I leaned my elbows on the shoulder-high perimeter barn wall. A laundry line strung between roof support posts held green, red, and blue horse bandages above my head. I settled beneath some dry red ones and looked out across the way, catching a breather.

Helen's Dream busted around a corner in Clements' shedrow, an alarmed exercise boy astride. He yanked her mouth, and she went straight up in the air and fell sideways into the wooden stall wall. The rider shrieked. A groom rushed up, grabbed Helen's bit. She lashed out with a front foot, knocking the groom to the side. Then she proceeded to buck and leap on down the shedrow, carrying her terrified rider out of sight around the far corner.

I shook my head, feeling bad for the rider. Was Helen's Dream a hopeless hellion, or did she have some physical problem like an abscessed tooth? Anyone with a bad toothache would go berserk if somebody shoved a piece of metal in her mouth and jerked on it. Equine dental problems weren't uncommon. Oh boy, here she came, cantering around the near corner, her saddle empty, stirrups flopping. Another groom joined the one she'd knocked aside, and together they managed to drag her into a stall.

Good thing those horse bandages partially hid me, because I couldn't drop the big grin off my face. The exercise boy reappeared and seemed okay, except Clements followed right behind, reaming him out, his voice loud and angry. This rider guy was having a bad day.

Suddenly he whirled on Clements. "I don't have to take this shit from you!" he yelled. I quit."

Clements raised a fist and I cringed, thinking he would hit the boy. But the kid turned and stomped away, cursing and muttering under his breath. Clements moved opposite Helen's stall, grabbed an empty bucket and hurled it inside. Helen responded by kicking the wall and shoving her head into the aisle way, ears pinned, bared teeth clacking.

I put my hand over my mouth to keep the laughter inside, mentally applauding her. Right then I renamed her Hellish.

Martha Garner emerged from Jim's office, spotted me and came over. "Honey, are you hiding under those bandages?"

"Oh no, just watching a horse in that barn lying catty-cornered to ours. She's a bad actor, but gorgeous as hell."

"My Ed used to have one like that. All the talent in the world, but more likely to misbehave than win. Drove Ed crazy." Martha stared over to Clements' barn. "Now there's a handsome one."

I felt his eyes even before I found the subject of Martha's interest. Jack Farino stood outside Clements' barn in the shadow of a hay truck. This guy always spotted me first, like he was spying on me.

"Look at him. Makes me think of those Gypsies," said Martha. "Kinda dark and mysterious?"

Farino knew he'd been noticed and eased around the edge of the truck, disappearing from our sight. "That one could steal your heart away," said Martha, "like a Gypsy in the night." This last part she sang out loud.

The old Martha had returned. I should have known when she'd shown up in a raspberry jacket.

"That's the second hunk I've seen today," she continued. "That Clay Reed stopped by here earlier. I think you were out with Kenny. Now he's a cutie pie."

"Clay, what did he want?" I didn't mention I had a date with him Saturday night, afraid Martha might expect girl talk and tell me again how I should put a hook in him.

"There's a two-year-old colt with two crosses of Destroyer in the pedigree, out of a nice mare. He thinks he can get him for a good price. Jim's going to look at the horse today, and if he likes him, Clay will seal the deal, and I'll have a new horse."

"That's great, Martha." I grinned at her enthusiasm and also with relief. We needed another horse in the barn, and I needed to get ready for Coca Mocha and the red dress.

I said goodbye to Martha and passed Clements' barn on my way to the car, wondering about Farino and what connection he had to Clements.

10

I stood before my bathroom mirror, amazed by the rounded cleavage escaping from my red dress, finally understanding why they called it the Miracle Bra. Slippers, fluffy and purring, hopped from floor to toilet seat to the counter, where he inspected the can of Spike! Earlier, inspired by Alfonso's magical ability to transform mediocrity, I'd groomed my kitty to cat-show readiness, maybe even Madison Square Garden. He'd almost purred himself to death when I did this, then spent time showing off his legs, which resembled feather pantaloons.

I'd done my best with my new makeup and mousse and thought I looked pretty good. I stared at Slippers for a moment, grabbed the Spike! and squirted a little onto my palm. I dabbed it on the top of his head and made a little point, which quickly stiffened, creating the illusion of a miniature knight's helmet. We both gazed into the mirror, in awe of our appearance.

Carla and Louis were picking me up and driving to Coca Mocha, where we'd meet Clay. This date was excessively arranged. I hadn't even spoken to Clay since I'd met him at the Laurel Jockey's Club, and to be truthful, the evening felt awkward. Yet a low level-hum of excitement pulsed in my core as I stuffed some essentials into my new black bag.

Someone knocked on my door, and I peeked through the view hole and saw Louis. I opened the door. Louis stood there wearing a loud blue shirt and gold neck-chain and cologne.

"She made you look gorgeous," he said. "I heard about the makeover. Carla sure knows her stuff. Is she amazing or what?"

Another one who needed to work on his delivery. Louis came in while I grabbed my bag and a lace shawl. Slippers strolled silently into the middle of my living room and sat motionless, gazing up at Louis.

"Does that cat have a point on its head?" Louis asked.

How do you explain putting mousse on your cat's head? "I don't want to talk about it," I said and closed the door behind us.

We climbed into Louis's Jaguar and headed downtown. Carla, who'd been waiting in the passenger seat, wore a leopard-print outfit that appeared painted on her body. Someday I'd figure out how she did this without looking cheap. Maybe the confidence and intelligence radiating from those brown eyes stopped disparaging thoughts cold.

But here I sat in a shiny Jaguar, feeling pretty and rolling into the big night out. Definitely cool. The Jag's engine purred as we motored downtown, city night lights reflecting off its silver hood. We pulled up to a ruby-colored awning with the words *Coca Mocha* lettered on the side in fancy gold script. A man dressed in white shirt and pants opened the car doors for Carla and me. A valet took the Jag and we went inside.

The room held a spicy, exotic scent and glowed with low, warm lighting. Club music blasted, and a dance floor pulsed with male dancers in tight pants and women in eye-catching cleavage. Louis conferred with the maitre d' and we were led away, past tables draped in ruby cloths, with candles burning in glittering red-and-gold jars. A woman in an astonishingly short skirt leaned over one table, using a miniature flame-thrower to light a man's cigar. I hoped she didn't lean over any further — I might embarrass myself by gawking. We rounded a corner and there, ensconced in a booth, lounged Clay Reed.

I'd forgotten how good he looked. Tonight he'd dressed in black, dynamite with his blond hair, and those blue eyes lit with pleasure when he saw me. My stomach lurched and my tongue tied up, not that it mattered with the loud music. We settled into the booth, and I sat, thigh to thigh, with a guy that probably broke hearts on a regular basis.

Clay ordered drinks, and the waiter returned with frosted glasses filled with pink foam, amber liquid and floating umbrellas. These things looked dangerous. I took a sip. Smooth and sweet, went down like honey. Definitely dangerous.

The music broke, and a bald man in a white silk jacket approached our table. His eyes bulged slightly over a nose as large as a horse's, only not as pretty. "Carla, sweetheart. Louis, a pleasure to see you."

Carla introduced him as Enrique, the Coca Mocha manager, and his gaze swept over us and came to rest on Carla with a look of adoration. Her blond hair tangled with the leopard print that stretched like skin over her chest and shoulders.

"Darling, you always look so fabulous." He turned to Clay and me. "This woman keeps our diners hungry for more. Her steaks and chops . . ." He rolled his protruding eyes toward the ceiling. "And her breasts. Carla, your breasts are so delicious."

"And for you, Enrique, they always will be," Carla said, with a slow smile.

I managed not to spit my drink out, but my eyes watered furiously. Carla glanced at me and burst out laughing.

"Chicken breasts, Nikki. We're talking about chicken breasts."

Yeah, right.

Clay grinned. "Such an innocent," he said. Come on, dance with me."

Since nobody has more aerobic stamina than a jockey, I wowed them on the dance floor. Besides, I'd acquired some good moves following my mom when she used to boogie around the rowhouse, where she weaned me on Little Feat and The Rolling Stones.

Later, sated with drink, laughter, and dancing, I figured I'd never had a better time. Clay had been funny, sweet, and attentive, and had never once looked down the front of my dress. But he moved closer now, caught my eye, and slid one arm around my shoulders, fingers lightly grazing my skin. An electric connection jolted me.

"You fascinated me the day I met you," he said close to my ear. "Beauty and bravery is a hard combination to resist."

My tongue refused to make words. I think I smiled.

"I'd like to talk to you, but this music. . . .," he made a frustrated gesture with his hand. "There's a place near here. You want to go?"

Like wild horses could keep me away. "Sounds good."

Clay said something to Louis, who sent me a vague wave. I wanted to say goodbye to Carla, but she'd gone to powder her nose and Clay's hand on my wrist was insistent. Outside a line to get into the dance club snaked down the block and disappeared around the corner. We stepped along the wide pavement, soaking up the cool, smoke free air, and talked about horse racing, a subject my tongue handled with agility.

A face near the end of the club line stopped me cold. Dennis O'Brien stood there sucking on a cigarette, his arm around a young woman. I hadn't seen him since he'd whipped a welt onto my face and pushed Flame Thrower into the rail. Maybe Jim thought I should let it go, but a hot eruption of anger produced a desire to tear into Dennis. I took a step toward him, but Clay touched my arm.

"What?"

"That guy over there," I said, my voice almost a hiss.

Clay scanned the line and his touch turned to a grasp.

Then Dennis saw me, his stance becoming arrogant, his lips smirking. "Hey, little miss Nikki. Lost any races recently?" He waved his hand through the air like he held a crop, until his eyes slid to my date and he suddenly looked worried. Maybe he should have noticed the stud before he whipped the pony.

"Look, buddy," said Clay. "Why don't you shut up before you get yourself into trouble?"

I thought Dennis would spout off at Clay — he was that cocky. But he surprised me by shrugging and turning away.

Clay's hold on my arm tightened. "Come on, Nikki, let's get out of here. You're way above brawling with trash like that."

I digested his advice. Maybe I'd continue this fight on the racetrack. I let Clay lead me away. We moved through a canyon of tall buildings, any available stars blanketed by the murky fog of light pollution. Instead, city lights twinkled from the canyon walls, street lamps loomed above us, and car beams bounced and dipped as they swept along the broken concrete of the downtown streets.

A small, posh hotel stood between two office buildings, an elegant awning and doorman drawing us in. Clay led me into a small, quiet bar with green velvet upholstered booths. In my red dress, I felt like a Christmas card as I sank into the cushy fabric. Clay surprised me by sitting close, on my side of the booth. A waiter appeared.

"Nikki, let me order you a nightcap?"

I didn't have to ride in the morning, but I didn't want to lose a day from booze indulgence the night before. "I've probably had enough," I said, hoping I hadn't just committed some kind of date-night faux pas. I'd learned fancy words like that from the rich girls who ate my mother's cooking at Miss Potter's School. I'd been exposed to their upscale chatter during riding classes. I'd also been exposed to their derision. My head felt spongy. How much had I imbibed? *Imbibed?* I giggled.

Clay grinned. "You are so adorable. One last drink won't hurt you, and this is a special night." His fingertips traced a small circle on my wrist.

The liquor accelerated the sudden eroticism that surged through me, headed south, and pooled as liquid warmth between my thighs. I met Clay's gaze and noted his quick intake of air.

"Bring us two champagne cocktails," he said, his fingers never leaving my wrist, his eyes stroking my lips.

Our drinks arrived, and I grabbed the glass like a lifeline. I couldn't remember feeling this aroused. I didn't even know this guy.

Clay straightened up, moving away from me slightly, as if sensing my confusion.

"I met Martha Garner recently. She thinks the world of you, Nikki. A shame about that stakes mare, Gilded Cage."

"That hurt a lot of people," I said.

"Someone told me you had her for the Venus. You must've been upset."

When I shrugged and looked away, Clay forged ahead.

"You're a talented rider — just need some good horses that'll let you show your stuff. I've got an excellent replacement in mind for Martha.

This guy's a two-year-old with pedigree up the ying-yang. He's about two works away from his first race and he just threw in a bullet. It's an awesome opportunity for Martha. You too, Nikki."

"I think Martha will get another horse when she's ready." She didn't need a horse pushed on her, not so soon after losing Gildy. And a bullet — the fastest morning work at a given distance, same track, same day — only rated if the competition was good. Suppose the horse produced a bullet work breezing against a bunch of cheap has-beens?

The waiter appeared with two champagne glasses effervescing with a concoction that seemed to glow. Clay leaned into me, sort of enthusiastic and bubbly, like the drink the waiter set before me.

"That's just it. If she waits, she could lose out. Talk to her Nikki, tell her you've heard great things about this horse. Don't blow this opportunity." His eyes shone with a driving intensity.

"Clay, I don't think so. I wouldn't be comfortable telling Martha what to do."

He looked a bit taken aback, then said, "No pressure, babe. I'll work another angle."

Somewhere nearby a familiar tune played. Wait, I knew that one. The lyrics "we're in the money," floated through my head. I watched Clay dig in his jacket pocket. He pulled out a cell phone, and it was still playing that melody. He must really like money.

He gave me a what-can-you-do look and took the call.

"Hey, buddy," he said, then listened. "Don't you worry, he's all but sold. Yeah, right." He grinned, "those two crosses of Destroyer will clinch the deal. Yeah, like we talked about. You're damn right that's good money. *Super* money."

He listened some more, a smug expression settling on his face. "Okay Yeah, later." He folded up the phone, and it disappeared into his pocket.

Hadn't Martha said Clay wanted her to buy a horse with two crosses of Destroyer? Was Clay brokering a deal at both ends, taking his five-percent commission twice? If not illegal, surely unethical? And he wanted me to help him? I pushed the champagne away and glared at him.

"What?"

"Martha told me you wanted her to buy a horse with Destroyer in the pedigree. Is that the same horse you're selling for your buddy here?"

A wary expression flitted across his face. "Not at all, Nikki. There's plenty of horses with Destroyer in the family."

"Yeah, but two crosses?"

He looked annoyed. "Nikki, this is my business, how I make a living, not some Girl Scout Cookie drive."

He had that right. "I don't like that your padding the price to line your own pockets. And Martha's the one paying. She's paid enough already."

"You're wrong, Nikki. There's two different horses. I wouldn't do that to Martha."

Why didn't I believe him? Maybe the earlier smug look, like a satisfied con who's pulled a scam. He reached for my hand, but I snatched it away, sad to feel the magic dissipating. I wanted that warm rush, that seductive thrill, but not like this.

"I want to go home," I said.

11

I took a taxi back to Laurel, glad I'd remembered to stuff cash into my black bag. The memory of Clay's chill expression and irritation was unpleasant.

"You shouldn't be so quick to judge," he'd said. "You've got me all wrong, but suit yourself."

I sighed and settled back into the taxi's bench seat. In the rear-view mirror, the eyes of the cinnamon-skinned driver watched me. Layers of black cloth wound about his head, making me feel like I fled America's capital with a terrorist disguised as a taxi driver. Of course, this man probably had me pegged as a rich party bitch. How do you know about people?

I should have seen the con in Clay from miles away, the way he'd schmoozed Janet LeGrange, given her that excited smile. The same smile that danced so recently on my lips. He seemed to genuinely like women — just didn't mind profiting by their inevitable attraction to his handsome face and flattering ways. Any man who took advantage of a woman like that dragged me right back to my stepfather, Stanley. I shuddered.

"You cold, missy?" asked my turbaned driver. He started to roll up the window that was cracked about two inches.

"No, I'm fine." The car had a peculiar odor, like stale sweat mixed with pungent spice. "Open is good."

He grinned at me in the mirror, and we motored out New York Avenue toward the Baltimore Washington Parkway. I arrived at my apartment after midnight, deflated, tired, and glad I didn't have to show up at the track by 6 A.M. I wasn't looking forward to relating the last part of the evening to Carla. She'd been so determined to fix me up with Clay. I'd probably downplay the con angle.

Slippers greeted me at the door, the little point on his head listing to one side, drooping.

"I know just how you feel," I said, and scooped him into my arms. We agreed to call it a night, purring and sleep being high on the agenda.

In the morning, a yearning drew me back to Jim's barn, a need to soak up those familiar racetrack surroundings. As I drove in around nine, my tension eased, the glitz and uncertainty of the previous night fading.

A horse van stood outside Clements' barn, and a reluctant Helen's Dream, or Hellish as I liked to call her, fought with a groom near the van's ramp. I parked and double-timed it over to the groom. He wasn't such a bad guy. At least he didn't beat on horses.

"Hey, Charlie. They shipping that filly out?"

The groom's pudgy face held a scowl, no doubt put there by Hellish. "Not soon enough for me. You wanna help me get this bitch on here?"

Hellish emitted a growling grunt and tried to leap backward.

"Here, let me have her," I said.

Charlie handed her over, and I eased up and scratched her neck, cooed a little, and she let me lead her into the trailer like a lamb. I felt smug.

"Where's she going?" Now that I'd helped, I knew he'd tell me. Before, maybe not. Clements tended to be secretive. Loose-lipped help received a quick slug of Clements' anger.

"Dark Mountain," he said with satisfaction.

My hand snapped Hellish's halter to the trailer tie and froze. A low-level dread spread through me. "Why?" I almost whispered.

"Don't look at me like that," said Charlie. "She's asked for it, nasty bitch."

"No one will buy her at Dark Mountain. She'll go to the killers." The town Dark Mountain, up near the Pennsylvania border, had a farm auction notorious for getting rid of unwanted horses. I'd never been there but I'd heard buyers from the slaughterhouses went there regularly to hook horses that couldn't find a new home.

"Look, it's not my problem," said Charlie. "I've got to load another one and drive them up to Dark Mountain for tonight's auction. Don't have another sale for two weeks, and Clements' wants them out of here, so don't give me a hard time." He couldn't hold my gaze and addressed my shoulder. "Could you stay with her while I get the other one?"

I felt like telling him to shove it, but nodded, realizing I wanted these few moments with Hellish. I scratched her neck some more while we waited in the trailer. Her breath was warm and fragrant. Charlie waddled out with a small gelding that limped.

"What's wrong with him?"

"Ah, he's got a microfracture on his shin. He's slower 'n dirt, not worth fixing up."

I'd seen this handsome little dude on the track and knew him to be a quiet, sensible type. They called him Silver Box, and he was cute, with a long forelock over a white blaze and showy white socks. A perfect Pony

Club horse for a teenage girl, he'd heal with a little time. He might find a good home. But Hellish . . .

I stepped off the van. Charlie raised the ramp and went around to the cab and climbed in. He cranked the engine, and when he rolled past me and I could see Hellish's head near a small, open window. She turned, stared right at me, and nickered. Sudden tears fractured my vision. *Enough.* This one wasn't going to die. I swiped at my eyes and hurried over to Jim's office.

I burst in, agitated, adrenalin pumping. Jim's gaze left his charts and veterinary records, registering surprise.

"I gave you the day off."

"Would you let me borrow your rig? I have to go to Dark Mountain."

"What the hell you want to go there for?"

I explained about Hellish, how I'd need a stall for her in his barn, how he had to lend me his truck and trailer.

"I probably should refuse you for your own good, but hell . . . you got enough money?"

I leapt around the desk and threw my arms around him. He stiffened and gave me a little half-push away. Then shoved his keys at me.

"You drive carefully now and don't be wrecking my rig." His voice sounded gruff, but a smile tugged his lips as I turned to run from the room.

Jim's red Ford 250 fired right up. I backed it up to the two-horse trailer, hooked them together, and took off up Route 1, merging onto Route 32, where I headed north. Almost two hours later, northwest of Hagerstown, the ground lost its lush green, rising rocky and bare-patched into low mountains. Jim's V-8 hummed up the steep inclines, the trailer rattling along behind.

I pulled into an Exxon for gas and coffee, then studied my map while I sipped hazelnut and bit into a chocolate bar that somehow followed me from the food mart. Heading out of the gas station, I felt the caffeine and sugar boiling in my system. I might tear the auction grounds apart looking for Hellish. Good thing I hadn't downed a beer — someone could get hurt.

My bravado and anger dwindled into surprise when I finally reached the sale. A huge circus tent rose behind the parking lot. Small pens holding sheep, donkeys, and goats flanked the tent to the right. A wooden barn, painted bright green, held position on the left. Ponies and horses watched with curiosity over stall doors as children and parents strolled the grounds, eating hotdogs and cotton candy. Wood smoke from a food concession wafted on a light breeze, bringing the smell of sizzling steaks and barbequed chicken, while the scent of popcorn and beer permeated the atmosphere. A musky scent of animal drifted through the grounds.

Beyond the horse barn, additional pens held cows, some llamas, and even an ox. The air buzzed with anticipation. Two bright-eyed boys rushed past clutching boxes with bunnies. What had I expected? Men in hooded black robes wielding sledgehammers? Well, yeah.

I fought the urge to rush into the barn to search for Hellish, and instead headed into the tent. I needed to find the office, learn about bidding requirements, auction rules and regulations. Through the tent opening, bleachers rose on either side of a long dirt runway. This path, enclosed by a sturdy post-and-board fence, opened at the far left end, where another tent door led toward the horse barn. An auctioneer's stand stood at the opposite end. Behind that I spotted a double-wide trailer rolled inside the tent. A sign labeled "office" hung over its door.

An excessively fat woman wearing a maroon cap and an extra-large Redskins jersey, had me fill out a form for my name and address. Her green-and-red name tag read "Bertha." She scribbled my driver's license number in a box at the top with one hand, while the other ferried corn chips from a plastic bag to her mouth.

"I only need this if you're paying with a check," she said, her voice a mumble of chips.

"No, I brought cash." Though not armed with Carla's expertise in per-pound meat prices, I figured Hellish wouldn't fetch more than $500.

After scurrying from Bertha's office into the roundtop, my attention was caught by a small crowd gathered around chickens in cages. Roosters crowed and preened. A man in a green cap led the people from cage to cage, his voice running in the auctioneer's singsong. I walked over there and immediately fell for a black-and-white rooster with fluffy feathers growing down to his toenails. His soft plumes and pantaloons reminded me of Slippers. An index card taped to his cage identified him as a "Barred Rock Cochin."

Time for a mental slap. I hadn't come here to buy a chicken. I bustled off to find Hellish, got almost as far as the tent door leading to the horse barn when I saw the rodent-like face of Dennis O'Brien.

He stood next to the bleachers studying an auction program. I didn't need a confrontation, didn't want him to see me. I scooted behind a family of five. The tallest two children, girls about 12, talked about the new horse they hoped to find for trail riding. Maybe a little showing. The father towed a small boy by the hand. The mother, in well-worn riding togs, led the way. I eased into the midst of this family as they moved through the door and headed for the horse barn. Dennis never saw me.

I sped up next to the woman. "Excuse me. If you're looking for a horse, there's a nice one here. He's quiet, kind, got an injury that'll heal, but probably keep his price down."

The woman looked a me suspiciously. "Are you selling him?"

Mistrustful of horse traders. Who could blame her? "No. I'm an exercise rider, seen him at the racetrack. Hope he'll find a good home." I threw a glance at the girls. "His name's Silver Box, he's real handsome."

Their eyes lit up and the mother sighed, "We'll look at him."

We moved into the barn. I spotted Silver Box right off. He poked his head into the aisle from his wooden stall, his rakish forelock partially hiding one mischievous eye. "That's him," I said.

One of the girls squealed, "Oh, he's so cute!"

I left them to it and searched for Hellish.

I passed some old scarecrows with hip bones and ribs sticking out, their eyes dull and patient. They'd reached the end of their story. I cringed at the thought of what awaited them. I couldn't save them all, but I could find Hellish, keep her from the butcher's knife.

I pushed on past stalls with ponies and dappled Percherons, rounded a corner and moved down a new aisle. A kind-eyed young man, tall and slender, paced before a group of about six stalls. He'd nailed up a placard that read, "Sensible, sound racehorses looking for a good home."

I hurried over to him. "I like your sign. Why are they for sale?"

He pushed some brown hair out of his eyes. "They've got a bad case of the 'slows,' but any of 'em would make a good riding horse. You interested?" He looked hopeful.

"Sorry, I'm here to save a rogue."

"Good for you," he said. "But if you change your mind . . ." He waved a hand at the horses.

I gave them a brief glance. They looked pretty good, mostly nondescript bays without much presence. A brief appraisal showed clean legs and healthy eyes. I wished them well and hurried on.

Ahead, a man shouted and yanked a small girl to safety as gleaming bared teeth threatened over a stall door. I caught a glimpse of a lightening-bolt blaze. Had to be Hellish. I reached her stall, found her glowering in the back. She had a white piece of paper glued to her hip with a big number 13 on it. Perfect. At least I knew where she fit into the schedule.

I needed to find a seat on the bleachers, get ready to bid. Slipping into the tent, I scanned the area for Dennis but didn't see him. They should be racing at Shepherds Town and Dennis usually scored a fair number of rides. His presence at a dog-and-pony-show auction made no sense. He didn't figure for a bunny-buyer.

I picked a spot up front near the auctioneer's stand, my fingers tap-dancing on my thigh, keeping time to a tune of anxiety emanating from my core. What if someone fell for Hellish's beauty and had real money to burn? The French consider horsemeat a delicacy. Who knew how much they'd pay? Did I really think I could train such a hellion?

I longed to get this over with and squirmed on my seat. A familiar prickle crawled down my back, that creepy feeling of someone watching.

12

Near the top of the bleachers someone wearing a blue baseball cap lurked behind a newspaper. A head edged over the top of the paper, and a pair of dark glasses studied me. Not a bad disguise, but the prick of this particular man's stare, the sharp cheekbones, and dark hair were all too familiar. Farino. I threw him a big smile and waved. He withdrew behind the news.

Both Dennis and Jack Farino? Too weird for me. I almost wished I'd worn a disguise. The loudspeaker crackled, and a man led a cream-colored pony through the side door.

"Folks, welcome to Dark Mountain Sales. Time for the horses and ponies, and we're starting with a real pretty one. And who'll give me one hundred dollars . . ." The voice took off in the almost unintelligible singsong I'd heard by the chicken cages.

Feeling like a sitting duck on the open riser, I drifted toward the side door to find a less vulnerable position. A small group of buyers and browsers stood outside the tent inspecting the line of horses parading from the barn toward us.

A young man and a girl, both in cowboy boots and western hats, strapped a saddle onto a sturdy bay horse. The cowboy swung aboard. He rode the horse into the tent as the cream pony came out. The cowboy jogged and cantered the bay for the crowd, then two guys in auction caps set up a rail, and the rider booted the bay on over the jump. The auctioneer dropped his hammer on a price of $950, and a starry-eyed boy watched his dad sign the ticket.

Someone had told me the slaughter price for a horse ran about $600 and I hoped they were right. I only had $785 in cash. I'd cleaned out my bank account before leaving Laurel and wished I'd thought it through, been less impetuous, and grabbed Jim's offer for money. Watching more horses sell, I realized the two men in auction caps were spotters, constantly watching the crowd for live bidders.

A man about 30-something hung in the doorway. He'd buzzed his blond hair into a severe cut, and wore overalls and heavy boots. The spotters' eyes constantly swept his way, as if he were a major player. I got a bad feeling about him. The fifth horse to emerge from the barn shambled by, old and thin, and buzz-cut locked right on him. The horse was barely in the ring thirty seconds before the blond bought him for

$750. Guy had to be a killer.

Panic surged through my gut. Hellish weighed more and stood over 16 hands tall. My cash wouldn't cover her. I looked in my purse at the rubber-banded bills. Shit! Lying useless in the bottom of my bag were the "essential" makeup items Carla insisted I carry. "You never know when you'll need them," she'd said.

Yeah right. If I hadn't spent all that money at the mall . . .

Horse number six plodded by about the time my brain rocked with a go-for-broke idea. I zipped into the tent, not caring who saw me. Dashing into the double-wide office, I halted before Bertha. She was fighting with the plastic wrap on a bag of cashews.

"Do you take . . . I think they call it an absentee bid? You know, leave money with you and somebody with the auction bids on the horse for me so I don't have to?"

Her plump hand, finally filled with cashews, paused, then rushed for her mouth. She held up a finger in a just-a-moment sign, and I felt like slapping her around.

She swallowed.

"Yes, ma'am. You fill out a form earlier?"

"Yes. Latrelle," I said, spelling it out.

"We need the highest price you're willing to pay in cash money, but my boys are fair. They won't bid the horse up. I'll phone your limit over, and you pay what the market bears."

I dug out my money roll and thrust it at her.

She took her time pulling off the rubber band and counting the bills. A frown produced a small canyon between her brows. "Miss, this won't pay for much more than a small pony. Is that what you're gettin?"

"Whatever, but she's coming up soon. Could you call that bid over?"

She drew back, gave me her hard stare. "Don't get your panties all bunched up. I'll take care of it." She reached for the phone with one hand, digging for cashews with the other.

I left Bertha, found a ladies room, dashed in and stood before a small mirror, cracked and scored with grime. I pulled out Carla's essentials, swiped mascara onto my lashes, dabbed concealer under my eyes and gel rouge onto my cheeks. I lined my eyes in black. Lipstick. Much better, but something was missing.

What would Carla do? I'd never tried this before, but when the going gets tough . . .

I grabbed toilet paper, wadded it into balls, lowered the half-zip on my cotton top, and stuffed my bra. The top's heavy fabric hid any lumpiness, and in the mirror cleavage erupted. Time to zip up and head out.

I jogged through the tent, heading for the meat buyer's hangout spot. He'd held his position, bidding now on a large palomino with a slow, crippled walk. Made me sick. I inhaled a quantity of air, slid the zipper back down, and eased over. "Feats Don't Fail Me Now," one of Mom's favorite songs, played in my head. I fixed a stare on the horse stumbling by and bumped into the man, dropping my bag at his feet.

He had plain, blue eyes, thin lips and a three-day-old stubble. His sleeveless tank displayed muscular arms, but his belly suggested a strong inclination to beer.

I tried to gaze at him like he was a rock star. "Hi," I said, drawing the word out, making my voice a little husky. "Sorry I bumped you." I got no reaction. Suppose he had no use for women?

Time to lean over and retrieve the bag. I pressed my arms against the sides of my breasts, and they obliged nicely, enhancing by at least a cup size. I rose slowly, to find the man's eyes locked on my chest. He ripped his gaze away and finished bidding on the palomino.

"What did you say your name was?" he asked with a slow smile.

If ever a woman felt like a piece of meat. "Dusty," I said. Hoping to beguile with a mask of lust, I sent him my best grin. In my peripheral vision, Silver Box ambled past us into the circus tent.

"Here's a good one," said Buzzcut.

My stomach clenched. Then I saw the mom in riding clothes, sitting in the front row of the bleachers. Her body line tense, she raised her hand and began bidding with determination. Relief flooded me when the family bought the horse for $800, outbidding Buzzcut. But he didn't drop out until $775, way too near my limit.

I moved closer to him, praying I could keep up my lecherous performance, amazed by my talent for deceit. My stepfather had jammed up my sexual flow years ago, and now this sudden capacity for acting lecherous, along with Clay Reed's ability to suffuse me with desire, surprised me. Then Hellish appeared, leaping and plunging as they tried to drag her to the tent.

Buzzcut examined the filly, then me. "Got two wild ones here today, and both just my type. Dusty, let me bid on this horse, then buy you a drink."

I struggled to appear relaxed and thirsty for sex. Hellish reared up, scattering shrieking children right and left. Fuck! What was I supposed to do?

Buzzcut put his arm around my waist and gave me a squeeze, his eyes glued to the area below my collarbones.

I pulled back. "That horse scares me. Couldn't we get that drink now?"

"Got a job to do, darlin', but I surely do love an anxious woman. Just give me a minute and I'll be done here."

And so would Hellish. I rose on tiptoes, leaning into the guy, brushing my breasts against his chest.

"Please."

"Oh, hell," he groaned. "Whatever you want." He forgot about Hellish and steered me in a lover's lockstep toward the beer stand.

Behind us I heard an announcement. "Folks, this filly doesn't wanna come into the tent, so were just gonna leave her outside for the bidding. Who'll give me one hundred dollars?"

I could use a beer.

13

A knot of people milled around the red Budweiser wagon. Fancy gold lettering decorated its wooden sides and the interior held squat, metal kegs that spouted foaming brew, permeating the air with the smell of beer. Buzzcut released me and ordered two tall ones from a man with a handlebar mustache and a yellow straw hat.

"I'm Butch," he said, handing me a plastic cup.

Maybe he should consider a name change, although butcher certainly fit his line of work. I couldn't think of anything to say, my brain too busy with escape plans. Like throwing myself on Hellish, bareback, and racing for the mountains. My ears strained to hear the auctioneer's hammer price on the filly.

Butch pulled me to the side and then behind the beer stand, leaning forward, tracing two fingers down my neck. He'd already downed half his beer, and I worried how much the full cup would accelerate this behavior. In the distance, barely audible, the auctioneer chanted for Hellish.

"You must really like horses," I said.

He blinked, then laughed. "Sure thing, darlin'. Horses are my business, got a whole trailer load of 'em. Got a nice little camper over there too. Wanna see?"

The alcohol on his breath, the escalating sense of being trapped, echoed a past I wanted to forget. The warm breeze shifted, carrying the auctioneer's voice our way. The bidding stalled a moment, then I clearly heard him: "I've got $500 who'll give me $550?" He repeated himself three times. An endless pause followed, then his hammer dropped on $500.00

"Yes!" My fist pumped in the air and I could feel the grin stretching my face.

"Baby, are you cute when you get excited or what?" Butch stared at me like I was a slice of birthday cake with his name on it. He grasped my wrist. "Are you excited?"

I snatched my hand away. "Not about you." I took two steps back. "Hey, thanks for the beer."

"Wait a minute." Dried foam clung to Butch's stubble, making him look foolish, but there was nothing comical about his narrowed eyes or the big hand that reached for me. "You're not leavin'. We've got some business to take care of." He grabbed my wrist again, only this time it hurt.

"No . . . we don't." I threw my drink in his face, jerked loose, and made a run for it.

"You cock-teasing bitch." His sharp words stung my back like darts.

My beer may have doused his fire, or perhaps the two bodybuilder types throttled his anger. They'd been watching from the beer wagon, and a last look back found them marching toward him, frowns darkening their faces. Whatever the reason, Butch didn't come after me.

I ran past a pen crammed with bleating sheep, startled to see Jack Farino lounging against its wooden rail, watching me, shaking his head. Could that be a grin tugging his lips? I moved too fast to tell and felt an odd regret that he might have seen me playing the tart. Why would I care? I sped even faster.

Back in the office Bertha sat behind the counter savoring a candied apple. She gave me another just-a-minute sign, wiping her mouth with a paper towel, laying the partially eaten apple on a paper plate. The tart smell of fresh apple and caramel made me realize I hadn't eaten since the chocolate bar at the gas station earlier. Some diet — coffee, chocolate, and beer. I was starving for something healthy, but first I had to settle up.

"Did I get number 13?"

"You sure do rush. Boys just brought a sheet over. Lemme take a look-see." She stared at the paper while I fidgeted from one foot to the other. She gave the apple a longing glance but restrained herself. "You're Latrelle, right?"

I nodded.

"You got her for $500." She paused, a puzzled frown flitting over her face. "Huh, wonder where Butch was?" she said mostly to herself.

You don't want to know. I felt a grin tugging my lips and inside my head I was dancing.

Bertha signed a release for Hellish and gave me my change, minus the auction company's 10 percent commission. I'd use the $265 to buy feed for Hellish.

I thanked the woman, headed for the barn, and ran smack into Dennis coming out the entrance.

"I know what you did," he said without animosity.

I tried to sidestep around him.

"I saw you up there with Butch. Girl, you know how to operate." He looked impressed.

How typical of Dennis that deceit earned his respect.

"You wanna watch out for Butch. He can be a nasty shit."

"Thanks for the warning," I said, surprised to get any support from Dennis. I moved around him and headed for Hellish.

"Liked you better with your top undone." His laughter chased me down the aisle.

A hot shower, lots of soap. Couldn't get home and cleaned up fast enough. Had to get Hellish first. I rounded the corner into the next barn aisle. The tall brown-haired guy stood next to his placards and equine sale prospects. I slowed and moved toward him.

"Any luck?"

"Yeah," he nodded. "Sold these three to one guy." He had a bag of apples and offered one to a fine-boned mare. "Said he's gonna turn 'em into show horses."

"Great." I moved closer, inspecting the three animals in question. Bays with no white markings, they wouldn't catch a judge's eye. They were quite plain, except for one fellow who sported a peculiar whorl down the left side of his neck. The hairs grew in opposite directions from the cowlick. The top hairs pointed to his mane, the ones on the bottom toward his legs.

I hurried on and found Hellish standing with her face in the stall's far corner. Her formidable hindquarters barred my way. I returned to the brown-haired guy and asked if I could borrow a lead shank and buy an apple.

He handed over a shank and the sack of apples. "Take the bag," he said. "I'm done with 'em."

"Thanks," I said, looking inside. Two shiny apples lay in the bottom. I bit right into one, double-timed it back to Hellish, and stood outside her stall, munching on the apple and ignoring her. I let the tart scent drift to her nostrils. She did a slow about-face, and pushed her head toward me, ears pricked, nostrils slightly flared. I held out the remaining half, and it disappeared into her mouth. While she snuffled at the remaining apple, I snapped the lead shank to her halter. Using the fruit as bait, I led her to Ravinsky's trailer, hoping we wouldn't run into Butch. She balked at the trailer ramp, and before she worked herself into a rage, I bit into the second apple, releasing more fragrance. She changed her mind and followed me into the rig. When I had her all fastened up, I fed her the remaining fruit as a reward. Time to crank up the Ford engine.

Threading Jim's rig carefully through the crowded parking lot, I drew alongside a big stock trailer. Someone had jammed horses and ponies inside without thought to safety or comfort. The bony horses with the old patient eyes I'd seen earlier stared at me through the open bars. The crippled palomino. Silently, I blessed the charities out there, like Rollin' On Racehorse Rescue and CANTER. They did what they could to save horses from slaughter.

An image of Butch appeared in my side-view mirror. He hadn't seen me yet. Time to leave. I promised myself — any future race won, any windfall that came my way, a piece of it would go to one of those charities.

A last backward glance. Through the bars of the stock trailer the mournful eyes of the palomino seared me, branding my brain.

14

Kenny Grimes and I rode back to Ravinsky's barn. Our horses' metal-shod hooves clip-clopped on the pavement, accompanied by the squeak of saddle leather. A horde of pigeons skittered along the roof ridge of a nearby building. Probably taking a breather after scrounging for grain. They liked to peck up anything spilled from a feed bucket, would land inside a bucket if a horse didn't clean up. Management kept saying they'd do something about the birds, but as far as I could tell the population continued to explode.

Kenny hummed a Sting song. I looked for something besides pigeons to help block out images of Butch's crowded stock trailer. Approaching Clements' barn, my inner radar began to hum. Jack Farino stood talking to Dennis O'Brien outside the hard-eyed man's section of shedrow. What brought Dennis here? I'd never seen him on the Laurel backside before. His presence irritated me, like a wad of gum that follows you around, stuck to the bottom of your shoe.

Kenny and I applied boot-heel pressure to urge our horses into Ravinsky's barn. Who could blame their reluctance to leave the air and sunshine? Inside, I handed my gelding over to Ramon. He'd tuned the radio to the Spanish station, cranked it to a high decibel. Salsa music blared, and Ramon sang along, painfully off-key. When he disappeared around the corner with my horse, I eased over and twisted the volume knob to a less excruciating level.

Curious about Farino and Dennis, I turned to the catty-cornered barn. Had Farino been at the auction *with* Dennis? I hadn't seen them together, just Farino skulking behind a news paper. Now he disappeared into one of his stalls, but Dennis remained, as if waiting for someone.

A flash of jagged white caught my attention. Helen's Dream, her head over the stall gate, looking around, bright-eyed and curious. I'd gotten her settled in the night before and fed her a bucket of grain laced with chopped carrots and apples. Now she saw me staring and pinned her ears, withdrawing back into her stall. God forbid anyone should see her looking happy. I pictured her life, a long road paved over hard by ignorance and human error. It'd be a while before she came around.

Clements appeared across the way, clutching a bottle of eye drops. He spoke to Dennis, who jogged off toward the gravel lot where horse vans parked. Farino emerged from his stall, stood next to Clements, said something. Thick as thieves.

I turned back to Hellish. She'd get a day off before going to the track. I checked her water, hay, and bedding. Keeping her stall fell to me, not Ravinsky's salaried grooms. Good horsemanship consumed time, took planning. I remembered I was supposed to give the filly a five-in-one shot. Who knew if Clements bothered to inoculate his horses against tetanus, flu viruses, rhino, or encephalomyelitis?

Only licenced veterinarians were allowed to give injections at the racetrack. Anyone else using a syringe broke racing commission rules and Maryland state law — a law seeking to keep Maryland free of doped horses and fixed races. But it didn't take a rocket scientist to realize vaccinations could be purchased through a catalogue and administered "privately" for a fraction of the vet's fee. Especially when talking upwards of 30 horses in a trainer's barn.

Jim had asked earlier if I'd inject some of his horses for a free dose for Hellish. I didn't have any problem with it since the inoculation wasn't a prohibited substance. Besides, who was I to frown on the practice with my past history of stealing food from convenience stores?

Kenny'd volunteered to help and appeared now with a box of pre-loaded syringes. They hid under a couple of brushes inside a tack box. He held Hellish while I slid the needle into her neck muscle and de-pressed the plunger. She took it surprisingly well, and Kenny and I went around the shedrow with Jim's list, Kenny holding and me sticking over a dozen horses. We finished up, and Kenny brought a half filled trash bag into the last stall, stuffed the box of empty syringes inside, and filled the top with an old newspaper and some 7-Eleven coffee cups.

The loud rumble of a diesel engine sounded on the pavement. Dennis pulled up in a four-horse rig, left the engine droning and climbed out. He dropped the ramp on the trailer. Clements joined him right about the time Kenny ambled by with his trash bag. Farino came out to give a hand. Then the three of them waited for Kenny to drive away in his Dodge truck.

They took three nondescript bay horses off the trailer and into the barn. I just knew they were those Dark Mountain horses, the ones sup-posedly sold as show horses. If so, Clements' had brought three horses that couldn't run worth a damn into his racing stable. What sense did that make? I was dying to hear any conversation, but fat chance with that diesel blasting. Besides, I had a race to ride later, needed to clean up and catch a nap.

*   *   *

I finished a good third, only a length off the pace that afternoon, in a maiden claimer. Afterwards a respected trainer asked if I'd ride one of his good horses in an allowance race the following week. Things were looking up.

On my way out, Martha Garner waved at me in the horsemen's parking lot. I hadn't seen her since my night out with Clay. She'd finished shaking that desolate expression that rode her after Gildy's death. She wore a magenta Nike outfit and squinted at me through a cloud of cigarette smoke. A huge pink diamond grabbed my attention, winking through the haze, lying on her right ring finger. I tried not to gawk at it while we exchanged greetings. I wondered if tobacco companies shouldn't roll out cigarettes in pastel papers. Women who liked their clothes and accessories to match wouldn't be able to resist. Might be a lot of money in pastel cigarettes.

Then I remembered Clay and the horse with Destroyer in the pedigree. "Martha, you ever find a horse you liked?"

"Nah, Jim didn't like that horse Reed was pushing." She started to say more, but broke into a series of coughs. She glared at her cigarette, dropped it on the pavement and ground it under her heel. "I gotta to give these things up."

"I'm kinda glad you didn't get that horse," I said. "I'm not sure I trust Clay."

Martha threw me a sharp look.

I hesitated a moment. "I think he might like money more than ethics." Was I out of line?

Martha's eyes danced with humor. "Lord, Nikki, I've got better sense than to trust a man that good-looking. What a charmer. You mark my words, honey, a man that charming's hiding a snake in a basket somewhere."

Her comment lit me up. I pictured Clay piping a tune for a big cobra and giggled.

Martha nodded. "We'd both do well to stay clear of him. Too bad he's so damn good-looking."

Wasn't that the truth.

I left Martha and drove back to Jim's barn. Though I'd set out a bucket of grain and flakes of hay for Ramon to give Hellish, I still had an itch to see my filly. Her stall probably could stand a little pitchfork work. Ramon had agreed to clean in the morning for six bucks a pop, but morning was a long way off.

Besides, curiosity about those three bays plagued me. Maybe I'd slip over to Clements' barn later and have a look. The trainers and stable foremen were rarely around in the late afternoon, unless they had a horse racing. Clements didn't. Of course, who knew when Farino might be lurking about, but I could always mumble something lame about searching for the barn cat.

The mindless work of tossing Hellish's stall allowed my thoughts to roam without direction, and they settled on Gildy's death. Seemed the apprehension of her killer lay low on the county law enforcement's priority list. That bird-like insurance investigator Beamfelter had finally okayed Martha's payout, and dropped me as a suspect. Clay Reed. He hadn't given up — had left a couple of messages on my phone, but I'd avoided him, fearing my attraction for him would override good sense. I could almost hear that sexy voice, feel those warm fingers.

I stabbed the pitchfork at a lump of manure.

Hellish avoided me by moving to whatever part of the stall I wasn't cleaning. Apparently we'd reached some sort of truce, as she kept her head facing me. I had great respect for that other end. Those hindquarters could drive metal-shod hooves in multiple directions faster than speeding bullets.

I thought about Gildy, the man running from her stall, Dennis and his "show" horses. A snake-like presence slithered somewhere on the Laurel backstretch. I could sense its evil influence, just couldn't see it. Probably coiled in somebody's basket.

I finished my work, hung the pitchfork on its nail in the tackroom, and studied Clements' barn for a moment. I sensed no movement, heard no voices. The place had a deserted feel. I slipped over there, ducked inside the narrow opening of a partially closed sliding door. Stood waiting for my eyes to adjust to the barn's low light. Odd that Clements had fastened the shutters above the low cinderblock wall so early in the year. Most trainers waited until later to close up against the winter's chill

To my left, Farino's small section was raked and tidy. His horses munched hay and examined me with alert eyes. As I moved into Clements' area looking for those three bays, I frowned in distaste at the heavy smell of dirty bedding. Horses skulked in the back of stalls, sour and uninterested in human contact.

After 10 minutes of creeping around Clements' shedrow, I found only one of the horses. A horse I recognized instantly with that weird cowlick running down his neck. The whorl had been on the far side when they'd led him into the barn earlier, and I hadn't seen it.

The bay wore a halter with a brand-new name plate that read "Noble Treasure." Yeah, right. Horse probably couldn't win a $2,500 claimer at Shepherds Town. Had I stumbled into the basket?

The metal frame shrieked as someone shoved the sliding door and moved into the barn. Overhead lights flicked on. I froze. Clements and Dennis O'Brien stared at me from the entrance.

"What the fuck?" Clements, loud, heading right for me. "What're you doing in here?"

His pale eyes were moist and cold, like melting ice. An involuntary half-step away from him put the stall wall against my back. I'd never been this close to the man. Those eyes.

I swallowed some air. "Our barn cat's been sick — he's missing. Thought he might've crawled in here."

"You're full of shit." Clements' face so near I could smell his breath. Cough medicine.

Screw this guy. "I told you, I'm looking for our cat. He's not here, so I'll leave."

"She was up at Dark Mountain," Dennis said.

"Shut up," Clements' hissed at Dennis.

I eased sideways and stepped around Clements. Probably stupid, but I couldn't resist pointing at the whorly bay. "Isn't this one of the horses you bought at Dark Mountain, Dennis?"

Dennis adopted his sneering punk face. "You stupid bitch. You think you're so smart."

Clements' low voice stopped Dennis like a wall of ice. "You don't listen, O'Brien. I told you to shut the fuck up. You're stupid as they come." Then he turned on me. "I got no horse from Dark Mountain. This horse came down from New York. Mind your own damn business and stay the hell out of my barn!"

Seemed like a good time to leave.

15

Had there been a noise, or only a sharp echo from a fading dream? My eyes cracked open, slid to the clock. Three-forty A.M. Too early to rise, but I could tell my brain was in full gear and on some level, disturbed. Memories of my last visit to Gilded Cage poured into my head. Finding an athlete with so much ability and heart, dead at the hands of a human. Though not my horse, her death had instilled me with a sense of guilt. Maybe I'd just go early and check on Hellish.

An odd connection to Hellish had driven me to rescue her from slaughter. Now her welfare lay in my hands. Though way too early to head for the track, some unknown fear for Hellish pushed me from my bed and into my riding clothes.

Outside the chill of a changing season tightened the air, bringing on a shiver. I buttoned my jean jacket, realizing Labor Day had come and gone, taking the August heat with it. The parking lot pavement glistened with dew. Drops of condensation clouded the Toyota windshield. I hit the wiper button, water sluicing left and right.

Ten minutes later I drove into the backstretch and slowed down to say good morning to Thelma, the security woman who stepped out of the guard house at the stable gate.

"Nikki, you're here early," she said.

"Couldn't sleep. Wanted to check on a new horse, maybe organize Ravinsky's tack room."

"You go, girl." She grinned at me, teeth white against her brown face. "And when you're done you can go on over to my house and organize there."

Waving, I drove into the dark, anxiety hurrying me to Ravinsky's barn. Devoid of the bustling activity that would gear up in an hour, the grounds were silent and deserted as I left the Toyota on the dirt apron. To the west, dim clouds riding the western horizon shifted to gun-metal gray. In the barn, I flipped the light switch outside Hellish's stall. She was fine. What had spooked me so?

The warm, soothing scent of horses filled the building, and down the long shedrow glossy heads contentedly tugged bites of hay from rope nets that hung outside each stall. The speckled Bantam rooster who ruled the stable flew down from his roost in the rafters and scratched in the dirt for grain. Two hens, still perched above, craned their necks, beady eyes watching to see if he got lucky.

Hellish had about emptied her hay net, so I walked to the end of the barn and around to the opposite side, heading for the room where Jim stored hay. This side of the building faced Bill Burke's barn. The darkness hid details, but Burke always kept a neat shedrow, his red buckets and feed tubs clean, his aisle way raked clean and smooth.

Since meeting the widow LeGrange and Clay in the Jockey Club, I'd noticed a number of race entries Burke had made for her. I still hadn't seen her sparkly diamonds around, but she had four or five horses over there and a couple of 'em were pretty good. Did Janet still cling to Clay's flattering ways? Did he deliver more than just compliments?

An odd popping noise sounded from Burke's barn, and my body stilled, the only things moving, my heart and the hairs on the back of my neck. My eyes and ears strained, and I thought I heard the sound of a sliding barn door, though the one opposite me remained motionless. I heard several anxious whinnies and a commotion of hooves. Sounded like horses over there were whirling about in their stalls.

My frozen stance broke. I ran across the pavement between the barns, tripping over a coiled hose, before falling against the sliding door with a loud crash. I rubbed a smarting elbow, then hauled the door open and stood listening, but only heard the sounds of nervous animals. The horses halfway down the shedrow appeared the most disturbed. The harsh crack as an animal kicked the wall almost stopped my heart. I darted down the aisle, pausing outside a stall where a horse stood bug-eyed. Two doors down an animal spun, then snorted. But the space between them was quiet.

A dark premonition washed over me. My fingers stiff, and awkward, searched the wood wall between doors for a metal connector box. I hit a switch and light flickered on, while my hands fumbled with the stall latch. I swung the door open and stepped inside. A bay horse lay lifeless in the middle of the stall, lit by a single, naked ceiling bulb.

Sinking to my knees, my fingers reached for his head. An eye devoid of expression stared at the ceiling. I pressed my hand against his neck where the head joined. The skin was almost cold. *Oh God, not again.*

My eyes focused on another object behind the horse. A man sat on the floor, leaning against the back wall. My breath sucked in.

"Are you okay?" I stood, shaky legs carrying me forward. Recognition prickled me. "Dennis?"

He couldn't answer. A small hole darkened Dennis's forehead, a trickle of blood dripped down his face and leaked onto his blue denim shirt. On the wood boards above his head, a thick smear of red, as if he'd slid down the wall and left a trail behind. His eyes were wide but unseeing.

Heat welled up in me, yet I felt clammy. Then the blood smell reached me, and I stumbled sideways and threw up in the straw. Agitation spurred me to leave, to get out. Something whitish in the straw next to Dennis caught my peripheral vision. I tried to observe, and not see Dennis. A plastic syringe, like the ones I'd used that morning. I moved toward it, then got smart. I wasn't going to touch anything, didn't need my prints on any of this. I whirled to escape and shrieked.

A man stood outside the stall. He spoke, his voice sharp and authoritative. "Stay where you are, Latrelle." Fred Rockston, the security guard who'd been around the night Gildy died, who'd been with Beamfelter when he'd questioned me in Jim's office. Now he'd found me with something way worse than another dead horse — he'd found me with a corpse.

He told me to stand against the wall, not to move. He sidestepped the horse, took a good look at Dennis, and his face paled. I feared he'd lose his cookies, too, but he was made of tougher stuff than me. He pulled out his radio, called in to the security office, told them to get somebody over here, call an ambulance, call the Anne Arundel County cops. He took me out, told me to sit on a nearby bale of hay and stay put. He paced, I waited, then the parade started. Track security guards came pounding down the shedrow, sirens wailed, blue lights flashed, and beat cops arrived, their radios squawking and hissing. More revolving lights reflected on the walls as an ambulance pulled up outside.

Queasy and fighting a growing headache, I dropped my head in my hands. My fight with Dennis at Shepherds Town. Who knew about that? Oh, Christ, who didn't? Had Dennis killed the horse, or had he surprised the killer and paid with his life? No, he wouldn't be in this barn unless here to do the horse. He'd never think twice about killing a horse for money. Who'd shot Dennis?

Hard fingers griped my shoulder. A tall, thick-necked black man in a gray suit removed his hand, straightened up and flashed a badge.

"Are you Ms. Latrelle?" His voice was rich and deep.

When I nodded, he said he was with Anne Arundel homicide. His face, as he stared at me, wore a jaded expression, like I was just another bad incident on a long warped road. No one had ever looked at me like this before, and I started to get scared. He said his name was Trent Curtis and introduced the shorter blond guy who stood behind him as Charlie Wells. Wells wore small rimless glasses, a drab blue suit, and a tie with tiny guns and handcuffs printed on it. His expression suggested he might still believe in innocence, and laugh lines cradled his mouth.

"Miss Latrelle?" Curtis asked.

"Yes."

"We need you to come into the Anne Arundel CID. We'd like to ask you some questions"

"What's a CID?" I asked.

"Criminal Investigation Division," Wells said.

I had nothing to hide and said I'd go.

A small commotion down the shedrow drew our attention. Bill Burke's foreman with a beat cop, probably arguing that he had to start the morning training, take care of his horses. Then I saw Lorna Doone edge past them and come hurriedly in my direction. A cop stopped her before she reached me. My gaze skidded to the blond-haired detective, Wells. "Please, she's my friend, can I talk to her?"

He considered my request, then said, "She can stand here." He indicated a spot to his side. "You can talk. Make it brief."

Lorna got as close as she dared, her eyes cutting from the cop to me and back again. "Dudarina, you all right?"

"Yeah. But I'm going to have to go with these detectives."

"Why?" Her voice held a strained quality, but she threw the detectives a defiant glare. "You didn't do anything, right?"

"Of course not. I said I'd answer their questions." Lorna's expression suggested she'd sidestepped into a scary mental place, but then I wasn't doing so well myself. "Listen to me Lorna, I need you to tell Jim what's going on, and ask Ramon to feed Hellish. Okay?"

Lorna snapped to attention. "Like, consider it done." She paused, shooting a worried glance at the two detectives. "Where are you taking her?"

"Crownsville CID," Wells said, eying Lorna's blue Pegasus tattoo.

"So, can I pick her up later?" Lorna put the question to Wells. Apparently neither of us wanted to deal with the cynical-eyed Curtis.

"It's up to you, Ms. Latrelle" When I nodded, he said, "You need directions?"

Lorna sighed. "I know where it is."

She did?

"You hang tough, Nikki," Lorna said. "I'll call, see when I can pick you up." With that she turned and sped away like she couldn't get out of there fast enough.

Curtis and Wells closed in around me, and I lurched to my feet.

Curtis stepped a little closer, his eyes unreadable. "Would you remove your jacket? I'll carry it for you. We're going to take you now."

Wordlessly, I took off my coat and placed it in Wells's outstretched hand. A beat cop stepped into the stall that crawled with crime-scene technicians and came out with a bag. My jacket disappeared inside, and the detectives ushered me into the back seat of an unmarked Crown Victoria. The engine turned over, and we drove away from Burke's barn.

Outside the cruiser's windows the familiar and normal world slipped away from me.

16

The detectives stayed quiet. Curtis drove, his wide gold wedding band glinting at me from his left hand on the steering wheel. The hair on the back if his head was trimmed neat and close. Wells had a bald spot beginning to show. Focusing on these little details kept me from shrieking and wrestling with the door handles. They hadn't put me in handcuffs, but they'd probably locked the doors.

The roads we traveled grew more narrow and closed in with gloomy trees. Why hadn't we just gone somewhere in Laurel? Where was Crownsville, anyway?

"Excuse me," I said. "Is it much farther?"

"Right up there," Wells said, pointing to the right.

We turned onto a narrow paved road. A selection of winding, circuitous lanes led to various brick buildings that looked like a campus, or perhaps an institution built early in the 1900s. We passed a building with a sign that read "Second Genesis." I knew what that was, a drug rehab with a tough reputation. We pulled into the lot of the brick building next door. A portico crowned the front entrance. Thin white columns supported its roof. The detectives got me out of the car, past the columns and up to an ugly gray metal door with a sign that said, "Ring intercom after 4:00 P. M." Inside, a pleasant lady who looked like someone's mom sat behind a bulletproof shield like a bank teller. Some reception. We passed her and came to another locked door, where Curtis used a key-card to gain entrance.

I guess I'd expected a crowded bullpen, ringing phones, desks heaped with files and littered with empty pizza boxes and discarded coffee cups. Instead, the area was spacious, neat and quiet, with pastel mint walls and soft, mottled-green carpeting. Probably trying to keep us criminals calm. I was looking around when we made a right turn, and found myself in a small room with two chairs and a table. Wells closed the door and left me in there with Curtis. Adrenalin surged through me, making my heart pound. A little late for the flight-or-fight reaction.

Wells came back with some cans of Coke, and they remained polite as they had me walk through everything that happened that morning.

"Tell us about your relationship with Dennis O'Brien." Curtis set down his Coke can. His big fingers had left impressions on the red-and-silver design.

I told them about the Shepherds Town altercation. If they didn't already know, they'd find out. I told them about the Dark Mountain horses, about seeing Dennis with Clements, and I mentioned Jack Farino. Their interest level in my different bits of information was impossible to gauge. They had the cop-face down pretty good.

"There were a lot of people who didn't like Dennis," I said. "Probably people who had more than one run-in. A guy at Shepherds Town, Will Marshall, mentioned Dennis was already in some kind of trouble. Marhall's a jockey. You could ask him."

Curtis's gaze remained impassive. Wells let me have a raised brow and wrote down Marshall's name in his notebook.

After an hour or so their questions wound down. Wells said he'd called an evidence tech from the state crime lab to do some testing. Unlike the questioning, the testing didn't appear to be optional.

"Such as what?"

"Fingerprints, gunshot residue," Curtis answered before he abruptly followed Wells out of the room and closed the door on me.

I had nothing to worry about, right? I hadn't touched anything, never even saw the gun. They'd left me in their interrogation room with a can of Coke and a little one-way mirror in the wall over my head. I thought about making faces at it but decided that was probably a bad idea.

A while later the technician arrived. He had a kit with him and pulled out some paper stubs that had sticky backs like you'd see on postage stamps or labels. He peeled off the slick cover and pressed the sticky part on my left palm. Another stub went for the back, then two more snooped along the sides of my hand. He finished up the right hand, then took my fingerprints.

"You know," I said, "everybody with any kind of license at the racetrack already has their fingerprints on file with the Maryland Racing Commission."

"We like to be thorough," he said, giving me a hard look.

"Right."

He left, I waited a while, then Wells brought in a document with my earlier words typed onto the paper. I read the statement carefully, signed it,and Wells said I could go.

"Your girlfriend, Miss Doone? She called, she's on her way."

Wells took me through the locked corridor,and suddenly I was set loose outside the gray metal door. I took a breath and sagged, realizing I'd been running on nerves and fear.

I looked around the grounds. The scattered group of buildings had a weird, disjointed feeling about them. Odd that Lorna knew the location of the county's Criminal Investigation Division. Maybe she'd lost someone in her family to violence or she had a brother who'd gone wrong. The CID and Second Genesis crowned a tall hill. Another brick building with a flat roof and darker bricks lay behind them, down the slope. Its sign read "Mary E. Moss Academy." What kind of an academy sits behind a drug-rehab center and a CID? I was doing it again, focusing on small questions instead of looking at the big ones, like who'd killed O'Brien and what was going to happen to me?

I heard a car engine and spied Lorna's battered red Jetta laboring up the hill. She waved at me and stopped the car at the curb next to me.

Cranking her window down, she said, "Nikki, dude, hop in. Let's blast you outta here. This place creeps me out."

My sentiments exactly. I climbed in, and the Jetta started rolling before I'd shut the door. Lorna was wearing a purple-and-orange tie-dyed T-shirt under a leather jacket. She'd added a purple streak to her red hair since I last saw her, and her face wore a defiant expression.

"Dudarina, how'd it go? They don't think you snuffed Dennis, do they?"

"It went okay. I don't know what they think." She didn't need to know the sorry details. Lorna might be a good buddy, but she'd probably find it irresistible to repeat everything I said to anyone who'd listen. I was under a dark cloud and needed to be careful.

"Everybody's like, wow, they've arrested Nikki."

"I have not been arrested." Fear made my voice spark with anger.

"Hey, like, chill out." She raised a placating hand. "Listen, I know evil, and you ain't it. I told everyone no way you did anything like that."

We both took in a little air and stayed quiet for a moment, while the hillside with its brick buildings faded into the distance.

"Thanks for picking me up, Lorna." I threw her a smile that felt lame. "How'd you know where the CID is anyway?"

"Oh, that whole place is like my, what do you call it, alma mother."

"Mater, alma mater," I corrected.

"Whatever. What I'm saying is, I went to school there."

What, for classes in crime? "What school, Lorna?"

Lorna didn't reply as we rode on a road called Generals Highway. She appeared to be concentrating on her driving. The Jetta sped downhill to a stoplight and there before us loomed the Annapolis Mall.

"Listen," Lorna said. "I'm starving. What say we get a pizza? They sell beer, too. Buy me a beer, and I'll tell you about my alma whatever."

The thought of pizza made me almost dizzy with hunger. The dash clock read almost noon, and as much as I wanted to get back to Laurel and Hellish, I wanted to run away. Time out with food and beverage felt like a reprieve, even if only temporary.

We found the restaurant close to the Annapolis Nordstrom's and slid into a booth that was butted up against plate glass, overlooking the mall corridor. Had it only been five days since I'd shopped with Carla? She'd left a message on my phone asking how my night with Clay turned out. I needed to call her. And tell her what? That I was being questioned regarding a murder?

"Like, earth to Nikki."

I focused on Lorna and realized a waitress had appeared. They both stared at me. Lorna was waving her hand slowly before my face.

"Right." Acting normal seemed problematic, but I gave it my best shot. "Can I have a large coffee and a double shot of Bailey's Irish?"

"Sure," the waitress answered, perky and smiling. Probably figuring a big tip might follow the double Bailey's. Lorna ordered us a specialty pizza and a beer for herself.

The restaurant's noisy crowd competed with the pop music pouring from overhead speakers. A brigade of young mothers wielding double and triple baby strollers rolled into the restaurant choking the aisle ways. Several of their offspring did their best to pierce my eardrums with those high-pitched shrieks they like to practice. Teenaged girls wearing incredibly low slung jeans and skimpy tops tried not to look self-conscious and failed. Men in business suits concentrated fiercely on their food, and frumpy women shoppers in sweats and comfortable shoes pointedly ignored a table of thin females in killer makeup and salon hair.

No one openly stared at Lorna's purple hair, body piercing, or blue tattoo. "So Lorna, you want to tell me about going to school at the CID?"

Lorna shrugged. "I got in some trouble in elementary school, lifted some stuff at a store. Used to get in fights with girls in my class. I was what they called a 'troubled teen.' They sent me to the Mary E. Moss Academy. It was that building down the hill, behind the CID?"

I nodded at Lorna. "Those buildings did look like an old campus."

"Used to be an insane asylum."

Nice. "So how was Mary Moss?"

"Grades nine through twelve. There were about 50 of us. We used to say anybody badder 'n us was behind bars. I met some rough dudes in that place, turned me on to crack cocaine, so I ended up graduating into Second Genesis."

My surprise must have shown on my face. I thought I'd had it bad.

Lorna put up that placating hand again. "Hey, Nikki, it's cool. Second Genesis was a bitch, but it straightened me out, helped me get the job at Laurel when I said horses were all I'd ever wanted. The track was pretty cool, except that Offenbach guy, works for the racing commission. He's a mean dude."

"The commission cop?" I'd heard he was like a Gestapo agent.

"Yeah, him."

Would he be on *my* case?

"So," Lorna said, studying a blue horsehead ring on her right hand, "they gave me this provisional license, found a trainer who was willing to take me on. Tested me for drugs. A lot. If I hadn't come up clean, Offenbach would've busted me, had the stewards rule me off. I've been clean for three years." She sounded proud.

The waitress appeared with Lorna's beer and my drink. Should she be having a beer? I figured she knew what she was doing. I grabbed the tall glass cup filled with coffee, slugged it with Bailey's and took a long swallow. Caffeine, sugar, and whiskey coursed into my system. No wonder people became addicted.

Lorna suddenly appeared dubious. "So are you gonna, like . . . not associate with me anymore?"

"Lorna, I was a runaway, used to steal food. I just never got caught."

"Awesome."

Our pizza came, its thin caramelized crust spread with warm goat cheese, field greens and grilled chicken. Large flakes of Parmesan decorated the top. Neither of us said anything for a while.

When our plates were empty, I felt more like myself, less like an escaped convict. Curious about Lorna's name, I said, "So are you named after a Nabisco cookie?"

Lorna pushed her plate aside, put her elbows on the table and leaned forward. "My Mom read some book about this princess. Think it was a romance with Scottish knights and stuff. Since she'd married a Doone, she couldn't help herself. Named me Lorna, after the princess."

I wondered if Nabisco would introduce the companion cookie, a chocolate shortbread, call it Scottish Knights? Where was my head? "Right," I said. "But I think Lorna Doone was actually a character from an English romance, set in the 17th century."

Lorna took a swallow of beer and gave me a suspicious look. "How do you do you know all this stuff? You have a pretty fancy education for a runaway. In fact, sometimes you sound like these girls at Mary Moss, tossed out of those la-di-da private schools."

I told her about my stint at Miss Potter's School for girls. How I'd been exposed to Muffies and Bitsies with their affectations and polished voices.

"They had summer reading lists," I explained. "I think one girl felt sorry for me. She gave me her books that first summer. When I read them all, she gave me more."

"So Lorna Doone was on her list?"

"Yeah. I love books. They're a wonderful escape, a way to turn off the bad times."

Lorna drained her beer. "There's a bookstore down the hall. You might want to buy some books."

17

Driving through the stable gate, Fred Rockston's close buddy, the security guard Pete, sent me a cold and distant stare. Usually he'd offer a friendly wave. The few people who noticed me in Lorna's Jetta stood still, their eyes following me down the road. I quickly learned to stare straight ahead. Lorna dropped me off just outside my barn. Before I climbed out of her car, I turned to her.

"Listen, you might want to keep your distance from me 'til this blows over."

She looked offended. "I'm not turning my back on you. Babe, I've been there. I understand. Totally."

She drove off, and I slipped into the relative security of my barn. I stuck my head in Jim's office. Might as well get this over with.

He sat at his desk studying the overnight, probably for a race he'd entered. He half rose out of his chair when he saw me, his brows climbing up his forehead. "You all right?"

"Yeah," I said sliding into a chair. "Sorry I wasn't here this morning."

He waved the comment away. "What's the matter with the cops thinking you coulda offed O'Brien? They give you a hard time?"

I relayed events, and read only concern on his face. I shouldn't have worried about Jim, he was a stand up guy. Still, finding Dennis had shaken me. I'd shied from the image of O'Brien all morning, dodged it that afternoon.

Jim slammed his fist on the desk. The electronic calculator next to him jumped, then whirred and clattered as paper fed through the keeper and ink was wasted on a series of zero balances. "I've never even seen you smack a horse." He glared at the calculator.

I leaned forward in my chair. "There was a dead horse in that stall with O'Brien. You know who owned it?"

"Huh?" He appeared to focus on my question. "Belonged to Janet LeGrange."

Why didn't that surprise me? "Don't you think it's kind of an odd coincidence that two horses are killed and they both belong to rich widows?"

"Nah, this place is crawling with wealthy women."

Women sure, but widows? And what were the chances that O'Brien would be in there with a plain bay horse? I'd lay odds it was a Dark Mountain horse. "What are people saying, Jim? Do they think Dennis killed the horse?"

"What is she doing here?" A voice so familiar but so changed. Martha Garner stood behind me in the door to Jim's office. "I know what you did." Her eyes burned with outrage. "You killed my Gildy."

"Martha, no. I didn't . . ."

"Shut up. I want her out of here." The woman's narrowed eyes fired electric bolts at her trainer. "I mean it, Jim. Get her out of here, or you'll never train another horse for me."

"Easy, Martha." Jim stepped from behind his desk. "Nikki would never do a thing like that."

"Don't you be so naive, Jim Ravinsky." Martha turned on me, her face bright pink. "Who paid you, you little bitch? How much did you get?"

"Martha, why are you so sure it's Nikki?" I knew that tone. Jim used it on frenzied fillies.

Her mouth set into hard, straight lines. "Janet LeGrange told me. She thought I should know. This person," she almost spit out the word, "has access to all your horses, Jim. What are you thinking?" Martha's smoker's cough suddenly consumed her, and it only flamed her fury.

I'd never been on the receiving end of anger so righteous and virulent. It impaled me with unwarranted guilt, fear, and a sense of impending disaster. Attempting to reason seemed futile. My eyes slid to Jim, my voice a grating whisper. "I'm gonna leave now."

Jim nodded. I sidestepped around Martha, who stood her ground, coughing and glaring at me, her gaze filled with hate, this woman who'd been my friend. I ducked out of the office, almost breaking into a run down the shedrow. I found Ramon, thrust a 20 at him, thanked him for feeding Hellish earlier, asked if he'd do it again that evening. "I gotta leave right now," I said.

"What happen? You arrested?" Wariness shadowed his features.

"No, just questioned." I slipped out the far end of the barn and avoided inquiring glances by studying my feet as they ferried me to my car.

At home, Slippers' friendly greeting almost confused me, it was so out of line with the rest of the day. "Don't you know I'm a suspect?" I spoke into the fur on the top of his head as I picked him up and closed my eyes. The cat's motor cranked into big-purr, and I held on to him as I sank to the couch.

How could Martha think I'd killed two horses? It had to have been O'Brien, at least for Legrange's horse, and probably for Gildy, too. Bastard. But I sure hadn't wished him the cards he'd been handed. Who was the dealer? O'Brien hadn't fired a bullet into his own brain, and whoever had was still out there. I shuddered, moved to the door of my apartment and stared at the motionless parking lot through my peep hole. I checked the door locks again, picked up the can of pepper spray I'd bought on the way home, then set it down it down and paced around my apartment.

The day's events overwhelmed me around seven, and I crawled into bed, falling into a deep sleep for nearly five hours. Just after midnight I heard Arthur Clements snarling that I'd better get the hell out of his barn or I'd be sorry. I couldn't see Dennis but recognized his voice. It sounded thin and wispy, like mist. "She was at Dark Mountain," the voice said.

I sat up in a rush, my eyes flying open, my hand groping for the lamp switch. In the sudden light the room was, of course, empty. Only Slippers glared at me from the end of my bed. He hopped from the comforter and stalked out the door, his tail an indignant plume.

Arthur Clements, yes. Definitely my first pick for murderer. I'd mentioned him to the homicide detectives. Had they listened? Clements was in on whatever this thing was with the Dark Mountain horses, and he'd been angry at O'Brien. Had O'Brien been killed so he wouldn't talk? About what? And that Jack Farino. He'd been there with them that afternoon.

I pressed my hands over my eyes, failing to block the image of Dennis slumped against the stable wall.

Kenny Grimes didn't show up for work the next morning. Jim said he'd been missing the day before, hadn't called in or responded to messages. I had to ride the entire morning schedule, and the horses just kept coming. Using my saddle and Kenny's, the grooms, Ron and Ramon, pulled me off one horse and threw me up on the next. I felt like a pogo stick. Before long I was reeling, wishing I'd gotten more sleep. Where was Kenny?

The morning sunshine hurt my eyes and was at odds with my mood. A warm breeze carried humid southern air. I got a short breather when they closed the track at 8:00 for the interim harrowing. At 8:30, when they reopened with a smooth surface, I was supposed to work a two-year-old filly named Lavender that belonged to Louis Fein. In the meantime I sagged on a hay bale with a bagel and coffee. My debut ride on Hellish would have to wait another day.

Fein's Jaguar eased its silver nose around the corner of the barn a little before 8:30. The incandescent blond hair in the passenger seat identified Carla. They came into the barn, and Louis disappeared into Jim's office. Carla spotted me and headed over. She said something about telephone tag, and asked me what happened after I left with Clay that evening.

"We didn't really hit it off that well." Did Carla know about the murder? Her expression was open and bubbly, sort of like the pink stretch top she wore over jeans and cowgirl boots.

"That's not the way it looked to me. You two couldn't take your eyes off each other."

"There might be more to him than I realized. Maybe not good."

"Tell me." Carla's brown eyes were bright with interest.

I told her about the phone call he'd received, about the horse with two crosses of Destroyer, and him taking a commission at both ends, padding the price, wanting me to pressure Martha into the purchase.

"But he's a salesman, probably just sees it as business. It's not illegal, is it?"

I sighed. "Not really. There's been publicity recently, an effort to curb games played at the bloodstock sales. Some agents and consignors can be pretty fraudulent. A group got together and wrote this code of ethics. I don't know how they'll enforce it. Too many different states, too many different laws."

We both moved against the inside wall as Ron came by with the last horse I'd ridden. Light steam rose from the gray's flanks and withers. Puffs of dirt followed his hooves. "Whoa, back," said Ramon, halting the gray beside a water bucket hanging from a screw eye. The animal grabbed a few thirsty sips before Ramon tugged him away and continued cooling him out. The horse knew he'd get more water next time around.

I turned back to Carla. "I hate to think Clay would sell a horse to Martha for way more than its worth." I still felt protective toward Martha? Yeah, I did.

"Clay's got so much going for him. I think it outweighs a little wheeling and dealing. That's how you make money, Nikki."

I let it go, too tired and worn down by recent events to stand up for ethics.

Jim and Louis emerged from the office. Ramon brought Lavender down the shedrow. The filly was a pretty-faced chestnut with a white blaze and a lot of blond in her mane and tail. Ramon gave me a leg up while Jim held the bridle.

"She's ready to go five-eighths," said Jim. "Might as well break her from the gate, see if she can get her card."

"What's a gate car?" asked Carla.

Louis rolled his eyes. Jim was busy adjusting Lavender's blinkers.

"A horse gets his gate *card* from the track starter once he's shown he'll load," I said. "Then, he's got to stand in there without going berserk, and zip on out in a straight line."

"They don't just do that?" Carla got a big eye-roll accompanied by an exasperated sigh from Louis. Trouble in paradise?

I jumped back in. "I've seen youngsters do all kinds of stuff. Refuse to load, rear up and flip over in the gate. Zigzag on the way out and trash whoever's in the next lane. The starter forces the rogues to come back to the gate until they get it right. Every once in a while a really bad actor comes along and flunks out." The last, I said over my shoulder as Ramon led me down the shedrow.

Lavender seemed precocious, willing to go with the program. She had potential. Jim had lined up another two-year-old from Burke's barn to work with us and I met the rider, Luke, outside the barn where we headed for the track. The work went well, Lavender exploding from the gate like a blond bullet, going head-and-head with Burke's colt, then opening up and outworking him by four at the wire. Galloping her out afterwards, I stroked her neck and told her she was a star. Luke had pulled up behind us and had already turned back for the barn.

Nearing the exit gap, I saw a group of watchers. Carla stood next to Jim, and Louis was huddled with Bill Burke and Janet LeGrange. A little pellet of dread sank in my stomach. This might not go well. I knew the gossip would be rampant by now. As we drew closer, LeGrange threw me a dirty look, her eyes even harder than her lacquered hairdo. Louis moved over to Carla and said something. Jim started tapping his lip, and Carla suddenly drew back from Louis and threw me a startled glance. Oh boy.

Normally I would ride closer, and we'd talk briefly about the work, but today I kept on going. In the barn Ramon waited for Lavender, and Ron held Bourbon Bonnet, all saddled and ready to go. I went, but not quite soon enough. Louis's voice, as he came in the barn, was quick and urgent.

"I'm not saying I believe it, Jim. I'm saying I don't want to take any chances. You know how much these horses cost me, and the mortality insurance is so high — they're all way under insured. I don't want her . . ." He grew silent when he saw me on Bonnet, turned, and walked in the other direction.

Carla's face wore an anxious, embarrassed look. She threw an uneasy glance my way, then followed Louis. My corner was emptying out fast. Jim, as I might have expected, disappeared into his office. I rode through the rest of the morning, acutely aware that many riders who'd normally call out a greeting or bantering comment, ignored me.

Lorna and a few others asked how I was doing and it worried me how much I clung to these small signs of support.

I slid from my last horse after the track closed at 10, cleaned both saddles and was wiping my hands on a towel when a heavyset older guy in a cap approached me and asked if I was Nikki Latrelle. He had nice eyes, but they weren't especially friendly.

"You got anyplace to go right now?"

I shook my head, wondering what this was about.

"Jerry Offenbach wants you in his office in the grandstand at 11. If I was you, I'd be there on time."

"Could I ask what about?" Meeting with the chief investigator for the Maryland State Racing Commission did not make my heart leap with joy.

"Well," he said,his voice edged with sarcasm, "it might be on account of you being found with two dead bodies yesterday?"

I closed my eyes for a moment. The man gave a curt nod and left. He moved across the pavement outside the barn, and I could see Arthur Clements' attention drawn by the investigator's departure. Clements was grinning.

I felt sick. A rabbit hole had opened up and sucked me in. It spiraled me downward so fast, my mind couldn't catch up.

A prickle of internal radar shifted my focus. Jack Farino stood across the way. The planes of his face appeared harder than usual. He stared at me, a knowing, predatory look in his eyes.

18

Jerry Offenbach's room hid inside the racing secretary's offices next to the paddock at Laurel. Just outside and to the right of these rooms, a ramp and small set of stairs led to the jockeys' room, and I wished like hell I were going in there — anywhere other than Offenbach's lair.

Inside the room a long counter faced me. The assistant secretaries sat behind this all day, accessible, and in plain view of anyone who walked in. The top-dog racing secretary had her own office.

They must have been taking entries for races later in the week, as the phones were ringing nonstop. A couple of trainers stood at the counter studying the overnight sheet, an essential piece of paper. It told them if the race they'd entered had gone or not, and, if so, what post position they'd drawn, how many they had to run against, and if the jockey they'd requested ended up on their horse or someone else's. When two or more trainers request the same jockey, the rider's agent usually makes the call. I didn't have an agent and could count on one hand the times I'd been named on more than one horse in the same race.

Eleven o'clock. I caught the eye of a nearby assistant named David, and in a low voice asked if the door to my left was the investigator's office. He gave a little start when he saw me. Cocked his head sideways and with unnecessary volume said, "Here to see Jerry Offenbach? Have an appointment? *Of course you do.*"

The two trainers at the counter turned as one and gave me a look. For some reason the phones stopped ringing, and I had everybody's attention. A vending machine out of sight around the corner clanked, rattled, and dropped some junk food. Arthur Clements appeared, holding a bag of chips. He stared at me, then glanced toward the security office and smirked. I wished that rabbit hole would swallow me up.

I knocked on Offenbach's door and heard a voice say to come in. I opened the door and stuck my head in. My body seemed disinclined to follow.

Offenbach sat at a cluttered desk to the left. He examined me with expressionless eyes. The man's features were strong but well made. His hair was clipped short, lightly sprinkled with gray. I couldn't guess his age. Probably over fifty.

"I'm Nikki Latrelle. Supposed to be here at 11:00?"

The man dwarfed his large leather office chair. He was that tall. I was real glad he was sitting down. He crooked a finger at me, flexing the joint to motion me closer.

"Come here."

I crept forward two steps.

He pointed at a straight-backed chair.

I obediently perched on its edge. The man studied me, maintaining a long silence. I fought the urge to squirm. When his gaze left me for a moment to open a drawer and pull out a notebook, I felt like he'd released a pin that had me fastened to the chair.

"Tell me about Dennis O'Brien." His thoughts remained hidden behind flat eyes.

"I only knew Dennis from the few races I rode up at Shepherds Town." The room was small, crowded with three desks and some filing cabinets. Though the other desks were in use, Offenbach was the only investigator in the room.

"But you had an incident on," he glanced at his notebook, "August 15?"

"I guess." Two of the walls were painted dark green, and one had a door that appeared to lead directly outside. Probably so the chief investigator could snake out a long arm and collar unwary jockeys suspected of drug use or race-fixing.

"The man struck you in the face during the eighth race, pushed your horse into the rail. Your horse fell in the stretch, causing his death and you to be unconscious. You never lodged an objection with the stewards. Why not, Miss Latrelle?"

He had my attention.

"You don't have an answer? Or did you have your own plan for paying him back?"

"No. That's crazy."

The door opened and the muted ringing of telephones grew louder. The assistant investigator who'd nailed me that morning came in. He was shorter than Offenbach, had warmer eyes. He sat at a nearby desk and rolled his chair to face me, said his name was Marvin Setz.

I'd heard they played good cop, bad cop. Not hard to peg the bad cop. The chief glanced at Setz. "I was asking Miss Latrelle about Dennis O'Brien."

For the next hour I was like a fish on a grill. They asked the same questions in different ways, loud and soft, harsh and gentle. Tried to trip me up. I kept repeating my story, from Shepherds Town to finding the dead eyes on Dennis O'Brien.

The only time I saw a shift in Offenbach's expression was when I brought up Jack Farino. His eyes moved to Setz, then snapped back to me, but neither investigator bit at my offering of suspects. Finally, I got mad.

"I keep trying to tell you that something's going on with Arthur Clements and this Jack Farino guy. Why don't you listen?"

Offenbach's eyes remained about as readable as a steel wall. He could make a living playing poker. "You're here to answer questions, not raise them."

When they wound down, Setz said they'd give their report to the racing stewards. I didn't like the sound of that. The stewards could do nasty stuff like suspend my license, rule me off the track. Setz interrupted my thoughts, nodding me to the door. The phone rang, and Offenbach answered as I stood to leave.

In the racing office, a group of jockeys' agents were hanging around like vultures. An interesting species, their habit was to promise trainers their top jockey, then often renege by putting their good rider on a better horse, the moment an offer came along. Next these guys tried to stick the first trainer with a second-string rider. When the musical rider's scramble came to a standstill, agents lurked about in the racing office, pouncing on any horse with a shot that came up riderless.

I'd seen this happen to Jim a number of times. He'd say no thank you to the second-rate rider and put me on. I had nothing against vultures. They'd provided me a number of rides.

I sidestepped the agents and slipped outside. The morning sun had given way to metallic clouds, heavy with rain. The wind had shifted to the north. Damp air brushed my back and clung like cold wet leaves. I suddenly realized Offenbach had been talking about me to whoever rang in as I left. He'd turned away from me, speaking quietly. Something about fingerprints.

19

"You got to hustle like yesterday," Jim said. "Kenny's still missing."

We were standing outside his barn early Friday morning, wearing jackets against the chill. Above us the stars faded to the west, and the sun painted promising streaks on the eastern horizon.

"I'm trying to line up another rider." He looked worried, brows drawn close, creating a furrow. If I got suspended, he'd have no rider.

I was afraid something bad had happened to Kenny. He'd been a good partner in the mornings. "Do you think he's in trouble?" I asked.

Jim pursed his lips. "Nobody's heard anything. I drove around to his apartment last night. His truck's not there, he's not home."

Weird. I thought how many times I'd watched Kenny scurry and hustle for extra rides, like he needed the money. Maybe he had a gambling problem. Then there was the shiny new truck. Those payments might be bleeding him. But where was he?

Ramon, with a new diamond stud earring, showed up with the first horse of the day. I zipped around all morning trying to get done by 9:30 so I could take Hellish out before the track closed at 10. I put her in the round pen filled with deep sand so she could buck and carry on, hopefully work out some kinks before I got on her. Then I whisked on a saddle and bridle. I added a martingale so I'd have a neck strap to hold on to. I left my stirrups long so I could get a good grip on her with my legs. Ramon tossed me into the saddle.

Hellish humped her back but went on down the shedrow without exploding. We made it to the track and went the "wrong way," my signal that speed wasn't on the agenda. She eased into a slow gallop, then extended into a long, ground-eating stride, the track rails sliding past us faster and faster. We passed Lorna on a two-year-old colt like they were walking. Wow. This filly had an engine. Reminded me of Gildy. *Gildy?* I fought the exhilaration and stood up to slow her down. She hadn't been out in a while, no sense in letting her do too much too soon. When I got her to a steady rhythm, we went along for about a mile, then headed for the gap leading back to the barn, back to her confining stall.

No. She wasn't having it. She spun and faced the opposite direction. I lost my stirrups, slid my feet back in as fast as I could. She reared, came down bucking and plunging. Oh boy. Another buck. One stirrup gone. A sharp duck to the left. I clung to the yoke of the martingale. She threw her hind end up in the air so high and hard I catapulted off like a pebble from a slingshot.

I hit the ground rolling, jumped up and watched she disappearing down the track. Dust on the horizon. Damn.

An outrider flew by in hot pursuit, and the track loudspeaker crackled,

"Loose horse on the track. Repeat, there is a loose horse on the track." I rolled my eyes.

A while later the outrider brought Hellish back and handed her over. "What do you want to fool with a horse like this for?"

"Guess I'm just crazy," I said, trying to keep it light.

"She'll get somebody hurt. Clements was right, sending her to that sale."

"Did I ask for your opinion?"

He gave me a cold look, but I turned my back on him and led Hellish away. I should have thanked him for catching her, but was too mad. I led her back to the barn and cooled her out. She was a sweaty mess and a little off in her right front foot. Great. Who knows how fast she'd gone?

"Nikki, dude, you two all right?"

I looked up from my kneeling position in the deep straw by Hellish's foot. Lorna stood in the stall doorway. Without her helmet I could see she'd exchanged her purple streak for two green ones.

"I'm okay," I said. "She overdid it. Has something going on in this leg. Can't tell if it's the foot or ankle."

Lorna knelt next to me. With her red hair I thought the green additions might work for the Christmas holidays. We stared at the leg. Hellish ignored us. After discussing cold-hosing, X-rays, and other options, I spread on a thick, heat-drawing poultice from above her knee down to her hoof. Then I packed the stuff into the hoof and left her to her hay.

Morning training over. The shedrow had been swept clean of straw, hay, and bits of litter. Ramon and Ron had used the heavy wide-rakes, leaving a neat zigzag pattern in the aisle way dirt. Lorna and I crept along the edge, trying not to disturb their design. The grooms had sprayed the dust down with a fine nozzle, and the smell of damp soil filled my nostrils. The sound of horse molars grinding hay, the occasional stomp caused by the crafty fly that got past the automatic insecticide sprayers, and the perpetual rattle of feed buckets soothed me like music.

The rhythm stopped. Marvin Setz stood at the end of the shedrow. Jim stepped out of his office, finger tapping a puckered lip, eyes concerned.

"You got trouble," said Lorna.

Lorna, rocket scientist. My stomach plunged. I moved toward them. Lorna hurried alongside.

The kindness had deserted Setz's eyes. Replaced by flint chips. "Morning, Miss Latrelle." He held a piece of paper in his hand, pushed it toward me. "Hearing notice. You're expected to appear before the stewards tomorrow morning at 10:30."

I blinked. My mouth too dry to form a reply.

"She'll be there," said Jim.

Setz shoved the paper into my hand and strode away, his job finished.

"Serious trouble in Candy Land," said Lorna.

Jim glared at the retreating figure of Setz, then withdrew into his office.

I got through the rest of the day on automatic pilot, my brain occupied with the next morning.

The paddock at Laurel was a pavilion-like building, with a tented roof and saddling stalls lining about a third of the rounded walls. A painted wood railing, where fans rested their elbows and programs, formed the rest of the structure's circumference. A raised wooden kiosk occupied the center, where before each race anxious owners stood and watched their horses parade past.

Tense trainers and grooms waited in each stall for saddling time, holding blinkers and bridles. The jockeys' valets brought in tiny saddles through a back door that opened between two of the saddling stalls. The riders were the last to arrive. Whenever I'd walked through that door I'd been determined to give it my best shot, hoped I could win, prayed I wouldn't get hurt.

The paddock had always reminded me of a merry-go-round. Horses continuously circling. All those people reaching for that brass ring.

At 10:25 on a Saturday morning the place was deserted as I walked past. Any lingering horse smell had faded overnight. A wood-chip and dirt mixture covered the floor of the building, its odor heavy and mulch-like. Moisture beaded on the paddock's wood railing, while above the sun struggled to break through a leaden cloud cover. I followed a path that wound behind the paddock to a locked door on the ground floor of the grandstand. Behind the glass I could see the track telephone operator look up from her cubicle. She nodded at me, buzzed me in. Through a small opening in her Plexiglas wall she told me the stewards office was just down the hall. I found it, a blank door in the wall, no windows, no way to see what lay in wait. I knocked and went in.

A small pleasant room. Forest-green carpeting, upholstered side chairs against the walls, three desks that looked like cherry veneer and a steward at each desk. Men, wearing coats and ties. They were all ex-jockeys, not like that would cut me any breaks. They looked small, nimble, and sharp-eyed.

I'd worn conservative navy pants and a navy peacoat. I pulled the hearing notice from the coat's pocket. "I'm Nikki Latrelle. Supposed to be here at 10:30."

The steward closest to the door pointed to a side chair that faced all three desks. "Sit there, Miss Latrelle."

The fabric on my chair matched the padded forest-green of the men's armchairs. I eased into it like it had teeth.

Jerry Offenbach crouched on a stool against the wall. Even sitting, he managed to tower over the rest of us, his face impassive, his body motionless.

The stewards introduced themselves, and we began. Round three. We covered the same old ground. They referred to Offenbach's typed report, asking familiar questions. I gave the usual answers, still trying to throw some suspicion on other players. They weren't interested. I had a strong feeling the meeting's outcome was already decided, a sense of just going through the motions for protocol.

The meeting seemed to stall. A silence hung in the air. The steward who'd told me to sit cleared his throat and placed his palms flat on his cherry desktop. Thomas Gorman. He had a long thin face, a matching nose, and heavy creases lining his mouth. He looked over at Offenbach and nodded. The air in the room tightened. A tension seemed to grasp the stewards as they turned in unison to Offenbach.

The chief investigator opened a folder lying in his lap, flipped out a piece of paper. "Miss Latrelle, this is a report from the Maryland State Crime Lab. Your fingerprints were on the syringe found next to Mr. O'Brien's body. You want to tell us about that?"

My stomach lurched. Fast pounding coursed through my body. "I can't tell you anything about it. I never touched it. I don't know how my fingerprints could be on there." That sounded lame. "Do I need a lawyer?"

Offenbach stared at me for a few beats. Maybe hoping I'd fold, confess.

Gorman appeared uncomfortable. He twisted in his seat, his eyes sliding to mine. One steward stared at a poster of the racehorse Cigar, and the other seemed fascinated by something over my right shoulder.

"This is not a police hearing, Miss Latrelle," Gorman said. "We are not formally investigating these crimes, nor is it our job to charge you with a crime. That's up to the Anne Arundel County Police. Our interest here is protecting the integrity of Laurel Park."

What about my integrity?

He cleared his throat again. "Miss Latrelle, we've reviewed this matter and we are going to have to suspend your license pending the outcome of the police investigation."

My mind reeled. Surely they would stop at a suspension, not rule me off? I searched their faces. Hard, implacable expressions. Gorman closing a folder that had been lying open on his desk. My right knee began shaking. I couldn't stop it.

"Because of the seriousness of this matter, you are denied access to Laurel Park. You are to clear the premises within the hour. If you attempt re-entry, you will be detained and subject to arrest. Do you understand?"

20

"What?" Jim stared at me from his desk. "You're white as a ghost. What happened?"

"They ruled me off." I'd headed for the security of Jim's barn in a zombie state. Now it hit me. There was no security. "I have to leave, Jim." I snatched back the cuff of my coat and stared at my watch. "In less than an hour."

"Those sons of bitches ruled you off?"

I nodded, feeling my upper lip go, the sting of tears in my eyes. I pushed the barn cat to one side of a nearby chair and sank into the available space.

"God damn worthless jackasses." Red spots flushed Jim's cheeks. "I got no riders, you got no job."

And Hellish. What would happen to her?

A timid knock on the door frame drew our attention. Lorna stood there with her green-streaked red hair catching light from the single window in Jim's office. She knew I'd had the hearing, had helped get some of Jim's horses out that morning. "What happened?"

I could tell by her expression she'd heard enough of Jim's ranting to have gotten the gist. I started a recount, only Martha Garner appeared in the doorway. She didn't see me at first with Lorna blocking the view. Then her eyes narrowed and she started shaking her head.

"Damn it Jim. You said you were getting rid of her. Little bitch kills horses."

Jim was half out of his seat, but Lorna had spun on Martha. "You old biddy. You're full of crap. Nikki didn't kill your horse."

Lorna was not defusing the situation. Martha took her old-lady pocket book and hit Lorna on the shoulder. Jim leapt across the room and got between them. I crouched lower in my chair, and the barn cat woke up, wide-eyed with alarm.

Jim made calming noises. Martha and Lorna faced off and glared at each other. Martha broke eye contact first, maybe intimidated by Lorna's gold brow ring. The older woman aimed her pink glasses at Jim. "I was going to talk to you about a horse. But I don't think I want one in your barn anymore."

"Martha," I said, "you'll be happy to know I've been ruled off indefinitely. I have less than an hour to leave, so if you don't mind I'd like time to make a few arrangements." I gestured toward Jim.

She stared at me, the animosity hot in her eyes. "Good. We don't need your kind around here." She threw a disgusted look at Jim and stalked away down the shedrow, fingers digging into her hard-cased purse, pulling out cigarettes and a lighter. So much for rules.

Lorna rolled her eyes, and in the distance the sound of coughing receded as Martha headed for her car.

I threw a guilty look at Jim, but he waved it off. Time was running out. I told Lorna about the meeting, asked if she'd ride a few for Jim until he could find someone.

"Sure," she said, "and I can take Hellish out on the pony, keep her going until you find a place for her . . ."

We looked at Jim, wondering if he'd be willing to keep Hellish. Who knew what law Offenbach would find for my filly?

Jim sighed and moved back to his chair behind the desk. "Nikki, I'll keep Hellish here for a few days, but you're going to have to find a place for her."

Where? I couldn't go to Pimlico or Bowie training track. I didn't have connections with any of the people that owned private farms. How would I pay . . . for anything?

A large shadow darkened the doorway. Offenbach. Lorna shrank against the wall.

"Hello, Jim," he said. His face held no expression, but his eyes bore into me like electric drills. "Miss Latrelle here has had her license suspended. I'm escorting her off the grounds." He crooked his finger at me, gesturing me out of my chair. "Let's go."

"I'm going." I slid from the chair, waiting for Offenbach to unblock the doorway.

"I'll just follow you out in my truck," he said, stepping aside, motioning me to move out.

"You've got a job here when this is over, Nikki," said Jim. "We'll work something out with Hellish."

Offenbach gave Jim a hard look. "I wouldn't be making promises you might not be able to keep."

Nobody said anything. I headed for my Toyota, Offenbach tracking me from the side. I splashed through a puddle of water where a hose had been left on. A scruffy, gray barn cat fled from beneath my car carrying an unlucky mouse. Offenbach pointed at it with his finger. I could almost smell the gun smoke.

An old black man was shuffling across the parking lot beyond my Toyota. He looked vaguely familiar. He had grizzled white hair, a shabby black suit jacket, and a red bow tie. His shoes were so old, a raised outline of bunions and knotty toe joints pushed at the worn leather.

"Hold up, Latrelle," said Offenbach. He stared at the black man. "Pinkney, you'll have to leave the grounds. Don't make trouble for yourself."

The old man turned toward Offenbach. His mocha brown face split into a smile, showing ivory-colored teeth. "Good day Mr. Jerry, sir. I just be leaving now."

"Why don't you just be getting into my truck," said Offenbach in a tone more amused than mocking. "I'll drive you out. We'll follow this lady. She's leaving too."

Pinkney's eyes settled on me a moment. "Sorry for your trouble, Miss Nikki."

How did he know my name?

Offenbach caught my expression and surprised me by acknowledging it. "Mr. Pinkney knows everything, don't you Mello?"

"I knows things, deed I do," he said nodding. "I know this be a good girl, don't deserve your kind of trouble."

"Come on Mello, in my truck."

We drove out in a procession. Thelma stood in the guardhouse at the stable gate. She didn't wave at me, but gave Offenbach and Mello Pinkney a curious look. I'd left the radio on earlier and the speakers were pouring out the Pretenders' song "Back on the Chain Gang." How appropriate.

I swung right, headed down Brock Ridge Road to 198. The chief investigator pulled up next to a bus stop, and I could see Mello climbing out of his truck in my rear-view mirror. What possible threat could an old guy like that be? Where would he go? Where would I go?

I drove to my apartment, realizing October rent was almost due. I'd spent that money on Hellish, then bought a supply of hay and feed for her. I had to get an income stream fast.

My phone started ringing as I wrestled the key in my lock. I grabbed the receiver just before the machine picked up. Maybe I'd been tracked down by a lawyer and was about to receive a large inheritance.

"Nikki?"

My body recognized the sexy voice before my brain did. A low level-thrill sped through me. "Clay?"

"Hey," he said, "I've missed you. Thought I'd take a chance, see if we can get together?"

"I'd like that," I said. "I might have jumped to the wrong conclusion." Or not.

"I heard you've had a rough time recently. Thought I could cheer you up."

"Clay, I think you should know I'm in some trouble."

"You're a suspect, right? That doesn't bother me."

I could hear another phone start to ring. He put me on hold, came right back. Said he wanted to take me to dinner but had to take care of a client on the other line.

"I'll call you, Nikki." And he was gone.

I stared at the receiver, then put it down. I had a lot of ambiguous feelings for this man.

The phone pealed again, and I jumped about six inches, then leaned over and snatched it up. Carla.

"How are you?" Her voice sounded nervous.

Nikki. Murder suspect. "I'm fine, Carla."

"Sorry I disappeared on you the other day. Louis wasn't exactly in your court. He was pressuring me not to talk to you, and I caved. I feel bad."

Was I supposed to make her feel better?

"Anyway," she said, "I thought I'd come to the track tomorrow. Maybe we could go to lunch afterward."

I took a breath and told her I'd been ruled off. I had to explain what that meant, then listen to a prolonged silence.

"Carla," I said, finally out of patience, "maybe you should wait until this blows over."

"Maybe I should."

"*Fine then*," I said, and hung up on her. Gee, I'd handled that well.

I sank onto my couch and rubbed my temples. Where was Slippers anyway? Too early for a beer, but I could use a purr. The cat was asleep on the pile of clean laundry I hadn't gotten around to putting away. It all lay in a heap on the end of my bed. Black T-shirts and jeans adorned with gray cat fur.

Damn if the phone didn't start ringing again. I threw myself on the bed and put some laundry over my head. Slippers started paw-pushing my head through the clothing. The machine picked up.

"Nikki, hi, this is Jack Farino."

Jeeez, the Gypsy. What did he want?

"Hear you've had some trouble at Laurel. I have a proposition you might be interested in. Give me a call." He left his cell phone number and disconnected.

I went to the refrigerator and pulled out a beer.

21

A pounding headache and anxiety chasing after too many beers awakened me at 4:40 A.M. I lay there in bed like I was somebody else. Someone with no job, no place to go. A murder suspect, with fingerprints on a syringe found next to a dead horse. A horse that was probably poisoned.

How the hell had my fingerprints gotten on that thing? Something about hypodermics floated on the edge of my mind, just out of sight. I'd gone over it the night before, hitting dead end after dead end, each roadblock demanding an additional beer. I abandoned the bed. Time to make coffee, find some solutions.

I put some laundry away, then hauled the pieces coated with cat fur and the previous day's clothes to the coin-operated machines at the end of my building. Got a load going, my mind flitting to other chores. Probably should get some cat food and other essentials at the all-night grocery on 198. I'd have to use my credit card.

The cold vinyl seat in my Toyota stung my skin right through the seat of my jeans. Condensation streaked the car's windows, the drops colliding and running in rivulets on the windshield. The western horizon glowed pink, and the radio announced the day would be sunny, a high of 70. The forecast ended, and the DJ put on that old Creedence Clearwater song "Bad Moon Rising."

The grocery was located in a strip mall, flanked by a darkened liquor store and a pizza parlor, still closed for the night. A pawn shop stood next to the liquor store. I might be forced to haul some things in there.

A man lay in the recessed doorway of the pawn shop asleep under a tattered blanket. His face had light brown skin. His head supported a mat of grizzled hair. Then I recognized a piece of red bow tie not covered by the blanket. That Mello Pinkney guy. Looked like he hadn't taken the bus. Probably hadn't made it past a bottle from the liquor store. Lot of that going around.

I still wondered how he'd known my name. I bought my stuff in the grocery and came out with two bags. Mello was sitting up with the blanket covering his shoulders.

"Can I get you a coffee?" Why had I offered that?

"That be mighty fine, Miss Nikki." His head nodding.

I dumped my grocery bags in the Toyota, slipped back into the store.

Put two coffees in a cardboard carton. Threw in some cream and sugar packets and went outside. Mello had folded his blanket into a neat square, straightened his bow tie and moved to a bench in front of the pizza parlor. I handed him the carton and stood stirring cream and sugar in my coffee.

His hands were long-fingered and nimble as they opened packets and fixed up his brew. I noticed his eyes were pretty clear for an old guy who was probably a drunk. They had an almond-shaped tilt at the outside corners. That tilt and high cheekbones suggested a probability of Native American blood in his veins. Maybe Piscataway.

"You be needing a place to stay," he said. His voice sounded thick but sweet, like chocolate.

"I have a place, an apartment."

"Yes ma'am. But you have a horse."

This guy knew too much. "Yeah, a filly," I said, staring at him like I could divine the wellspring of his knowledge.

He took a sip of coffee, leaned back into the bench, stretching out his legs. "I has a nice place, barns and a training track. They even has a starting gate."

Doubt was an understatement. "Where's that?"

"Dimsboro."

Ah, jeez. I'd heard of that place. It was for horsemen ruled off the main tracks. People stamped with felony convictions. An unacceptable last resort. It used to be one of Maryland's racetracks until a previous governor got in trouble, some sort of scam with the place. Then the grandstand "mysteriously" burned to the ground.

Anyway, I was pretty sure with Jim's help I could get a job at one of Maryland's private farms up in the northern part of the state. There were some beautiful operations up there, and good exercise riders were hard to come buy. I drained my coffee.

"Mr. Pinkney . . ."

"Peoples call me Mello."

"Okay, Mello. Why would I want to go there?"

The old man leaned forward. "Didn't Mr. Jerry show you the way out? Down at Dimsboro we calls it 'Jerry's escort service.' You a member now, jus like us Dimsboro folk."

Right. "Thanks for the offer, but I've got a place in mind."

"Sure you do," he said. Then he cackled. Sounded like the brown hen that hung out in Burke's barn.

"I knows things," he said. "I'll fix up a stall for that chestnut filly. I be waiting for you. Won't let you down, Miss Nikki."

I sketched a wave and beat it back to my car. Who'd told him my filly was chestnut?

Back at my apartment I fed Slippers, changed the litter box and attacked the bathroom with scrub cleanser. Finished that, and looked for more before I caught myself. Enough with the procrastination. I called Jim. He said he knew the managers at two farms. He'd get back to me. Yes, Hellish was fine.

Curious about Jack Farino, I punched in the number he'd left and got voice-mail. Didn't leave a message. If he was involved in Dennis's death, maybe better not to talk to him. But anything pointing a finger at someone else would only help me. Being ruled off, I couldn't spy on him or Clements at the track. Not anymore. So where did they live? Dragged the phone book out, found an address for Clements. Nothing listed for Farino. I had nothing against tech but hadn't spent the money on a computer. I was probably the last person I knew to get a cell phone. And that mostly stayed in my car on a charger.

Maybe Lorna could find a home address for Farino on that barn computer. Not sure what I'd do with the information, but it beat sitting in my apartment.

The phone rang. Jim. "Got a pen?"

I did and he gave me the name of two farms he'd contacted, and directions. I'd call, see if they needed a rider, see if they'd let me bring Hellish, and work off her board through the riding.

"What I can do, Nikki, if you make a connection, is load Hellish on my rig and meet you outside the stable gate, let you drive her up there. Sorry, but I need to get her out of here. I made up with Martha, but somebody told her Hellish belonged to you. So . . ."

I told him I understood, thanked him, and disconnected. I'd forgotten to ask about Kenny. I was beginning to wonder if he was dead.

22

The engine of Jim's red Ford purred as the truck climbed an incline on the narrow country road. To my right the land rolled up a long gentle slope. A stone barn sat up there, topped by copper cupolas oxidized down to pale mint green. A stand of trees, their leaves still predominately green, protected the steepest part of the slope from erosion. A few bright spots of red and orange had begun to dapple the foliage.

Jim's rig crested the top of the hill, and down to my left, through a sturdy post and rail fence, a dozen or so broodmares grazed. Most of them had foals nearby. Thoroughbreds. Maybe I'd ride one someday. Not a weed in sight. The grass was shamrock green, the sun bright, and I couldn't imagine having the money to own such a place.

I reached over, my fingertips searching for the piece of paper with directions. "Poplar road/over the creek with wood bridge/ turn to left." Okay. I swung downhill and below me trees crowded against the road. Massive trunks of an old-forest stand and the dark green of pine and holly. Ahead a wooden bridge with a "Single Lane" sign led over a large rushing creek strewn with smooth rocks. I slowed, making sure no one was approaching from the opposite end, slid the electric window down and listened to the water roar, inhaling damp earth and cedar. The rig rattled over the bridge, and I looked left.

There. A small sign. I made the turn and headed up a steep hill thick with timber and evergreen. A few moss-covered boulders lay along the edge of the road. At the top of the hill the ground opened sharply, the panorama ahead making me slow the truck. A sign with red lettering read "Balmora."

Historic-looking Maryland brick home to the left. Box bushes, brick walk leading to the house. Horse barns ahead, vast fields of grass to the right, horses grazing, and in the distance on the left, a racetrack, maybe a half-mile around. Steeplechase jumps set up in the infield. Money, lots and lots of money. Could I get a job here?

I rolled down to what appeared to be the main barn and climbed out. Hellish knew we'd arrived somewhere and started stomping, impatient to be set free. She could smell the horses, and she'd been shut up in the trailer for almost two hours. I hoped she wouldn't explode, and walked into the barn.

Wide center aisle. Clear solid wood-paneled stalls with black iron railing from shoulder height up to about 10 feet. The buckets, feed bins, and tack boxes shining in turquoise and red. Snappy. Glowing coats, bright eyes on the horses. A guy about 25 grooming a horse in a stall halfway down the aisle. Bales of sweet, dark-green alfalfa formed a neat stack to my right, the guy just ahead on the left.

"Excuse me," I said. "I'm looking for Mr. Boucher?"

They guy paused, resting the hand holding the curry comb on the horse's withers. Handsome, light brown hair, thin and very fit. "Senior or Junior?"

"Senior." Like I had a clue.

"That would be my dad." He gave me the once over. "Are you Nikki Latrelle?"

I said I was, and a kind of resistance settled on his features. He came out of the stall. "I'll get him for you, but I don't know how much good it will do you." He walked away down the aisle and disappeared through a door on the far left.

Not encouraging. The horse he'd been grooming ambled over and shoved his head toward me over the stall door. I moved to him and stroked his neck without conscious thought.

An older version of Junior came quickly through the door and jogged toward me. He was lean, his face planed sharp from hard work.

"Miss Latrelle." His accent clipped and British. He shook my hand rapidly, his face already negating my employment. "We agreed to help out, but Jim didn't tell me you're involved in a murder. Sorry, you've got too much notoriety attached. It wouldn't do for us."

He raised a brow and jutted his head forward.

Yeah, I got it. "Thank you. I won't take any more of your time." I turned and walked away. Could feel my face burning, hear his footsteps retreating. Figured he'd already forgotten me.

The second and last place on my list was another hour and a half away, near the West Virginia border. I'd better get going. Hellish already had the trailer swaying as she moved restlessly inside. She'd started whinnying. Other horses began answering, and she got more worked up by the second. I jumped in the cab, cranked the engine and pulled out, hoping the rhythm of movement would calm her down. At least she'd stop thinking it was time to unload.

The Robersons' place wasn't a movie-set like Balmora. Fences needed repair. The barnyard was littered with straw and bits of trash, and a number of pesky vines attempted to strangle the locust posts in a nearby paddock. To the west of this place the mountains near Harper's Ferry, West Virginia, were gilded by the late afternoon sun sinking steadily into a dark cloud bank that stirred on the horizon. The radio had warned of a cold front, rain, heavy at times.

Sally Roberson was tall and thin, maybe 65. She looked tired. Her face suggested resignation — etched by the accumulation of too many disappointments.

I stepped away from Jim's truck and headed toward her where she stood in the entrance to an old wooden barn, its red paint long overdue for a touchup. A short, round-bellied man stepped from the shadows behind her and stared at me. His mouth turned down.

"If you're Nikki Latrelle, we're not buying . . ."

The tall woman raised a sharp arm, her hand slicing the air near his face, fingers splayed. "I'll handle this, Dundle," she said, her eyes never leaving me.

"You tell Ravinsky he's got some nerve sending you up here. We may live in the sticks, but I have connections. I graduated from the Madeira School in Virginia." She pronounced it "Vah-ginia" and stood up a bit straighter.

Oh, right, that school where the head mistress murdered the Scarsdale Diet Doctor in 19-whatever.

Sally glared at me. "Same school as Janet LeGrange. I used to be somebody," she said bitterly, her head whipping to stare at the round-bellied man. He retreated back into the shadows.

I pictured Janet with those big diamonds and designer duds. If they'd been social equals, Sally had suffered a long fall.

"She still calls me. Happens she called today, told me about you being a serial horse killer."

This was going well.

"I know what you are. Get the hell off my land!"

"I'm gone," I said.

"Sally, you want this?" Round-belly had reappeared with a shotgun.

"You just hold that right on her, Dundle, until she gets her ass in that truck and off our farm."

Hellish was screaming at some other horses and the trailer was lurching from side to side. *Jesus Christ.* I jerked the handle on the cab door, threw myself inside and got the hell out of there.

23

A hard rain from the west struck Jim's rig as I motored down the ramp from 270 where it connects with the Washington Beltway near Bethesda, Maryland. A sudden gust drove sheets of water sideways, causing the trailer to sway. Hellish fought back with a lurch that shoved the trailer into a fishtail. An 18-wheeler rode alongside us down the sharp curve, blinding me with spray from its big tires. I struggled with the wheel, correcting against the skid, pumping the brakes.

Through my left window, the right rear tires of the huge truck appeared, sliding toward me, an avalanche of water. Panic grabbed my stomach. Then Jim's Ford steadied. Separated by inches, the big rig drew ahead as I continued dampening my speed.

Could this day get any worse? Don't ask, I thought. By now I'd slowed to a crawl, gaining control over Jim's rig, the tractor trailer barreling on ahead, finally out of spray range. The moment past, but my knees kept trembling.

I merged onto 495 and worked over to the slow lane. Hit the tape "play" button to see what Jim had on there, and Sinatra joined me in the cab. That was cool, he was an upbeat guy, kind of soothing.

I'd been putting off admitting it, but I was going to have to check out Dimsboro. I'd called Jim on my cell phone after leaving the Robersons' place.

"You can't bring her back here, Nikki. If Mello says he has a stall, he's got one. He may be a drunk, but he keeps his word."

Great.

"And he knows things," Jim had said.

"What does that mean, exactly?" I asked, but must have hit a dead cell zone. Jim never answered, and I couldn't get him back. Now I concentrated on the wall of rain, and the river on the highway. Rough enough that cars had pulled from the highway onto the shoulder. Under an overpass five or six of bikers sat on their Harleys, waiting it out.

I headed south into Prince George's County, took the Route 4 exit and hydroplaned toward Pallboro. Funereal sounding name. I drove into the town, amazingly quaint for being so close to D.C. I passed an ancient brick church. Wet English box, hollies, and tombstones crowded the churchyard. The brick walk to the building was sunken and old. I crossed over Tavern Branch, the creek so swollen with rain it surged and splashed up through the bridge's metal grating.

Some cops were at the crossing with sawhorses and battery-lit signs, getting ready to close it off. Figured I'd just made it. I'd heard that back in the 1800s this creek was so deep and wide, big ships could sail up from the Patuxent River and Chesapeake Bay. Cargo boats would navigate up Tavern Branch to deliver goods and pick up Southern Maryland tobacco in Pallboro.

Ahead, to the right, I could see an arena run by a division of the Maryland State Park. Along with the sports center they'd inherited the racetrack, which lay to the left. Rumor was the park service was doing everything possible to make the track fail. Probably wanted to use the land for some money-making scheme. Nothing like letting in a bunch of felons to help its demise. I couldn't see too well in the deluge, but even in this torrent a well-maintained track shouldn't look like a lake. Sharks could swim out there.

I followed the road along the track to the backside. It turned right and ran parallel with a row of barns. Their blank ends faced the road. The track stretched away in the gloom to my right. It was late, getting dark, becoming almost impossible to make anything out in the rain.

I heard, then felt a growing rumble. A speeding light approached from beyond the barns. When I recognized the long notes of a train whistle, I let go the breath I'd been holding. Probably just the moisture in the air, but the barns seemed to sway as the train lumbered through. I eased the Ford to a stop and cut the engine. Sat there a moment, feeling exhaustion sweep through me. Cold vapor from the rain seeped into the cab. The train whistle grew distant.

I let loose a scream as a face materialized outside my window. A Latino stared at me, his face streaked with water. The silver of a teardrop tattoo glistened beneath the corner of his right eye. A prison tattoo. He was naked to the waist. Maybe some drug kept him comfortable. The long ropy muscles of his arms were stained with reptilian tattoos.

I smashed my palm onto the lock next to my window and thought about firing up the Ford's engine. The man pointed at me with a long fingernail. A flashlight approached, and with a mental sob I recognized the voice of Mello Pinkney.

"What you doing, Vipe? You'll scare her to death."

"Screw you, old man." The Latino turned abruptly and moved away. A dark ponytail sprouted from his head and snaked between his shoulder blades. The night swallowed him.

"That you, Miss Nikki?" Mello shone the light in my face.

I raised a hand against the piercing beam and slid the window down a few inches. "Yeah. I got the horse back there. Is there a place for her?" *Mental prayer of supplication.*

"Got a stall all fixed up. Don't you worry about old Mello." He was wearing a black rain hat. A see-through plastic-coat covered his thread-bare jacket. A glint of red bow tie somehow brightened my night.

Hellish came off that trailer in a rage, her metal shoes crashing on the ramp, a deep, angry whinny erupting from her chest.

"Oh my lord," said Mello. "We'd best get her in the barn." He hurried away.

I followed him between two barns. Water sluiced along the pavement and gurgled down a drain. These barns, like Laurel, had a roof overhanging the open-sided shedrows running outside the stalls. Unlike Laurel, the roofs leaked. Water dripped on the covered dirt paths on either side of me. There weren't enough buckets in Prince George's County to catch the flow.

Mello stepped into the aisle on our left, ducked an ambitious leak and moved to the end of the barn. Water lay in the aisle way, and I splashed through with Hellish. The path inclined upward near the end, the dirt becoming dry.

Hellish bulled along, dragging me after Mello, like she was trying to catch up with him. He disappeared into a stall, Hellish hot on his heels. Inside, she stopped. I took the lead off and stepped back, astonished.

The stall was clean, dry, knee-deep in fresh yellow straw. A hay rack in the corner held a cornucopia of sweet-smelling alfalfa and timothy. Full water buckets hung on the wall, and a feed tub brimmed with grain. But it was Hellish's deep interest in Mello that stunned me. She moved over to him, ignoring the amenities, and shoved her nose against his chest.

The old man stilled. His eyes lit with recognition. A mocha hand rose, trembling fingers traced the filly's finely-made head. "Gallorette," he whispered.

24

Sheltered from the wind and rain, a whiff of Mello's liquored breath curled past my nostrils. What was the old man going on about? Famous and a champion, Gallorette had died decades ago.

"Her name's Helen's Dream," I said. "But I call her Hellish."

"Call her what you want," he said. "This be Gallorette. She's come back to me." He crooned unintelligible words to the mare. Hellish raised her head, slid it over Mello's right shoulder and arched her neck. Her gesture pulled the man in close.

Gee, it had been a long day. Had Tavern Branch overflowed? Was I stuck in this place for the night? I rubbed my eyes with my knuckles, worrying about getting the rig back to Jim. No time to stand there listening to nonsense. Sharks were circling outside.

I stepped back against the wall and sank into the crisp straw, elbows on bent knees, head in my hands. I felt my cell phone digging at my hip through the pocket of my jeans. Pulled it out, tried to speed-dial Jim. A flashing sign on the face indicated no service. Of course not.

Mello was still making a fuss over Hellish. I watched them, shaking my head. The old man looked over at me, a dreamy smile lazing on his lips. Catching my expression, his eyes narrowed. "Don't you believe in the reincarnation?"

I made a *yeah-right* face. But the hairs stirred on the back of my neck and my scalp prickled. Didn't believe or not believe in reincarnation. Who knew about these things?

I ended up sleeping in Hellish's stall. Mello'd said the bridge was shut down, he'd see me in the morning, then had disappeared into the rain. I could have locked myself in Jim's truck, but I felt safer with Hellish and made a little nest of straw in the corner. Bedded down like I'd done almost eight years ago at Pimlico. Fading into an uneasy sleep I felt like I was falling downhill uncontrollably until I jolted awake. In the darkness I could just make out Hellish's lightning-bolt white blaze. Her presence comforted me and I finally slept.

I awoke in the pre-dawn hours thinking about fingerprints, remembered dreaming about white plastic syringes. A memory pricked at me like a needle. Kenny. He'd helped me give those flu shots to Jim's horses that morning before Dennis was murdered. He'd put the syringes with my prints all over them in a trash bag, then supposedly taken them to the dumpster. Had he been paid to hand them over? Or had someone taken them from him? That hypo I'd seen lying next to Dennis had to be from that bag. Nobody had seen Kenny since. *Damn.*

Hellish wandered over to my corner, stretched her neck down and investigated me with warm breath and whiskers.

"That tickles," I said, sitting up. No chance of going back to sleep. The rain that had pounded the roof all night slacked off, then shrunk to the sound of trickling gutters and dripping downspouts.

Might as well clean the stall, feed Hellish an early breakfast, check out the bridge.

I went out looking for a ladies room and actually found one. I pushed open the door and a gush of heated air hit me. Things were looking up. Inside a young woman with platinum zebra-like streaks in her dark kinky hair was asleep on a futon under a burgundy velveteen blanket. The blanket was folded away from her left side, revealing a low-cut, gold lame-top, significant breasts. She hadn't washed off her makeup from the previous night. Lot of eyeliner, gold sparkle on her eyelids. Her skin a smooth, taupe brown. A pair of shoes with mud-caked stiletto heels lay next to her. Runaway and hooker came to mind.

I tiptoed into a cubicle, used the facilities and flushed. When I emerged, the girl was sitting up, hair sticking out every which way. She rubbed at her eyes, making them racoonlike. A wild young animal.

"Hey, girl," she said, yawning. "Who you?"

"Nikki. You always sleep in the ladies room?" Maybe I should watch my tongue.

She didn't seem to mind. "Got heat, a shower, dressing room. And it don't cost nothing."

I couldn't argue with her logic.

She stood up and draped the blanket over her shoulders. Big surprise — she was wearing a gold skirt, about ten inches long. She moved over to one of the two shower stalls built against the far wall. Each one had an extra cubicle attached to the front with a cloth curtain. She leaned inside, pulled out a black vinyl suitcase, and rummaged inside. Her hand emerged with a terry sweat suit and she began to peel off her skirt.

"I was just leaving," I said, scooting for the door.

"You need anything, sugar, you just ask for Chocolate."

"Right," I said and slipped outside. The rain-washed air felt cool and fresh. Dawn revealed puddles hiding in potholes on the pavement between the ladies' bath and the barns. Jim's rig was right where I'd left it, scattered beads of water forming a decorative web on the red paint.

A thin, sandy-haired white boy rode past on a dark horse headed for the track. Something about the horse's neck. That big cowlick. The bay horse I'd come to think of as Whorly, the gelding from the auction. The one that had shown up in Clements' barn with the fancy new name.

I called to the rider, "Hey, is that Noble Treasure?"

The boy's head whipped around, eyes wary. "You'd have to ask Vipe. I don't know anything. Just ride what I'm told." He urged the horse into a trot, moving into the sand chute leading onto the track.

Vipe? The scary guy with the prison tattoo? How was he connected to Whorly?

Some of the barns were beginning to stir with activity. Figures hauling buckets were silhouetted by the sun rising behind the railroad tracks. A man ferried a wheelbarrow to a manure dump. Two African-Americans wearing dreadlocks emerged on horseback from a nearby barn.

Back in Hellish's stall I found Mello at work with a pitchfork. "You don't have to do that," I said.

"I'd do anything for Gallorette."

Mello appeared sober, even had on a new orange bow tie, brown nylon stable jacket. I'd hoped with morning sobriety he'd forget that reincarnation stuff, but the filly hadn't. She was following the old man about the stall, pressing her nostrils against the back of his neck.

"Sure, thanks," I said. "Uh, Mello, who's that Vipe guy?"

Mello set the prongs of the pitchfork in the straw, turned toward me. "He be trouble, Miss Nikki. Don't be messing with him."

"How do I keep him from messing with me?" The guy had been so threatening the night before.

"That do be a problem," he said, nodding his head.

Dimsboro was a problem. Crawling with ex-convicts charged with God knows what crimes, ruled-off horsemen exiled from the main tracks, hookers in the ladies' room. A place that was shunned, rundown, and seedy. Where better to hide a horse with fake papers?

I got my cell phone out and reached Jim. Explained what had happened, where I was. Said I'd have the rig back by noon.

Jim said okay, paused a couple of beats. "There were two Anne Arundel County cops looking for you, Nikki."

"What'd you tell them?"

"The truth. I had no idea where you were."

"They say what they wanted?"

"Course not. Those types keep it real quiet."

Probably about the fingerprints, I thought. I wasn't going to tell Jim my theories about Kenny Grimes. "Do they think I ran?"

"Nah, I explained about you being ruled off, looking for a home for your horse."

We said goodbye, disconnected.

Mello had found a curry comb and was working on Hellish's chestnut coat with surprising energy. She was nodding her head up and down in time to his rubbing, a blissful response I'd never received.

Out on the track three riders were hobby-horsing their mounts around, and no doubt, they were being paid to do it. I balked at the thought, but I had to have cash.

"Mello, do they need riders here? I've got to earn some money."

He looked surprised. "They don't got nobody here can ride like you. You get plenty of work. Best say you only takes cash. Up-front. We got some slippery folks here." He went back to cleaning.

I could see he'd already taken care of feeding Hellish. I had to *pay* him. Took a breath. "Who should I talk to about work?"

He gave me some names and barn numbers, pointed at some buildings. I stepped out into the morning light at Dimsboro, skirting puddles, keeping a watchful eye out for snakes and other reptiles.

25

The large black man I talked to first was called Bubba Lard. Mello had indicated Bubba paid well, in cash. I recognized him. He'd run horses from time to time at Laurel, wasn't ruled off. So why was he at Dimsboro? Probably, I didn't want to know.

"You're Nikki Latrelle, right?" His eyes lit with interest.

I said I was, and peered around, taking in his barn. Looked like he had the whole building. Pretty well fixed up, too — fairly clean. No moldy or sour odors.

"I've seen you ride. You're good. What you doing here?"

"I've had a little trouble. Been suspended for a while."

He wheezed a low, slow laugh. "How the mighty hath fallen."

I stood there, taking it. "So, can I get some work riding for you, or what?"

"When the Lord provides, I don't turn away." His voice rolled loud, like a reverend.

"What are they paying for freelance at Laurel?" he asked, sliding his hands into the pockets of his large black jacket, a shiny nylon worn over gray track pants. New Reebok trainers on his feet.

"Ten a ride," I said.

"I'll pay you seven." An arrogant smirk curled his lips. "You won't get more from anyone else here. Not unless I says."

I dug my finger nails into my palms. "When can I start?"

"Right now." He looked down the aisle, an impatient expression settling around his mouth. "Junior," he bellowed. Some grooms poked their heads out of a couple of stalls to see what was going on. They stared at me, various piercings glinting gold from nostrils, lips,and eyebrows on their dark skin.

An immense young man waddled out from what appeared to be the barn office. Wasn't sure how he'd fit through the door. He worked his way up the shedrow. He wore a clean white sports jersey the size of a dining table. It advertised him as number one. His pants were royal blue nylon, loose and wide, the crotch suspended somewhere near his knees. A gust of wind blew from behind him. and I was afraid he'd set sail and run us down.

"This is my boy," Bubba said. "Junior, get over here."

The kid rocked a bit, increasing his pace, reminding me of a runaway

Winnebago.

"Wha's up?" His voice somewhere between a wheeze and a gasp.

"Go tell one of them," Bubba waved in the direction of the glinting metallic faces, "to get Andy Blue ready. This girl's going to take him out."

The kid's eyes got real big. Not a good sign. He turned and lumbered toward the grooms, working hard to build momentum. He didn't strike me as lazy, just fat. I kind of felt sorry for him. Had a nice face. Why would you let that happen to your kid?

Andy Blue. A large bay gelding with an oversized, common-looking head. I got the son of a gun out to the track only because he had Junior for ballast on the end of the shank. The kid let Andy go in the deep sand. The horse tensed, ready to explode. Wanted to misbehave in a bad way. I tapped with my whip. "Move out," I yelled, scared. The horse reared up, reached his zenith and sailed over backward. I bailed, pushing off his withers with my hands, fast and hard. Watched him crash into the dirt. Crushing the saddle beneath him. I grabbed the shank from Junior. Clipped it to the ring on Andy's bit before he scrambled to his feet.

I was mad. Of course an audience had gathered to see the girl get trashed by Andy Blue. "You," I yelled at a guy with a ring in his nostril. "Give me a leg up on this son-of-a-bitch."

Junior held the shank. Nose-Ring threw me up.

"Let him go!" I said.

No time for any of that Monty Roberts, Horse Whisperer shit. I pointed Andy's head down the track and whipped him hard. He started bucking, but at least he was moving. He leapt up. I kept a death grip on the yoke to keep from falling off backward. He plunged down, throwing his hind end up in the air, and I had my feet on the dashboard, straight out in front of me. He wasn't sending *me* over his head. He continued bucking. My whip kept flashing.

Now the horse was truly irritated. Wasn't used to stubborn riders. He almost threw himself on the ground in a tantrum. I whipped harder. And just like that, he gave in. Went on around the track two times in a smooth gallop, walked back to the barn like a stable pony.

Bubba looked real pleased when I returned. "Changed my mind, Latrelle. You did a $10 ride." A low laugh rumbled from his chest. "That old Andy, he was *so mad.*"

Junior, wheezing and wordless, took the horse back to its stall. The grooms with gold piercings stared at me round-eyed. Respectful.

Bubba gave me a couple of tame ones to ride, paid me cash. Thirty bucks.

"You come back tomorrow, I'll have more," he said.

I followed directions to another barn on Mello's list. A short, sly-looking man with a pencil moustache appeared when I asked for the head man. He had natty hair slicked back with shine enhancing pomade. Raymond Marteen. He gave me a couple of appraising looks.

"You ride or what?"

"Ride. I'm looking for work," I said.

He stared at me, apparently thinking about it. His barn aisle held water from the previous night. The horses that looked out at me appeared ratty and underfed. A flagstone walk had been laid along the edge of the barn and turned in at the end. I could see a new piece of roof had been added down there. The last third of the barn aisle had been closed in with heavy, pressure-treated plywood. A red door, apparently leading to the built-in area, blocked the end of the shedrow. The door hung next to a miserable looking gray horse in the last stall. He was "weaving," shifting his weight from one front leg to the other, swinging his head back and forth without pause.

The red door opened with a grating sound, and Chocolate strolled out, still in her sweat suit.

Raymond's eyes assessed me. "You're a fine-looking woman. You ride anything besides horses?"

"I don't think so," I said, my glance drifting to Chocolate, back to Raymond. "You need someone to exercise your horses or not?"

"I might." He wouldn't hold my gaze. Slippery fellow.

"Okay," I said. "Ten dollars a ride."

"I'll pay you ten . . . when our big horse comes in."

"Forget it," I said and walked away. That old line. Pay me when their good horse won a race. People who wouldn't pay their help never had a "big" horse.

I stalked back toward Mello's barn. Went past a storage shed, and a man in dark glasses stepped out, blocking my path. His hand snaked out fast, fingers gripping my wrist. I saw an edge of silver teardrop beneath the glasses. Vipe. Hadn't recognized him with a shirt on.

"Hey, chica. I got los caballos de carrera. You wanna ride for me?"

Telling me he had race horses. Like I cared. "Ah, no thanks. Think you could let go of my arm?"

"Sure, pretty lady." He smiled, revealing a gold tooth, dropping my arm. His body seemed too thin, unhealthy. A druggie. "So you kill a man? I hear this," he said. "Is true?"

My eyes squeezed shut. "No, not true. Excuse me." I tried to push past him.

His hand flashed in and out of his jeans pocket. Sharp click. A long blade reflected the morning light. Vipe had a big knife.

26

"You don't walk away from me," he said, his voice a hiss. "And you mind your own business, yes?"

"Yes." I stood rooted. His liberal use of cologne only worsened a stench of unwashed body.

He recognized my fear and laughed, a high girlish sound. He had what he wanted, folded the knife. "You go now, you have my permiso." Up close his olive-toned face revealed an underlying pallor.

I stepped backward. Carefully. *Get me out of here.* Made tracks to Hellish's stall, noticed a hose and twisted the nozzle at the end. Sprayed cold water on my hands and wiped my face.

Mello sat on a broken-legged stool that at one time had been painted yellow. He'd placed the stool before the filly's stall door. Hellish's chestnut face peered out above Mello's gray hair. She had an orange baseball cap in her mouth that she'd probably snatched from Mello's head. She looked real pleased with herself.

Maybe I should gallop her before I returned Jim's truck. In her stall I knelt in the straw next to her front legs, looking for evidence of heat or swelling and found none.

I got my gear from the storage compartment in Jim's trailer, and Mello helped me tack up Hellish. His quick hands moved in familiar territory as they slid the bit into Hellish's mouth, buckled bits of leather, adjusted the saddlecloth. He walked out ahead of us to the track, and the horse followed him like he was a grain wagon. Once we stepped onto the track, he pushed Hellish's head away and gave her a light slap on a hindquarter. She jogged off, eased into a gallop, neck arched, chin almost tucked into her chest.

About half way through our circuit, she took off and I had trouble holding her. The filly had a talent for speed. Not that it'd do me any good if she remained uncontrollable. When I finally pulled her up I felt a trace of soreness, her rhythm off a half-beat. Still something in that right front leg. I had no money for X-rays, but she wasn't lame, just off a hair. Light training, if I could just hold her to it, shouldn't hurt her. But if I was serious about racing her, I had some things to figure out.

I emerged from my apartment bathroom in clean clothes around one that afternoon. Someone was knocking on my door. Nearby my phone flashed with red message lights I hadn't bothered to play. Earlier I'd met Jim outside Laurel Park, returned the rig and driven my Toyota home. Slippers had met me at the door howling. I'd fussed over him, checked his dishes and plunged into a hot shower.

Now the cat trailed me to the door, watching me squint through the peephole. Cops. The Anne Arundel homicide detectives, Trent Curtis and Charlie Wells. I opened the door.

"Miss Latrelle," said Curtis, "we've been trying to reach you."

I'd forgotten the deep resonance in Curtis's voice. I stepped back. They moved in. Wells gave me a quick smile. A tight pattern of teeny silver bullets decorated his blue tie. Wells' big shoulders stretched a brown suit jacket, while his thick neck strained the collar on a cream-colored shirt.

"A lot's happened," I said.

"So we hear," said Curtis. "Can we have a seat?" He gestured at my couch, sat on the edge. Slippers went right for his brown suit pants. Rub, purr, rub.

Wells chose a wicker chair. I remained standing.

Curtis impaled me with a hard stare. Those jaded eyes. Wished he wouldn't look at me like that.

"You know," he said, "your fingerprints were on that hypodermic we found near O'Brien's body. State lab found remnants of insulin inside. Nice way to kill a horse. Doesn't leave a trace, either. But you probably know that."

Gildy. Dr. Dawson saying he'd found no traceable toxins. "*No.* I didn't know that." I stepped back and sank onto the other wicker chair, then stood up again. Maybe these guys would hear me out. "I figured something out last night."

"I'm listening," said Curtis.

I told them about Kenny and the syringes. How Kenny had disappeared. Sketched Clements and Farino back into the picture. When I started in about Whorly and Vipe, I lost Curtis. He came back at me.

"You kill Kenny?"

My jaw dropped.

"Ah, give it a rest, Trent," said Wells. "Maybe she's got something there with this Clements guy. We could run priors on the bunch of 'em."

More good cop, bad cop?

The two of them hung around a while longer, digging at me for answers I didn't have. With hard looks and a warning not to go AWOL again, they left. I snuck a peek out my window to make sure they drove away. Curtis stood with one foot raised on the bottom stair step, picking at a fringe of gray fur blossoming on his pants leg. Served him right.

The phone shrilled. I grabbed it, heard the voice that always stirred me.

"You doing anything tonight?"

Sleeping, I'd hoped. "An early evening might work." The sudden proximity to Clay sped me up, pushed sleep down my priority list.

"Great. Let's grab an early dinner. Got a flight to Kentucky tomorrow morning at seven. How about Mama Stellina's? Meet me at six?"

I said I would and hung up. Looked at the blinking message lights and turned my back on them. Went to the bathroom and rummaged for the can of Spike!

Clay stood in the foyer at Mama Stellina's with his back to me, but I knew those wide shoulders and narrow hips. He turned, saw me, and smiled. A glow of heat spread through me. So he wasn't honest to a fault. Who was?

A stout woman with dark hair pinned high on her head showed us to a table covered with a standard red-and-white checkered cloth. A Chianti bottle, partially buried under wax drippings, stood at the center of the small round table. A candle sprouted from the bottle's mouth, flickering hot with yellow flame.

We sat in wooden chairs. I set my elbows on the table and reached for a menu. Clay's hand closed over mine. "What would you like?"

Oh boy. "Chianti's good," I said, pointing to the centerpiece.

A waitress who might have been related to the hostess came by with a notepad. Her hair was pinned up, teased, and sprayed. Little plastic butterflies, flowers, and barnyard animals nestled in her beehive. Like the hostess, she was mid-40s, same dark eyes and generous figure, with the addition of heavy makeup. She gave Clay the once-over, taking in the streaked blond hair, the good face bones, intense blue eyes.

Clay smiled at her. She fluttered. He ordered wine and asked if she'd give us a few minutes.

A silly smile grew on the woman's lips. "Sure, honey. I'd give you as long as you wanted. Anytime." She gave me a wink and minced away, hips swaying.

After we'd ordered and I'd worked partway through a plate of shrimp scampi, our conversation changed direction. We'd made small talk about the Kentucky yearling sale Clay was attending and the upcoming Maryland Million stakes races.

Now, as Clay sopped up the remnants of his thick tomato sauce with crusty Italian bread, he gave me an intent look. "You've been through a lot. Was it hard finding O'Brien like that?"

"Wasn't pretty," I said.

"Is that the same guy we saw outside Coca Mocha that night? Made you angry?"

More incriminating evidence. "Guy almost got me killed at the races. Anyone would be mad."

"Hey, take it easy," Clay said. "I haven't mentioned it to anyone. Wouldn't do that to you."

A row of Italian opera singers in full costume gestured from picture frames on the wall behind Clay. A dark-eyed young man in a white apron rushed up with a pitcher of ice water, frosted over with condensation. He tumbled water into our half-empty glasses.

I pushed a shrimp around my plate. "It's been . . . humiliating."

"I'm sorry." He sounded sincere, like he felt bad about my predicament. "Do the police have any leads?"

"Only the ones I've given them."

"Really?" He looked interested. "Like what?"

I gave him the rundown on Clements, Farino, Kenny and the syringes. Decided to leave out Vipe and the horse with the strange cowlick. Too much information.

Clay looked curious and started to ask another question.

"Look," I said, "this whole thing has ground me down. Can we talk about something else?"

He shrugged. "How about we share a tiramisu?"

Our waitress brought the dessert on a plate with two forks. She hung around until Clay forked a mouthful of chocolate and whip cream through his lips. She shivered and rolled her eyes, animals and insects bobbing in her beehive. I was afraid a cow might fall into my half and pulled the plate away from where she hovered near the table edge.

Clay hid a smile, turned those baby blues on the waitress. "Thank you. Could you bring us a check?"

By the time we went outside I was beginning to wish we hadn't driven there separately. But I'd asked for an early night.

At my car Clay's hands closed around my forearms, slid down and held my wrists. He pulled me in, the light in his eyes close enough to burn. He brushed his lips against mine, drew back and studied my expression. Smiled.

I wasn't exactly beating him off.

The man leaned in, kissed me, and I felt his tongue flick into the left corner of my lips. Surprised, I realized I wanted the warm, wet surge of a French kiss, but Clay only teased at that crevice with slow strokes, never slid his tongue inside my mouth.

Imagining how that would feel made me shiver.

He wrapped his arms around me, held me close. "We'll do this right," he said. "When we have time."

Remembering those words on the drive home, I almost whimpered.

27

I loathed the Washington Beltway, thought of it as the "Death way." Even at five A.M. I preferred commuting to Dimsboro by taking Route 197 to 301, then rolling south to Pallboro.

New development crowded up to the pavement, suggesting the long anticipated housing collapse hadn't yet reached the area. Probably wouldn't, what with all the companies that fed on government contracts protecting the local economy.

I'd read an article in the *Washington Post* interviewing a Prince George's County group. They'd complained about overcrowded schools, highways, and strained emergency services. One man had asked how it was that developers were allowed to shove in poorly planned housing, get out with *their* money, and leave the county holding the bag for additional infrastructure and social service expenses. "Look at the results," he'd said. "Gridlock and higher taxes."

As I motored down 301 at dawn, I felt empathy for the guy. Vinyl-sided housing mushroomed on gentle hills where only months before cows had grazed on open green pasture. Where would they stash all the cars that came with the houses? How many more fast-food factories and strip malls would spring up to feed these people's appetites?

I wondered how the area had looked in Mello's time. When I'd called Jim the previous evening, I'd asked him about the old man.

"Has trouble with the bottle, but he knows his horses," he'd said. "Must be up in his 80s."

"He thinks Hellish is a reincarnation of Gallorette."

"Huh."

"Why does everybody keep saying Mello knows things?"

There was a two-beat pause, then Jim had said, "Lot of people think he's got the second sight."

"You believe in that stuff?"

"Nikki, if you're in horse racing long enough you'll believe anything. Things happen you can't explain."

Gee, that had cleared everything up. Now, as my car bumped over the Tavern Branch bridge, my mind drifted back to the previous night, memories of Clay outside Mama Stellina's. I went right by the turn into Dimsboro and had to make a U-turn to go back.

I'd brought a bottle of Acepromazine with me, hoping a small dose of the horse tranquilizer might calm Hellish, allow her to be more businesslike in her morning gallops. Mello wasn't around, so I cleaned the filly's stall, fed her breakfast, then headed for Bubba's barn.

The early morning still retained a cool, freshly washed quality from Sunday's heavy rain. The previous day's paper containing the development article was stuffed in a nearby trash can. I searched for the date. Monday, September 28. October 1 would arrive Thursday. How would I pay rent? My feet double-timed it to Bubba's barn.

I found him and Junior in the office. The room was neatly organized and large enough to accommodate the big men and two boxes of doughnuts. I didn't think there was room in there for me, so I stood in the doorway

They were both talking on cell phones, Bubba seated at a metal desk next to the door, and Junior on a sturdy oak bench. A flat-screen TV with a cable news station droned from a wall shelf, and down the shedrow the grooms had a radio playing loud hiphop. Bubba nodded at me, stuck his head into the aisle and hollered. The boy with the pierced nostril brought a gray horse around.

I rode four for Bubba, got forty bucks, and found two more Dimsboro outfits willing to pay cash. They'd heard I'd mastered Andy Blue and brought me their hard cases. I got through it, but riding horses like that, it was only a matter of time before I got injured.

I pocketed ninety in cash and went back to my filly. I put a needle on a syringe, slid the thin steel through the rubber cap on my Acepromazine bottle and drew out three ccs of tranquilizer. Pulled the needle off the syringe, put it away and got a hold of Hellish's halter. She dragged me around the stall, not wanting any part of the syringe in my other hand.

"Stop fussing," I said. "You'd rather me stick you with a needle?" Mello appeared outside the stall, a timely distraction. I zipped the syringe into Hellish's mouth and squirted the drug on the back of her tongue where it could absorb.

"Gotcha," I said. Any round won with Hellish was a victory.

I thought I'd ask Mello about Gallorette while we waited for the drug to soak into Hellish's system. This morning he sported a bow tie in maroon with old stains. His almond-shaped eyes looked tired, one hand trembled slightly.

"Mello, why do you think she's a reincarnation of Gallorette?"

He scratched at his cheek. "I don't thinks it. I knows it."

I squinted one eye shut. Okay, I'd bite. "How do you *know* it?"

"Because I knew Gallorette," he said, like he was talking to a half-wit.

There it was again, the "k" word. "You saw her at the races when you were a kid?" I asked, hearing the sarcasm in my voice. "You met her in a dream? What?"

"Don't be gettin all fluffed up with me, Missy. I worked for Mr. Christmas. Trained Gallorette. Back in the 40s." His head nodded, then turned toward the plaintive sound of the freight train's horn as it headed through Pallboro.

Mello's eyes took on a faraway look I hadn't seen before. "Time was, you could board a train right here in Pallboro. Ride on into Baltimore, Washington. Anyplace. One time Mr. Christmas put me on a train with Gallorette. Rode up to Long Island for the Brooklyn Handicap. Beat Stymie by a nose that day."

I thought Jim had a picture of that very race on the wall in his office, but I'd never read the fine print, never heard of anybody named Christmas. Hadn't seen any commuter trains come through, either, just the freight trains with coal cars and containers, like the one that rumbled through now.

"Christmas?" I asked. "Like Santa Claus?"

"Like Jesus," he said. Anger transformed his gentle voice into a rebuke from the pulpit. "And don't you be such a doubting Thomas. Christmas is a fine old name in Maryland trainers. Donnelson, Edward, Yancey. Those gentlemen knew how to train. Not like folks today — every kind of drug made legal, sneaking stuff that ain't. Who knows what all?"

He was really fired up. Then his shoulders sagged, and the bright light from a distant fire receded into the old eyes of a man with a drinking problem.

Hellish yawned. The Ace had hit her. I got her tacked up, and she galloped along agreeably. Truth was, even without Ace, she seemed calmer at Dimsboro. Maybe it was the quieter location, perhaps Mello's presence soothed her.

Riding back from the track, we passed Marteen's barn of sorry horses. Chocolate was crawling out of a huge black Mercedes. She stood on the gravel, stretched and yawned, the top on her hot red outfit riding up to reveal a ruby-colored jewel in her navel. Another girl with pearl white skin, long legs, and a shiny black leather getup staggered out behind her. Looked like they'd had a long night. They made for the red door in Marteen's barn and disappeared. One of Marteen's grooms slouched behind the Mercedes wheel in a black cap. He drove the car out of sight behind the barn.

I didn't want to know.

I spent the drive back to Laurel worrying about my October rent. I had visions of an eviction notice, my furniture and cat on the pavement, a big guy with a shaved head repossessing my Toyota. I hoped to find a solution, didn't want to ask Jim for a loan.

At my apartment I stretched out on the couch. Slippers purred on my stomach while we listened to phone messages. Three old ones from Trent Curtis before he'd found me, an electronic solicitation from a dry cleaners, and a call from Lorna. I'd hoped for a message from Clay. No dice. I called Lorna back.

"Wonder dude," she said.

"What's up?" I didn't feel much like talking.

"My big sister. She's making me homicidal. Blows in from Florida. Big divorce settlement. Lah-di-dah. Moves right into my room 'til she finds a place to live. I have no closet."

Being only 18, Lorna still lived at home with her parents. A small house, built in the 50s when they didn't know about walk-in closets and big bathrooms.

An idea floated by, and I grabbed it like a life preserver. "Think your sister'd like to sublet my apartment?"

Lorna squealed. I held the receiver away. Slippers flattened his ears and hissed at it.

"I'll ask her! Call you back, Nikki."

I sorted through my clothes, trying to decide what to take with me. Most stuff could be stored in my extra closet if Lorna's sister, Lucy, moved in. I had to sublet, if not to Lucy, then to someone else. Couldn't lose my home, face a new security deposit somewhere else. Hoped Lucy would go for it, take care of Slippers for a reduction in rent.

But where would I go? I might have to sleep in Hellish's stall for a few days. This thing had to blow over soon, right?

28

Wednesday afternoon. Checking phone messages. No news from Lorna. No call from Clay. That stung. It had been 36 hours, not that I was counting. The morning at Dimsboro had gone well. I'd made another 50 bucks, Hellish had behaved, and Vipe hadn't shown his scary face.

The phone rang. I grabbed it. Lorna.

"Nikkarina, you're in business. Lucy wants to come over right now and check your place out."

A brisk knock on the door came about 15 minutes later. I swung the door open. Could this be Lorna's sister?

Lucy Doone stood on the landing outside my apartment staring at a pot of withered Petunia remnants. She was slender with silky red hair, no freckles, no tattoos. She wore a black knit suit with splashy gold buttons and carried a shiny black leather pocketbook. She looked about 30.

I remembered Lorna saying something about being a change-of-life baby. That her two siblings were older. This one turned and swept me with haughty green eyes. Lorna hung back, a couple of steps down the staircase.

"Hello," Lucy said, holding out a thin, manicured hand.

I shook her hand, and she withdrew it quickly. Fine by me, felt like holding a dead fish anyway.

"Lorna said you might sublet for a month while I look for something suitable."

The way she'd pronounced "Lorna," made it obvious she didn't consider her little sister "suitable." I probably didn't rate, either.

"Come have a look," I said.

She came in and seemed to tolerate my blue batik slipcovers and straw rug. Slippers appeared, tail plumed, eyes bright.

"Oh. A cat." Slippers sauntered over to her, purr motors in full throttle. He sat at her feet and gave a silent meow.

Traitor.

"He'll have to go," Lucy said.

Lorna and I exchanged glances.

Lucy marched around, said she'd take the place on a month-to-month basis. "How soon can you get out?"

"Tonight," I said. I stared at my cat.

Lorna caught my look. "I'll take the cat. Mom won't mind."

We settled the deal, got the cat carrier, litter box and bag of Iams. Then the Doone sisters left, arguing about the howling cat and who'd sit where in the Jetta.

After they took Slippers, I had to fight tears. I was in a bad way. Forced myself to sort clothes, make a list, start packing.

Around five that afternoon I heard a knock on my door and my heart kicked up. Had to be Clay. But Louis Fein stood on the other side of the door's spyhole, wearing a downcast, miserable expression.

"Louis," I said, opening the door, "what happened? Looks like you lost your last friend."

"I lost Carla," he said, and started to cry.

I grabbed his arm, pulled him into my apartment, pushing him toward the couch. "Sit," I said, snatching a Kleenex from the bleached-wood counter that separated the living room and kitchen. Louis used the tissue with a loud honk. His black silk shirt appeared to have been slept in, his eyes were bloodshot, his face as rumpled and creased as his shirt. Not a hot dog today.

A momentary fear washed over me. "Did something happen to Carla?"

"She dumped me." Now he was blubbering.

A sour booze scent clung to him. I didn't feel sorry for him. He'd been a rat, jumping ship on me when the first cloud of suspicion darkened my head. Why had he come crying to me? "She broke up with you?"

"She called me last night from Kentucky. She's there with him. For three days." He waved his sodden tissue at me, tears streaming down his face.

I grabbed the whole Kleenex box and shoved it at him. Knew the answer but had to ask anyway. "She's with who?"

"She's running with that Clay Reed."

How could Clay be with Carla? Had I imagined Monday night? "How long has she been seeing him?"

Louis stared up at me, a child who needed comforting. He'd have to get in line behind me.

"She told me . . . on the phone," he wailed. "Said she'd met someone else. I was mad, kept asking her. Finally she told me it was Clay."

Outside the dump truck had arrived and was lifting the garbage container. A succession of booms sounded as it dumped the container, vibrating my apartment, rattling the dishes in the kitchen cabinets.

"Louis, I know it hurts, but why are you telling *me* this?"

"Because you're her friend. You probably know what's going on."

"I haven't a clue. Haven't talked to her since the two of you bailed on me at the first sign of trouble."

He drew back. "Oh, that."

I was disgusted with all three of them. "Louis, I've got no job, can't pay the rent, and the police are hounding me." I boiled over, yelling now, "I DON'T CARE ABOUT YOUR PROBLEMS."

He grabbed a handful of tissues and made for the door.

That night I moved into Dimsboro.

29

A yellow harvest moon was rising in the east as I hauled a sleeping bag, the futon I'd bought at Wal-Mart, and a small bag holding toothpaste and other essentials over to Hellish's stall.

The sound of car tires on gravel turned my head. Marteen's black Mercedes rolled by, the tinted windows and deepening dusk making it impossible to see inside. The car slowed, a rear window hummed down, and Chocolate's face appeared. She was wearing a red hat. A veil sparkling with red-and-black sequins covered her dark eyes. A shiny layer of crimson lipstick coated her mouth.

"Nikki, sugar," she called. "You moving in with that horse?"

"'Fraid so."

"Honey, we got an extra bed over at Marteen's now. You wanna stay there?"

"Gee, thanks, Chocolate. But I'm fine."

I thought I heard something about "shouldn't be sleeping with no horse" as her window powered up. The Mercedes receded into the distance. What was with her and those outfits anyway? I was beginning to think Marteen's barn must be a cover for a stable of call girls.

Hellish was thrilled to see me. She pinned her ears and shook her head in a menacing manner when I opened the stall door, pitchfork in hand. We ignored each other while I cleaned her stall, paying particular attention to my corner. I told myself this was great. I wouldn't have to drive back and forth twice a day to take care of her.

I lay out my futon and crawled into my sleeping bag. Couldn't help thinking about Clay . . . and Carla. Wondering if I'd been too hard on Louis as I closed my eyes. Eventually, the sound of Hellish munching hay lulled me to sleep.

A familiar noise jarred me awake. I didn't move, just listened. The latch on the stall door grated. Someone was sliding it open, slowly. Hellish, partially illuminated by moonlight, swung her head toward the sound. The door squeaked open, the silhouette of a dark, thin figure appeared in the doorway. The person's head turned sideways, as if listening, and I saw the outline of a ponytail. Vipe.

My hand crept to the can of pepper spray I'd put in my sleeping bag. I needn't have bothered. Hellish's bared teeth glimmered in the moonlight, she grunted and charged Vipe, teeth clacking. He drew back and slammed the door shut, cursed in Spanish.

I saw the glint of metal over the stall door. This jerk wasn't going to cut my horse. I grabbed the pepper spray can and erupted from my sleeping bag, scuttling through the straw on hands and knees, popping up over the stall door, fingers ready on the can's nozzle. Vipe was gone.

In the morning I rode four for Bubba, and picked up another three at a different barn. My last horse, a truly contrary individual, had thrown me on the path leading back from the track. My neck and back stiffened up as I waited for the ornery horse's owner, a squat, tight-mouthed woman, to pay me. She resented paying cash even more than my neck resented forced rotation. Since she'd never see me again if she didn't pay, she handed over the green. Compared to what was available at Dimsboro in the way of riders, having me in the saddle was like having Chris McCarron show up.

I was just five when McCarron won the '87 Kentucky Derby on Alysheba. My mom jumping up and down in front of the TV set, yelling her heart out for those two, had made a memorable race indelible. I'd seen replays since. The thrill's still there as Alysheba clips heels with Bet Twice and stumbles badly, a wall of horses looming behind. McCarron, with the agility of a high-wire artist, picks his colt's head up, steadies him, changes lanes to clear Bet Twice and sprints on to win the Derby.

Such dreams were far removed from Dimsboro, especially after another night of sleep deprivation. I was beyond ready to crash when I dragged myself back to face Hellish, wishing someone else had to climb on that recalcitrant horse's back. And was there any point with her only a step away from lameness?

There was no light in her stall, so I went down the shedrow to flip the electric switch. Came back to find the dim bulb revealed a dark-haired man kneeling in the straw by Hellish's front feet. I suppressed a cry, my brain scrambling to remember where I'd left the pepper spray.

"Thanks," said Jack Farino. "Wondered where that switch was."

"You scared the hell out of me. What are you doing here?" I could feel my hands clenched into fists, made an effort to relax them.

"You're jumpy as a stray cat. You never returned my call . . . about a proposition I've got for you."

"You've got no right to be in here with my horse." Anger sharpened my words. Who the hell did he think he was anyway?

He stood up. Those eyes — sharp, but hooded. Like a bird of prey.

"Nikki, this horse has been sore on and off since I came to Laurel. You're in a tough spot. I've got an offer that might help you, and since I was in the neighborhood I decided to look you up. I used to be a farrier and when I saw Hellish —"

"You just waltzed in and started working on her without permission?"

"Look, I tried to find you, you weren't around and she was pointing with that right front."

His mention of "pointing" diverted my anger. A lot of horsemen say when a front leg hurts a horse will push it forward and turn it out slightly, taking some of the body weight off. The action relieves pain, and the result is the foot looks like it's pointing at something.

"I'm just trying to see if the trouble originates in the foot. I'm trying to help you."

I sighed. "Okay, but if your hurt her . . ."

He turned his attention back to Hellish, leaned over and lifted her right foreleg. Hard to ignore the way his black jeans molded over a tight butt. I snapped my eyes away before he caught me staring. The curved metal and sharp, tapered end of a hoof pick glinted in his hand. Scrapings from inside her hoof already sprinkled the yellow straw. I could smell the odor. Pungent, like strong cheese.

But mostly I registered surprise at Hellish's calm behavior beneath Farino's hands. Maybe she was a sucker for those dark, Gypsy looks.

Farino straightened, removed his jacket, revealing a white sleeveless T-shirt. His arms had the long hard muscles of a man who rode and did hard work. Not like the guys I'd seen strutting from gyms with puffy muscles, often overlaid with fat. His thin cotton outlined pectoral muscles, a flat abdomen. I'd lost control of my eyes. They slid south. Oh boy.

"Come here," he said. "I want to show you something."

A vague alarm sounded in my brain. A warm tingle surged through my core.

Farino folded his jacket.

I took a step backward.

He turned and moved into a dim corner and lay his jacket next to a metal farrier's box I hadn't noticed before. He reached into a canvas bag and drew out a rawhide apron, like the blacksmiths at the track wore when shoeing. He slipped it on, picked up a trimming knife and slid it into the apron's pocket. He rattled around in his tool box and withdrew a pair of steel pull-offs.

Obviously, he planned to work on Hellish. I felt disappointed. Had I thought he was going to work on me? Had I completely lost my mind?

"What are you doing?" Did he know what he was doing?

"If you'll stop dancing around over there and come here, I'll show you."

30

Farino bent over, grasped the filly's right front foot. Both Hellish's knee and ankle joints were bent so the bottom of her foot now faced up. I stared, fascinated as always with the spongy, V-shaped frog. Centered, taking up about a third of the foot bottom, the frog acted as a cushion when the hoof struck the ground.

"See this metal here?" Farino tapped the front end of the shoe with a forefinger.

The aluminum racing plate was nailed into the outside of Hellish's hoof wall, an action I knew caused no more pain than a person trimming the tip of their fingernail.

"Yeah," I answered, wondering what he was up to. Get to the point, Farino.

As if he could sense my impatience, he raised his head and silenced me with those gypsy eyes. Looked back down. "See this sole?" He tapped the flat, hard-as-leather section lying between the frog and the hoof wall. "Whoever shod her last time left the metal pressing into the sole."

Clements' blacksmith. I got closer, focused, could see the inside rim of her shoe pressed hard against the sole. Didn't look that off to me. "That could make her sore?"

"Hell, yes, and this foot's worse than the other one." Using the steel pull-offs, he grabbed the shoe and pried it off. Dropping the metal tool into the yellow straw, he pulled the trimming knife from his pocket. "We've got to trim back the sole enough so when we put the new shoes on there's no contact."

He'd brought me new shoes? How would I pay for this? Yet the man seemed to know what he was talking about. The way Farino bent over near me, the thick, wavy dark hair covering his head was close and extremely touchable. I admonished myself for such a foolish thought, and watched him peel away layers of my filly's sole. I knew he'd have to go deep before he hit nerves, caused pain or drew blood. He placed the shoe on her foot to check its proximity to the newly pared foot bottom.

"That should do it." He dug around in his tool box and pulled out two new shoes. They came with horseshoe-shaped yellow rubber rim-pads. "This will give those front feet some cushion." He took out a metal rasp and filed her hoof some, then smoothed the sole. I couldn't believe how willingly Hellish accepted his actions. Her eyes were half closed, her body relaxed.

Farino rustled around in the toolbox some more, pulled out a farrier's hammer and shoeing nails. These last he clamped between his front teeth, leaving his hands free. Strong hands. He set the shoe, pad side first, against the hoof, pulled one nail from his mouth, and lightly tapped it in place. Checked to make sure he'd angled the nail properly, then drove it home with swift, hard strokes. *Sexual.*

Where had that come from?

I took a step back, watching those hands bend back, then clench flat the nail ends where they pierced through the outside of the shoe. He rasped them smooth, then reached for the filly's left front foot.

About the time he finished, Mello's lined, nutmeg-colored face appeared over the stall door. He sniffed. "'Bout time somebody dug in that foot." He squinted at Farino and a faint stirring of recognition moved across his face. "Do I know you?"

Farino's head swivelled toward the old man, his hawk eyes blank mirrors. "No, sir, don't believe I've had the pleasure." He stood up, pulled a rag from his jacket pocket, wiped his hand, and stepped forward to shake Mello's.

"You Jake Farino's son?" asked Mello.

I was amused and pleased to see the startled look in Farino's eyes.

"Mello knows things," I said.

Farino waited a couple of beats. "My *grandfather* was Jake Farino. You knew him?"

"Sure," said Mello. The lines around his mouth crinkled deeper as he smiled. Smoke from that long ago fire filled his eyes. "He trained up at Belmont back when Gallorette was running."

"Mello's convinced Hellish here's a reincarnation of Gallorette," I said.

Farino rubbed the small of his back. "Thought her name was Helen's Dream."

Mello placed his elbows on top of the splintery wood door. "Nikki here don't want to be reminded of her mama every time she sees this horse."

My jaw dropped in astonishment. "Hellish fits her," I muttered.

Farino grinned. "Whatever you're talking about, Mello, you just hit the nail on the head."

"Some things you can't help but see." Mello picked at a long, pointed splinter coming loose from the wood. "Don't matter what you call this filly. She be Gallorette."

"Huh," said Farino. "She's got the white rings around her feet, the strong bones, but I don't believe Gallorette had any white on her face."

"Don't be fussing 'bout that. Gallorette was fast as lightning. This one here's got the mark right on her face, is all." Mello stepped back from the wood door and shuffled away. "You'll see," he said, his voice fading as he moved down the aisle way. "She gonna be Nikki's dream."

I shook my head. Didn't appreciate false hope. Too much of that in the racing game. Farino gathered his tools, stowed them in his box.

"Thanks," I said. Hellish was prancing in place, ready to get to work. I could hardly wait to take her out, see how she moved with her doctored-up foot.

"Let me ask you something." Farino's eyes held that speculative look, like the first time I'd ever seen him staring at me from the catty-cornered barn. During the last few minutes he'd been so kind and decent, but now something wolflike crept into his expression. "Mello's right. Not about the reincarnation," he said, catching the look on my face. "Her ability. She's got speed. Saw her run in New York as a two-year-old. You seem to have a way with her. She'll come right for you."

His words flattered me. I stepped right in it. "There was one day I galloped her, she felt like a stakes horse. She's been abused. It's like nobody knew what they had."

"Exactly," he said. "She gets no respect. When you run her, I'll help you in any way I can . . ."

"I've been ruled off. I can't run her, ride her or anything else." I clamped my eyelids shut for a moment, opened them to find Hellish staring at me, reacting to the emotion in my voice. I slid my hand down the silky fur on her neck. Pulled a loose strand of mane hanging near her withers.

Farino stepped closer. "When this mess you're in blows over, and it will, you'll run her. She'll be a longshot."

Why was he so sure my dark cloud of suspicion would disperse?

Farino locked his eyes on mine. "But you hold her first time you run her, make sure she puts in a bad race. Next time out she'll be the longest shot on the board. Then . . . you *send* her." His mouth curved in an unattractive smile. "They'll be shoving piles of money at us through the betting window."

Was he like Clay? Thought I'd run a con? I could feel my jaw tighten. "That's called fraud. I don't do that."

A movement at the base of the wall to my right pulled my gaze off Farino. A mouse scurried along in the straw, squeaked, then dove into a small hole in the corner. The mouse didn't bother me, but I was mad as hell at the rat standing in front of me.

"Sorry to disappoint you," I said, pulling cash from my coat pocket. "How much do I owe you?"

"Forget it," he said. He got a better grip on his toolbox, shoved the stall door open and left.

I couldn't figure him out. He seemed so sure I'd be cleared. Was it because he knew who killed O'Brien?

31

"They got free food over at the arena today." Chocolate lounged against the door frame next to Andy Blue's stall, inside Bubba's barn. She wore a black track suit with gold running shoes. Black swooshes decorated the sides, and gold threads were braided into her black-and-blond dreadlocks.

"I like your hair," I said, unbuckling the girth and sliding the saddle from Andy Blue's back.

She twisted a braid against her neck, pointed a long gold finger nail at the horse. "I heard he's a mean sucker." She threw the horse a nasty look, then broke into a smile. "But you fixed him *good*."

"Just got his attention." The horn of the freight train sounded from the south. Must be 10 o'clock. I hollered down the aisle at Bubba's boys where they were jiving and listening to a rap CD. One of them sauntered over, led Andy Blue away.

"Who's having free food?" I asked.

"One of those conventions. Food sellers or some such. Heard last year you just walked in, they was handing stuff out. Real food. Chicken. Beefsteak."

As the train drew near the engineer blew the horn. The loud rumble increased, kind of like the one in my stomach. I'd gotten too thin, could use some food. Who knew when I'd ever have to worry about racing weight again?

"So," I said, "walk over with me when I finish with Hellish?"

She said she would, and I headed for my barn wondering if Farino's magic trick would still work. Had there really been no kindness of heart behind Farino's exceptional work on the filly? His only interest setting up a betting scam? When he'd left the previous morning, I'd ridden Hellish out to the track, amazed to find the little hitch in her stride had evaporated. She'd felt eager, yet relaxed. I'd been real careful not to let her get into full gear, didn't want her running off with me, especially not at Dimsboro. The track suffered from hordes of small rocks and uneven dirt that could damage her legs at a canter, let alone racing speed.

Mello stood outside her stall with a shiny metal horse bit in his hand. He held it up. "You needs to use this." He had on his shabby black jacket and a polka dot bow tie.

"What kind of bit is that?"

"This be Gallorette's. Polished it up this morning."

Didn't know if I believed him, but my scalp prickled anyway. I touched the gleaming bit where it hung from Mello's hand, free of leather reins or bridle head piece.

Most of the bit was standard — a couple of two-inch rolled and curved metal pieces joining together to form what's called a "broken" snaffle. The outside ends were joined to three-inch rings that would hang from the cheek pieces of a bridle. When fully assembled reins would also be fastened to these rings.

An unusual rolled metal piece, shaped like a W atop a small oval, attached to the center of the bit where the snaffle pieces came together.

"How's this work?" I pointed to the odd-shaped portion.

"This here," Mello wiggled the part, showing it rotated on the snaffle, "go over her tongue, like so." He moved the bit as if sliding it into a horse's mouth, using two fingers to show how both the snaffle and the "W" would rest on the tongue.

The dreaded occurrence of a horse "getting his tongue over the bit" came to mind. I realized the additional piece could keep the horse from doing just that and said as much.

Mellow stroked the metal, nodding. "Gallorette always ran off with the boy 'til we got a holda this. She won't be able to get away from you so easy now."

It made sense. "I'll try it."

I dosed Hellish with tranquilizer, put the new equipment on and rode out. She took right to that bit. Her head came down, her neck extended, and she galloped along like a stakes horse. When she'd cooled out and was back in her tall, I stood outside staring at her. Between Mello's Gallorette mythology and Farino's magic, this filly might come around.

Chocolate showed up, and we left for the arena. Close up I read the marquee: "Welcome D.C. and Baltimore Area Food Wholesalers."

"Chocolate," I asked as we pushed through the double glass doors. "Do you work for Marteen, or . . ."

"We're in sales," she said, her shoes squeaking on the arena's smooth concrete floor. She grabbed the handle of a metal door, pulled it open, and stepped through. "Look at this."

I moved through the door to find myself in the stadium's crow's-nest. Cement steps, flanked by rows of padded seats, dropped down to the convention floor below where platters of food on draped tables were surrounded by placards, banners, and people in white aprons and chef's hats. Thronging about them were guys in business suits and women in skirts and jackets, all jamming food into their mouths. The smell of steaks and baked bread almost made me swoon. Chocolate bolted down the steps; I dashed right behind.

We didn't look too businesslike, but nobody seemed to care. At the closest booth a man carved pieces from a tenderloin he'd just pulled off a gas grill. His partner offered us a platter of sizzling meat studded with toothpicks. We got busy. The two men wore badges advertising "Potomac Beef and Poultry." Next door a woman tossed a pan of garlic shrimp beneath a "Metropolitan Seafood" sign. Hot sliced bread sat on a platter with butter.

Chocolate dove into the bread, then resurfaced, her lips shiny with butter. She rolled her eyes. "I'm gonna have an orgasm."

"You might want to save that for later." I speared a shrimp as the tantalizing scent of ribs reached my nose. I moved down the aisle, spied a slab of barbequed beef ahead and made tracks.

Carla Rubin stood behind the booth's counter slicing into the ribs.

How could I have forgotten she sold wholesale meat? "Carved any hearts lately?"

She looked up, her expression warm with recognition. "Nikki! Your phone's been disconnected. Are you okay?" Then my words registered. "What did you say?"

"Louis tells me you've been running around with Clay."

Carla's brown eyes narrowed. "That piece of crap. Did he mention I found him naked on top of a redhead?"

Hadn't told me that. "I asked you about Clay, not Louis." An edge of anger roughened my voice.

Chocolate appeared beside me, grabbed a rib from Carla's white ceramic platter. She took a bite and watched us like she was at the movies.

The booth lights lit Carla's hair to a luminous blond. Her eye makeup was perfect. At that moment I hated her. "Think you can have any man you want? No matter who gets hurt?"

She appeared confused. Then awareness widened her eyes. "You're still interested in Clay."

I stared at her.

Chocolate jabbed a partially gnawed rib bone at Carla. "Girl, don't you be taking Nikki's man. She got enough troubles."

"Stay out of this," snapped Carla. She turned back to me. "You told me you didn't like Clay. Remember? After the date?"

"That changed."

"Well, it's news to me. Clay told me you weren't interested. Didn't you turn him down?"

Two men in navy blue suits eased up to Carla's booth. Both held plates loaded with food. They listened to our heated exchange with open interest. Chocolate picked up a fresh pineapple garnish, then started on a second rib.

"Clay took me to dinner," I said. "The night before he left for Kentucky. Heard you went along . . . for the ride."

"Clay had dinner with you *Monday* night?"

I nodded, remembering how I'd almost whimpered at his seductive words about doing it right, taking the time. My face must have mirrored the memory. Carla's anger visibly defused.

"Nikki, I'm sorry. I didn't know."

Chocolate set her hands on her generous hips. "Huh."

One of the two guys in blue suits seemed compelled to rush to Carla's defense. "Hey. She said she didn't know."

What was it about men and blondes? "Whatever," I said. "You know what? Clay's a liar and a con artist. He's all yours."

"Sounds like sour grapes to me." Carla tossed her hair.

I wanted to say something smart about her roots showing, but of course they weren't. Like a prize show horse, I couldn't fault her. No wonder Clay moved on.

Chocolate put her hand on my arm. "Come on, Nikki, let's get away from this trash." She pulled me down the aisle. "They got pastries and ice cream over there." She pointed to the opposite side from where we'd entered.

"I've kinda lost my appetite."

"Girl, don't let that bitch get you down. She ain't nothing." Chocolate still had a hold on my arm, tugging me toward the dessert section.

I stopped cold. Two booths ahead Vipe lounged against a counter, decimating a wedge of pie. A turtleneck hid his snake tattoos. His oily ponytail glittered under the arena lights.

My abrupt halt broke Chocolate's grasp. Her gaze followed mine. "What's with that Vipe guy?" I asked.

"He a trainer."

"They'd never let him on the Maryland tracks. Isn't that a prison tattoo under his eye?"

"Uh-huh. Served up at Jessup."

My eyes slid from Vipe to Chocolate. "For what?"

"Rape."

I felt a chill. "He tried to get at me the other night. I think."

"What you mean, you think?"

We'd stopped in the middle of the aisle, and people flowed around us on the gray concrete floor. A woman with a briefcase gave Chocolate a curious look.

"What I mean is, he must keep horses for someone who's not on the level. Maybe someone who needs to keep them out of sight. Got one in his barn I know is a ringer." Is that why he came after me? "Who's he work for?"

Chocolate took a half-step away from me. "I don't know nothing about any of that. That man scare me." Suddenly she looked very young. "And he lookin at us right now. Why you wanna get us in trouble?"

Vipe dropped his plate into a trash can. Slipped his hand into his pocket, came out palming a closed switchblade. His lips spread into a nasty smile, his gold eyetooth winking as he headed our way.

"Shit, Nikki." Chocolate clutched my wrist.

My glance darted around the exhibit units, display walls, and crowds of people, searching for a way to run. A cop crossed through an intersection of booth aisles about 30 yards away. Not a rent-a-cop, either. A fully loaded Prince George's County police officer. He wore the big utility belt. I could make out the handle of a revolver.

32

A week after I'd run to the cop for help, I gazed at the distant rectangle of the arena's service door on the far side of Dimsboro's racetrack. With the county cop hard on his heels, Vipe had slithered through that door and disappeared like a snake in the water.

After losing the Latino, the officer, Jacob duCellier, had hustled back to get our names, made us stand beside his squad car while he radioed checks in on the two of us. And Vipe. Chocolate and I had shuffled around uneasily, worried information might broadcast back featuring one of our names. The radio squawked about an outstanding assault warrant for somebody named Ricardo Margoles. Vipe's real name? More garbled words caused officer duCellier to give Chocolate a hard look, but I'd gotten lucky. Apparently, Anne Arundel wasn't sharing information with Prince George's County.

I stood outside Hellish's stall waiting for Lorna, the mid-October sun trying to reassure me with its Indian summer warmth. I knew better. The increasing chill of the past few nights held a warning. Winter, with icy claws, crouched just beyond the northern horizon.

In the distance, Lorna's battered Jetta turned into the Dimsboro entrance near the arena, and I stood up, stretching out some kinks left over from the Dimsboro horse that had thrown me. Earlier in the week I'd finally driven up to Laurel to visit Lorna and my cat, check my mail, make sure sister Lucy wasn't trashing my apartment. After a show of indignation, Slippers had finally climbed into my lap at the Doones' kitchen table. I'd told Lorna about the Vipe incident, and how Clay had taken Carla to Kentucky. Lorna had promised me a return visit.

Now her red Jetta bumped over the gravel lot and stopped next to my car. Swirls of dust from the dry ground rose beneath the tires leaving a thick coat on both our vehicles. Lorna slammed her car door, crunching gravel as she walked toward me. "Nikki, dude, seen any vipers lately?" She had a great smile, and those silly green streaks still curled through her mop of red hair.

"Nah," I said, giving her a hug. "He's disappeared."

A bright reflection caught my peripheral vision. A black Mercedes with glossy chrome nosed around the turn into the backside. "We might have a visitor." I turned toward the car.

Lorna squinted, read the tag. "Vanity plate says Carla 1. Nice wheels."

"Too bad the driver isn't." What was she doing here?

"That's *the* Carla?" Lorna drew herself up and glared at the approaching car. "She's got a lotta nerve showing up here."

The Roadster stopped next to Lorna's Jetta and more dust swept up, forming a column of particles floating in the hard noon light. Carla stepped from her car, a butter-soft black leather jacket wrapping her breasts, her favorite pair of cowgirl boots accentuating her long legs.

"Oh." Lorna sounded deflated.

"Yeah," I sighed. "I know."

"Before you say anything, Nikki," Carla said, striding toward me, "you're right and I'm sorry."

Though I'd had a week to cool off, anger and hurt welled up inside me. Still, I was curious. "Go on."

Carla's eyes searched my face. "Clay lied to me about you, but I should have checked with you, not taken him at his word."

"Duh," said Lorna.

Carla took in Lorna's red streaks and brow ring. Restrained herself.

"He took me to this elegant restaurant. Dinner, champagne, the whole works. Then this older man joins us for dessert." She stopped for two beats, a grimace twisting her face. "Guy's a name-dropping jerk who made sure I knew he was rich. Next morning Clay calls me about how anxious he is to sell this guy a racehorse. Wants *me* to go out with the old goat. Schmooze him into buying the horse. Can you imagine?"

Carla looked so appalled and astonished, I burst out laughing. She almost swallowed her tongue burying a comeback. She waited a few beats. "I guess I deserved that."

Unspoken words hung in the warm air. Behind me Hellish rattled her empty feed bucket. In the silence that followed, a man pushed a squeaky wheelbarrow piled high with dirty straw toward the nearby manure pit.

Carla shrugged. "I guess there's nothing else to say." She turned away from us.

"He's a real piece of work, isn't he?" I said.

She swung around, a glint in her eye. "Total prick."

Lorna chose that moment to ask the question I'd burned with. "So did he stud you with his heavy metal?"

Carla's eyes drifted briefly to the ground. A warm pink colored her cheeks. I had my answer.

"Lorna." I made a placating motion with my hand.

Carla dove into the awkward silence that followed. "I'm finished with him. He knows it." She took a breath and looked around for the first time. The broken pavement, decayed wood, rotten roofs. Several abandoned cars and a tractor that looked like it had been rusting since the 60s. "What's with this place? Why are you here?"

As I recapped events leading to my arrival at Dimsboro, the three of us began to relax. Starting with the cold shoulder I'd received at the Maryland training farms, I ended with my arrival at Pallboro.

Carla's gaze swept across the decrepit Dimsboro grounds. "I wouldn't send a serial killer to this place." She stared at an old metal shed on the other side of the potholed car lot. Three seedy-looking guys sat in there playing cards, passing a bottle. "What have the cops found out?"

"Ongoing investigation," I said.

"Nikki, you can't sit in this dump waiting for them to clear your name."

"She's right." Lorna favored Carla with a hesitant smile.

Where had my fire gone? I'd planned to find out where Clements and Farino lived, spy on them, but had never followed through. Dimsboro had enveloped me with a lethargic hopelessness. I had to fight back.

"I think there's a betting scam going on," I said. "A guy named Arthur Clements, maybe a guy named Jack Farino, and —"

Carla jumped in. "Farino. That sexy guy, looks like a gypsy?"

I started to add my two cents on Farino but Carla was on a roll. "Wait. Let me tell you. He has a new owner up at Laurel. You should see it. Old lady on a walker, has a big Mercedes with a driver."

No doubt she was a widow. I exhaled some air. "He's one of them." A ring of thieves. The three of us shook our heads. Why did all the hot men have to be scum bags?

"There's another guy. Lorna knows about this other creep called Vipe," I said, nodding at her red head. I quickly rehashed the Vipe story for Carla. "But there's this connection between all three of them and those Dark Mountain horses."

"Like what?" Lorna's eyes glowed wide and round.

"Remember the horse I called Whorly?" When Lorna nodded, I turned to Carla and brought her up to date on Hellish's Dark Mountain rescue. "So this thin boy that worked for Vipe always rode Whorly. Still works in Vipe's barn with some Latinos. I nosed around, asked who paid their salary. If they'd ever heard of Arthur Clements or Jack Farino. They clammed right up."

"I don't understand," said Carla. "What do you think these people are doing?"

"Suppose," I said, "they have Whorly and another bay horse with a cowlick? Suppose both sets of Jockey Club papers simply state, 'single whorl on left side of neck, no white markings.'" I glanced at Carla. She appeared to be following.

"So," I said, "the second horse might not even need to have an unusual cowlick, just one on the left side. Let's say they run Whorly at Laurel, Delaware Park or Charles Town, and he has a bad case of the slows. He gets lousy speed and performance ratings."

"Wait a minute," said Carla. "Doesn't somebody check these horses?"

"Totally," said Lorna. "There's this guy called the identifier. He's got, like, this booklet, describes blazes and socks, whorls, any odd markings and the tattoo numbers — for all the horses running that day." Lorna's short-sleeved shirt revealed the Pegasus tattoo on her forearm. She tapped it with her right index finger, emphasizing her point. "You've been to the races, Carla. Didn't you ever see that guy, stares at every horse, gets a hold of the upper lip, reads the tattoo number underneath?"

"Didn't notice," said Carla.

Lorna rolled her eyes.

"Okay," I said. "Let's call the other horse Rocket. Suppose he's a good horse, they fake his papers up, and can find a way to get around the tattoo ID? Rocket can impersonate Whorly for the day."

Lorna's eyes gleamed. "And the bad dudes bet big bucks and Whorly, who's really Rocket, comes in, pays maybe 90-1."

Carla frowned. "But Louis told me if you win a big pot, the IRS is waiting for you. They're stationed right behind the betting windows. Everyone would know."

"Right," I said. "But there are so many gambling outlets now. You can bet on the phone, the Internet, overseas. They'd spread their bets. Hell, there's even offshore betting accounts now."

Carla, raised an eyebrow. "Seen any fast bay horses around here?"

My breath caught. "As a matter of fact . . ." I stared toward Vipe's barn.

Told them how I'd seen another bay breezing around the Dimsboro track one morning like he was running on rocket fuel.

The thin boy had ridden him.

"I'm going over there later, take a look at what's in that barn. Then I need to figure a way to look at those horses' papers."

Lorna all but squealed. "Vernal, my buddy in the secretary's office. He could take a peek in Clements' file. Check out the papers on any bays."

Carla looked clueless, so I said, "The track identifier keeps a folder for each trainer. Any time a trainer runs a horse, the papers have to be in that folder, available to track ID. Most trainers leave 'em there. It's more convenient, unless a horse is racing out of town."

"Yeah, but that's totally discouraged." Lorna nodded knowingly. "They're always threatening to take stall allocation away if you race out of town."

Carla's eyes started to glaze over. Too much information.

"Clements wouldn't keep both sets of papers in that file," I said. "He'd pull the old switcheroo. I need to get into his office. If I could just figure a way to get back inside Laurel." I closed my eyes. God, how I longed to return to Laurel.

"Louis may be a two-timing piece of crap, but he bought me a Maryland owner's license," said Carla. She turned those brown eyes on me. "I can get you in. The rest is up to you."

"Better be careful, Nikki." Lorna looked worried. "These could be seriously dangerous people."

Later, I'd remember her words. Wish I'd taken them to heart.

33

I walked toward Vipe's barn that afternoon, attempting to look casual — just out for a stroll. The building stood next to a sagging chain-link fence separating Dimsboro from the railroad behind. On the far side of the tracks a steep bank dropped into the unadorned backside of a Food Lion strip mall. A hole in the fence and a well-worn footpath provided access to a number of shops, the liquor store and Chinese takeout being the most popular.

Vipe's barn upheld the Dimsboro standard. His shedrow wasn't neat, his buckets didn't match, his aisles weren't raked, and, of course, his roof leaked. But his horses were well fed. If someone directed this scam from the shadows, they were sly enough to supply the speedy "Rocket" with the necessary fuel.

Past training hours, but too early for evening feed, the barn appeared free of humans. The Dimsboro shedrows lacked the customary concrete half-wall perimeter. Instead, wood posts and waist-high pine-rails confined the horses to the dirt paths running before the stalls. People said the state park stapled sheets of plastic over the wood frame in the winter, and I could just imagine the stuff tearing and flapping in the northwest wind.

I eased into the aisle facing the track, looking for the two plain bays. The horses I found had white markings. At the last stall on the aisle I turned left and moved around the barn's end on to the side facing the strip mall.

I spotted Whorly's unusual arrangement of twirling neck hairs in the first stall. Four doors down I found Rocket. The two horses were about the same size, with similar head shapes. Rocket's muscle structure was more developed than Whorly's, and his eyes held the proud determination that good racehorses so often have. He obliged me by thrusting his head over the stall door. I slid my hand onto the left side of his neck and scratched. His pleasure was evident, the way he pushed against my hand, nodded his head in time to my rubbing. I gazed at the neck fur, finding a single cowlick. Stepped sideways and inspected the right side. The fur ran smooth and even.

My heart kicked up. I looked around, didn't see anyone. I slipped into Rocket's stall, grasped his halter and led him away from the door. With my other hand I got a hold of his upper lip, tried to curl it up, read his tattoo number. He resisted. I needed two hands and glanced around the stall walls. In the back a tie chain hung from a screw eye. I led Rocket over and clipped the snap on the end of the tie chain to his halter ring.

This time I got his lip up and stared at the number: 0120661. That meant he'd foaled in '01, and his specific Jockey Club number was 20661. Tattoo numbers become worn and harder to read as a horse gets older, but these were fairly clear, didn't appear to have been tampered with. I released Rocket and headed for Whorly.

I heard a rattling sound and froze. Stood motionless a few moments, my ears straining. I heard nothing more and crept into Whorly's stall. Being more of an old plug, he let me fold his lip up and read the number. My heart hammered harder in my chest as I stared. The exact same number, only the sixes were fuzzy. Did it look like the sixes were previously eights? Like the one was a seven with the top knocked off? I thought of Vipe's prison teardrop, of the lasers that could remove tattoos. How hard would it be to change an eight to a six, a seven to a one?

Proving my theory left my hands shaking. I'd thought maybe it couldn't be true. Time to get out. I slid from the stall into the aisle, my eyes searching. Hurried down the shedrow, ducked under the rail and moved away, slowed as the sensation of watching eyes reached my back. Turning around, I saw someone staring from the track side of Vipe's barn.

The thin boy. Damn. Where had he come from? I walked on as if unconcerned. Had he seen me come out the far side of the barn?

That evening, Lorna called, told me Vernal had found one set of papers in Clements' file in the Laurel Park ID office. The document described a bay horse with one left-side-of-neck whorl. "Did you get the tattoo number?" I asked.

"My brain didn't come from Wal-Mart. Of course I did." I heard her rustling paper through my cell phone. "Here it is — 0120661."

"And I bet the name on the papers is 'Noble Treasure'?" Holding my breath.

"How'd you know that?"

I explained about the name I'd seen on Whorly's halter after Dennis brought him into Laurel. Told her about my recent sleuthing in Vipe's barn. I needed to talk to Carla and began winding up the conversation, but Lorna wasn't finished.

"Nikki, didn't you say something about an insurance scam going on, too?"

Mental head slap. "*Yes*. I didn't think about it when the three of us were talking. Remember the Dark Mountain horse that turned up dead with Dennis O'Brien's body? Belonged to Janet LeGrange. She probably had insurance, like old lady Garner."

"You mean like Gildy?"

A spurt of fear hit me. Was there a connection I couldn't see between the betting scam and the horse fatalities? "Yeah, like Gildy." A heavy feeling washed over me. I paused a beat. "Lorna, what are the chances of two rich widows winding up with two dead horses?"

"Wouldn't get my two bucks," she said.

We disconnected with me thinking how I never got beyond Martha admitting to her insurance policy on Gildy. I felt she had more to tell me. Hell, she wouldn't give me the time of day now.

I reached Carla. Told her I needed to pick her brain. We decided to meet the next day at Annapolis Mall, a halfway point between Dimsboro and her Baltimore wholesaler's.

In the morning I realized Hellish was coming around. Before long I wouldn't be afraid to drop the daily dose of Acepromazine. She'd been like a human with a nagging headache. Cranky. But since Farino worked on this filly, her anger was slowly dissolving. She realized galloping didn't hurt anymore. The urge to run had been bred into her for centuries. Who could blame her for being frustrated when the thing she'd wanted to do the most caused pain?

Jim always said a happy horse will run to their potential, maybe beyond. I skipped the grinding routine of the racetrack for the day and rode Hellish down a dirt path beside Tavern Branch, letting her canter near the water's edge. Mist hung over the creek in the morning chill, and a few Canada geese spooned their bills into the mud on the bank. As Hellish warmed up I could smell her sweat vaporizing into steam. She rolled along effortlessly, rocking me into a state of calm euphoria.

On the way back we slowed to a walk, stopping to watch some teenage goslings waddle behind their parents. The family slid down the bank and splashed into the branch, honking about it and waggling their tails. A fish flipped out of the water, then folded back into the stream, leaving only a ripple to mark its brief emergence.

I gathered the reins and my thoughts, and headed back to our barn.

Carla and I worked on vanilla lattes at one of the small round tables on the white tile floor near the coffee bar outside Nordstrom's. Skylights lit the high ceiling overhead, and a fountain splashed and soothed in a stone basin nearby. We studied a lined pad where I'd drawn the tattoo numbers and a picture of the whorls. Below that was a notation on the single set of papers in Clements' ID folder. Then the words "Dennis brings three Dark Mountain horses to Laurel."

I swallowed some coffee and swiped at a trace of foam on my upper lip. "Whorly is one of the three. The horse I found dead with Dennis is number two. I don't know where the third one is."

"It's not the one you call Rocket?" Carla's elbows rested on the shiny table surface. She wore the soft leather jacket and a short black skirt.

"No way. He's the real deal, wouldn't have been sent to that auction. Bet his name really is Noble Treasure."

Carla studied the page, frowning. "You said there's more. Something about insurance."

"We have two dead horses, Martha's Gildy and Janet's Dark Mountain horse. I have to find out that horse's name, see if he was insured and for how much. Martha told me she had a policy on Gildy for $150,000."

"Did she collect?"

"Finally." Seeing her next question forming, I said, "No I don't think Martha's the bad guy, and I have no idea how someone else would benefit."

I turned at the commotion made by a woman shouting after a small boy who pounded away from her, making a beeline for the fountain. The woman rushed with a baby stroller containing a plump infant who soaked up the sights and sounds of the mall like a sponge. Her face relaxed when she realized the water's fascination had checked the boy's flight. She caught up with him and gave him some pennies to toss in the fountain. The baby stared at the splashing water, mesmerized.

"You know," said Carla, pulling my mind from the fountain. "Anyone can take out a life insurance policy on just about anybody. What about equine insurance?"

"I don't know." But I sure as hell needed to find out.

"I'll go online, get the name of an equine insurance agent, call and pretend I've bought a horse. See if I can get an answer." Carla studied me a moment. "I know how to get you into Laurel Park."

A shadow darkened the skylights above, graying the white tile floor, removing the warmth of the sun. I remembered Carla saying earlier that she'd get me in, but the rest was up to me. She sat opposite me, supportive and loyal, while nearby the small boy gurgled with delight at the fountain. So why did I feel so alone?

34

Carla met me at the Silver Diner in Laurel for a late breakfast the following Monday. A hostess walked me past a row of blue-padded counter stools into the dining area, and pointed out Carla, who sat in a booth upholstered in blue vinyl with retro silver flecks. She'd already ordered us pancakes, crispy bacon, orange juice, and coffee. A waitress with masses of mascara showed up right behind me with the food. Conversation waited while Carla dug in. Being nervous, I tended to pick more than dig.

Carla slid her plate aside and drained her juice glass. She heaved a shopping bag onto the Formica tabletop, pushed it across to me. Red print on the silver paper read "Baltimore Stage and Costume."

I peeked inside, and pulled out a Baltimore Orioles baseball cap with a curly blond wig sewn into the lining. The hair appeared real. Folded in the bottom of the bag were a matching nylon jacket and running pants.

"The kind of stuff you'd never wear," Carla said.

I'd kept on my fleece vest from the morning, a perfect match to the Oriole red. I pointed to my vest, held up the ball cap. Carla ignored me.

She waved a wand-type lipstick. "You need to let me put this on you." I squinted at it, made out the name "PuckerUp" in purple letters.

"This is the greatest stuff. Permanent lipstick, has to wear off," Carla shook the product, and I could hear a hard mixing ball rattling around in there. She unscrewed the top, pulled out the wand to show me the color on the sponge tip, then examined the label. "They call this Hearts-in-the-Snow. It'll look great on you."

This was so Carla. "You want me to look good to sneak into Laurel?"

"You should always look good." She pulled me into the ladies' room, had me clean my mouth with a wet paper towel. With precise strokes, she painted on the red, going just over the edge of my lips, making them appear fuller. She accentuated the cupid's bow, then studied her work. "Didn't I tell you? Great lips. A man could die for those lips."

"Let's hope no one else has to."

The words startled Carla. "Maybe I should have used a different expression. You're going to be careful, right? Just waltz in, look at a file cabinet and get out. Right?"

"Let's do the wig and the other stuff," I said. "I want to get this over with."

I left my car at the diner. While Carla drove the short distance to Laurel Park, I pulled down my visor and peered into the mirror glued on the back. A cute blonde with big lips stared back at me. Didn't look like anybody I knew.

Gucci sunglasses covered my eyes, and my head was buried in a fashion magazine when Carla stopped at the stable gate to show her license to Fred Rockston. My body tightened as his gaze swept over me, but his eyes held no recognition. Carla and I slapped palms as we left the security guard behind. I still wondered about Rockston's appearance at both crime scenes. Always found it hard to believe in coincidences like that.

Monday was a "dark" day at Laurel Park, which meant no racing. We'd picked the middle of the day because there wouldn't be much going on, and hopefully no people in Clements' barn.

Almost three weeks since I'd been escorted off the grounds by Offenbach. A wave of nostalgia swept through me as I looked at the horse paths leading to the track, the attractive barns with their tight, secure green roofs. I missed Jim Ravinsky, the fat tabby cat, and the stable pony, Mack. Missed the daily wisecracking and gossip, the Mexican grooms with their laughter, flashing smiles, and gold earrings.

"Nikki." Carla pulling me into the present. "I'll park by the track kitchen, wait there. You've got your cell phone?"

I felt in the pocket of the new jacket and found the phone, held it up. Slipping it back, I felt a small object push against my fingers from the pocket of the vest underneath. Something from Dimsboro, no doubt.

"The Phillips?" Carla asked.

I withdrew the screwdriver from the jacket's other pocket. Lorna had talked to a guy from her pre-rehab days. Apparently a thief, he knew how to pick locks and get into places. He'd told her to check out Clements' office door, and after her description of the hasp and Yale padlock, he'd said a Phillips would do it.

Carla's brown eyes were solemn. "Watch your back, Nikki." I threw her a smile, grabbed the magazine, and climbed from the car.

Weird, being in disguise. I passed a few grooms who lived in the track's backstretch housing on my way to Clements' barn. I knew one of them, but he stared like I was a stranger.

Jim's stable roof rose in the distance, and closer I could see Clements' barn arranged in that catty-cornered angle. I headed for the rear side, not wanting to get near Jim's, thinking I'd either be recognized or unnerved. I reached the entrance, leaned against the outside wall, and leafed through the magazine. My ears strained to listen, my peripheral vision surveyed the surroundings, and some extra sense kicked in, scanning the barn for human presence. At midday the big sliding metal doors remained open. When convinced anything alive in there had either four legs or feathers, I closed the magazine and stepped into the barn like I had an appointment.

To the right a row of stalls stretched into the distance. To my left was the short end of the long rectangular barn, its dirt aisle making a quick right turn over to the barn's opposite side, and another row of 30 stalls. Farino's space occupied the far end, where the metal door facing his stalls provided a view of Jim's operation.

My interest lay in this end, where three doors opened into small rooms generally used for office, tack, or feed storage. Clements' lair occupied the middle spot. Pausing outside his door, I listened. Horses stomped, munched hay, and bumped the occasional feed bucket. A few pigeons preened and pecked for grain, but most of them remained half-asleep in the rafters. The barn's sour odor still festered beneath the rich scent of horses.

I turned, studying the hinged metal hasp. The end securing the padlock had a slot fitting over a metal loop. The Yale lock hung from that loop, closed down tight, unbreakable. But the other end of the hasp . . . I almost laughed. The Phillips screws fastening it to the doorframe were totally accessible. Oversight or arrogance? Whatever, I took out the screwdriver and removed the little buggers, then yanked the hasp off the frame, rendering the lock useless. I turned the knob and went in.

Clements' office was surprisingly clean and neat. Probably on account of his allergies. A row of plastic eye-drop bottles, inhalers, and prescription pills lay on a stand directly behind his wooden desk. Horse periodicals and stallion directories filled a bottom shelf. I went for his metal filing cabinet, and jerked open the top drawer. Folders labeled with horses' names in alphabetical order stuffed the inside. My fingers flipped to "N," found "Noble Treasure."

My heart raced as I pulled the horse's file. His Jockey Club papers lay between some vet records. The neck whorl description matched my memory of Whorly's spiraling cowlick. The name, registration number, date of birth, and breeder were identical to those of the horse I called Rocket. I folded the certificate into my coat pocket, thinking they'd done a good job, the papers looked genuine.

Pigeons flew up from the dirt to my right, their wing beats loud and startling. I grabbed some air and tried to replace the first screw with nervous fingers.

Soft Spanish words drifted from the corner to my right. My heart jigged, the hand grasping the Phillips felt suddenly weak. A young man with fussy blond hair came around the corner, something about him familiar. I dropped everything and took off.

"Hey!" The guy pounded after me.

I reached the left corner and bolted to the right down the long side of the barn. Footsteps hammered behind me, swift and closing. I didn't waste time looking over my shoulder, just ran full-out. Daylight spilled through the metal door down in Farino's end. I sprinted toward the sunlight, almost reached its safety, when Arthur Clements rounded the far corner and blocked my path.

Surprise killed my momentum, and the blond smacked into me from behind. We crashed in the dirt, a tangle of arms and legs. I got my hands under me, struggling to rise. He clubbed the side of my head. Grabbed my shoulder, rolled me over so I faced him. Those *eyes*. I knew this man, but the hair was wrong.

"Hold her down." Clements' voice.

The blond gripped my wrist, twisting it to a painful angle. I tried to knee him in the privates, but he caught my bent leg and flipped me back into the dirt.

A heavy boot pressed against my neck. Clements. He stood over me, his face dark with some emotion. The blond straddled my legs, snatched at my arms. We struggled until Clements shifted all his weight onto my neck, cutting my air. I stopped fighting.

"You stupid bitch," he said. "Couldn't leave it alone, could you?"

A memory raced through my brain. Clements shouting at Dennis that he talked too much. Panic churned my gut.

"This chica, she think she know everything. I know girls had same problem." He grinned and pulled a knife from his belt.

Vipe's knife? My eyes found the prison teardrop, faint under some kind of greasepaint. Recognition froze me like a wave of ice.

"You like my disguise? Is good, no? Yours, not so good." With an odd giggle, Vipe snatched the cap from my head, ripping hairs as Carla's pins gave way.

"Put that back on," snapped Clements. "I don't want anyone recognizing her. We gotta get her outta here."

Vipe pushed the tip of his knife against my cheek. My eyes slid shut. "I want to play with her. You no let me play with her?"

"Stop it, Vipe. You've already got her hairs all over the dirt. You think I want her blood?"

"Okay, man. Chill." The knife eased away.

"Get some baling twine, tie her hands and ankles. Do it!" Clements' angry shout almost sounded tinged with fear.

Vipe trussed me up like a Christmas goose and sealed my mouth with duct tape. Clements removed the crushing leather boot. I coughed, trying not to gag behind the tape. Clements pulled Vipe aside, whispering.

The Latino's laugh made my skin crawl. "You wait for me there, chica." He grinned like he'd made a joke. "I hurry back with something you like."

I twisted, searching Clements' face. His expression was like a door slamming shut.

Outside I heard a truck's diesel engine clank by. I tried to make noise through the tape but Clements slid his boot back onto my neck and I gave it up. Vipe reappeared with a small plastic grocery bag. He knelt next to me, rustled in the bag and withdrew a small glass bottle and a syringe.

I exploded. Clements dropped to the ground, shoving one hand on my neck, pinning my left arm with the other. Vipe sat on my thighs, pressing the inside of my right forearm until the vein popped. He held up the needle, stared at it lovingly, then drove it into my arm.

I could feel their anticipation. The bastards were enjoying it. In seconds a warm, hot rush coursed through me. My head wanted to explode, then I sunk into an unseeing daze. I sensed them untying me, felt a sharp sting as they ripped off the duct tape. They must have half-carried, half-walked me out the door. I remember my arm over Vipe's shoulder, him kissing me and laughing at someone, saying something about me liking to get drunk early. Then I was in Clements' truck, wedged between them, incapacitated, slipping away.

35

I surfaced from somewhere deep, aware of engine vibration, the motion of a car. Dirt, or maybe chips or gravel, dug into my cheek. I lay on my left side, listening to the sounds of the highway, some instinct whispering for me to stay still.

Thirst dried my tongue. I needed more air, because something covered my lips, and I realized I couldn't move my hands. Memory rushed back, causing a wild hammering of heart. I slit one eye open. Metal parts, rubber flooring, the kind of trash that collects under a car seat. Clements' truck.

I'd been folded into the fetal position, head shoved against the passenger door, wrists handcuffed against my abdomen. My bent knees blocked sight of my ankles, but I could feel something gripping them together. The odor of horse manure, dirt, and oil rose from the rubber mat beneath my face.

A wheezing cough brought both my eyes open. Clements' legs, I recognized the brown boot on the gas pedal. Partial relief flooded me. Vipe wasn't in the cab. It didn't last. I was bound, gagged, woozy, and pretty sure Clements' would kill me if he could.

The light outside the overhead windows slowly faded as I lay there motionless. Did he plan to dump my body in some dark, lonely place? Oddly, a mental image of Hellish bloomed, then faded.

The truck slowed, turning onto a bumpier road. My fingers scratched at the fleece vest I'd put on that morning. Something hard pressed into my side. I crept my fingers to it, recognizing the small object I'd felt in Carla's car. Something from Dimsboro . . . something about Hellish. Memory flashed . . . the unused syringe of Acepromazine. Hellish had come around so well, we'd gone to the track that morning without the drug. She'd behaved like a pro, allowing me to dream. Tears stung my eyes. Not now, not with tape over my mouth. Clements flipped a turn indicator. It dinked as the truck slowed and swung onto a gravel surface. He switched on the radio to a pop station, cranked the volume up, and stopped the truck. I could smell fuel, but the radio blast locked away any sounds from outside.

I raised my head a bit, darted a glance and saw Clements going at it with his eyedrops. I lowered my head, and, above the wailing of some *American Idol* drama queen, I heard him blowing his nose.

A rush of cold air and the rocking of the cab told me he was getting out. For gas? He slammed the door closed and something fell on my knee and bounced near my hands. The damned eyedrops.

The idea hit fast. I closed my fingers around those drops, unscrewed the top and squirted the bottle dry. Set it down, then went for the pocket with Hellish's syringe. Hard to reach in there with cuffed hands. My fingers fumbled and dug, racing against Clements' inevitable return.

A dim thunking sound and vibration suggested Clements had shoved a gas nozzle into the truck's tank. Would he sit in the truck while it filled? Please God, let him need the bathroom. I waited a few precious moments then scrabbled for the hypo. The radio song crescendoed into a shriek, then a man reported weather for the Chesapeake Bay area. I was still in Maryland. My fingers touched plastic, curled around the cylindrical shape, prying it out. I pulled it clear, gripped the plunger between one thumb and index finger, and removed the plastic needle guard. Slid the thin steel into the allergy sprayer's opening and shoved the plunger. And just like that Clements' eyedrops were loaded with three cc's of Acepromazine.

I withdrew the needle, screwed the top on the bottle, tossing it over my bent knees, hoping it would land someplace he'd find it. Shoved the hypo in my pocket.

Not two minutes later another thump, chilly air, and that bouncing motion as Clements climbed into the truck. He cranked the engine, turned off the radio, and drove out. I waited, willing his eyes to itch, anything to make him reach for that medication. Waited a lifetime. Had Carla called for help?

A hand groped along the bench seat. "Where'd it go?" he muttered. He swung the truck to the right and stopped. Through my lashes I could see him bent over, reaching, grabbing for his drops. He set them on the seat. Didn't use them. His next action startled me. He leaned over me toward the glove box, and I had to fight the urge to shrink from him. He grabbed something from the box.

A hard object jabbed my right hip. Impossible not to jerk and stare up.

"Knew you were awake. Not for long." His pale eyes frightened me. The waning light reflected a metallic glint from the gun in his hand. He tapped my hip with it and smiled when I flinched. "You got any more snooping to do, you can do it under the ground."

My reaction amused him. No. He wouldn't shoot me in the truck. He'd take me somewhere, get me outside first.

Clements set the gun in his lap, made a gasping sound and sneezed.

He rubbed the knuckles of one hand into his eyes, then groped for the eyedrops, squirting a dose in one eye, frowning.

Fear nipped at me. Would he know what I'd done? I held my breath. He dosed the other eye. I'd gotten drops of the stuff on my hands before. It wasn't oily, and I didn't think it would sting. I took a breath, watching. Damn if he didn't double-dose, squirting the stuff in each eye again. Irritation heated his face.

"The fuck you looking at, bitch?"

The venom in his voice made me cringe, snap my eyes shut. He pulled the truck onto the road, accelerating.

No choice but to lay on a mat that felt more and more like a rubber coffin. Time stretched and shrunk, stretched and shrunk.

He slowed to a crawl and bounced over what felt like a curb. Sudden bumps and dips, the sound of the tires told me we were off-road. I stole a glance at him. His eyes drooped, he looked dopey. A silent prayer whispered through my brain.

His head nodded. The truck rolled down what felt like a slope, gaining momentum. I reached my hands under the seat, grasping a metal rod, bracing myself. The rolling grew wild, the truck lurching and rocking until we smashed into something unyielding.

The crash threw me under the dash, then whipped me back into the seat. My grip on the rod lessened the violent contact to my forehead. I may have been stunned for a few moments. I remember a warm trickle down one side of my face. Blood. I had to get out of there.

I wiggled body parts, relieved things moved without much pain. Snuck a glance at Clements. His face pressed against the steering wheel. The dash lights were still on. Something dripped onto his legs. A cold gleam near my knees, the gun's snout protruding from beneath the truck seat. I inched my fingers to it, closed them over the metal, aiming the barrel away from me as I dragged the thing closer. The revolver was heavy with bullets, the ends of their copper casings glowing dimly in the dash lights from the gun's cylinder.

Clements moaned, started moving. I scrambled to my knees. Shuffled forward. Still clutching the gun, I got my hands on the door handle. Pushed it down. The door flew open, flinging me into the dark.

36

Pain shot through my hands and knees. I pushed through it, rolling into a sitting position, eyes searching and finding the gun nearby. I stretched my arms and fingers, reaching for whatever bound my ankles. Bailing twine. My kingdom for a knife, but fingernails would have to do. Pick, pull, pick. The handcuffs hindered me, sending waves of frustration. The knot loosened. Flying fingers forced the twine apart, while my ears listened for Clements.

Standing, I kicked the gun under the truck, ripped the tape from my mouth, sucked in fresh cold air. The scent of salt water and pine permeated the area. Evergreens, darker than the night sky, climbed toward the stars. One headlight still shone, highlighting a tall pine embracing the truck's hood. I searched for other sources of electric light. Only the natural glow of a clear night appeared around me.

I heard Clements trying to open his door. It sounded jammed, which might give me a few seconds head start. The incline we'd raced down seemed the logical path, and I worked my way up it, picking my steps, trying to hurry, praying the crash and Ace would shred Clements' ability to hunt me. At the top of the slope I could see farther. A distant glow of manmade light drew me like a beacon. I walked as fast as I dared, relieved to see a streetlight illuminating a small road and the curb I assumed Clements had driven over. Drawing closer, I made out some kind of entranceway with a closed gate and a sign.

The longer I moved through the crisp night, the clearer my head became, and by the time I got to the lights and sign, I was jogging. I stopped to listen for sounds of pursuit. Didn't hear anything. The nearby sign read "Sandy Bay State Park. Closed until March 15." Must be close to the bay, not far from Annapolis. Studying the dark horizon, I made out a glow of suburban light to my left. I stepped onto the pavement and made tracks down the road, hugging the shoulder so I could disappear into the pines if I heard Clements.

I crept along the road, fighting head pain and a longing to lie down and close my eyes. They'd taken my watch, and unmeasurable time crawled down the road with me as the pavement wound and curved through a pine forest. I heard a car approaching, saw its lights through the trees around a bend. Instinct and fear scuttled me off the road, into the trees and onto the ground where I remained motionless. The car swept past with a distinct rattle, as if the muffler were loose, leaving me to wonder if I'd been cautious or foolish to hide. My eyes were so heavy, the pine carpet so soft.

I don't know how long I slept, but I awakened when a car with the same rattle returned, rushing past me in the opposite direction. My head felt better for the sleep, and once the car's engine faded to silence, I moved back onto the road. Small night sounds surrounded me, a snapping twig, a rustle in the leaves shed by the deciduous trees among the evergreens.

Around another bend a small gravel road opened to my right. The chrome and waxed paint from a big SUV shone in the ambient light. The driver had backed the vehicle into the trees, as if hiding. The windows appeared foggy and music drifted out. The shadows of the road edge concealed me, where I remained motionless. Soft moans of a woman's voice mingled with the music. Oh boy. I relaxed, recognizing the sounds of pleasure. These were not bad guys, more likely a couple out looking for love on a lonely road.

Hated to interrupt. . . .

I stepped from the shadows. "Help!" I called. Don't think they heard me. *"Help!"* I yelled. Heard a small shriek, voices, rustling from within. Their headlights swept over me where I stood on the gravel, clothes torn, face bloody, shackled by handcuffs. A young guy rolled his window down, but only halfway.

"No," he said, as I started toward them. "Stay where you are. You in some kind of trouble?"

"Yeah, I need help. Man's after me."

He gave me a weird look. After all, I was the one wearing handcuffs. He grabbed a cell phone.

"I'll call 911." He sounded irritated. Then he was talking to someone, giving a location. "They're coming," he said and took off, leaving me to hide in the pines.

When the county squad car showed up, relief hit me so hard my knees buckled. A young cop, about six-foot-two with wary eyes, called in for backup. Ten minutes later, Detectives Trent Davis and Charlie Wells barreled down the road, siren screaming. Hard to imagine I could be so happy to see them.

The evening stretched into a festival of flashing blue lights from county cop cars, a wailing ambulance and even a fire truck. I couldn't see the need for the fire truck, but the more rescue types that appeared, the better I felt.

From inside the warmth of Davis's car, I rubbed my wrists where the handcuffs had been, watching some cops search Clements truck — inside, outside, and under. I'd told them about the gun. They bagged a few items, spread out, apparently searching for Clements, but he'd disappeared.

A glance at car's dash clock told me it was only 8. Felt like 3 A.M. to me. Davis and Wells came up from the truck, folded themselves into the car, and eased into a question-and-answer session. No more accusations. I told them everything I could remember, finishing with the car that had rushed in and out of the park.

"Maybe Clements was picked up," Davis said.

I sagged into my seat, hating to think Clements was loose.

"How's that forehead?" asked Wells.

"I'll live."

"Yeah," said Davis, "but you need to have that looked at."

"The ambulance medic already did," I said. "Who do you think put on this bandage?" But they walked me to a squad car, urging me to go to the hospital with the young officer who'd first responded. I stood in the cold air shivering, arguing that I was okay and should get going.

Right about then Carla and Lorna showed up. Turns out Carla had hounded the cops ever since I'd disappeared. She rushed up to me, pulled off her jacket and hung the butter-soft leather around my shoulders. She started crying. Lorna looked fierce, like she wanted to fight somebody. The three of us started jabbering at once, until I noticed Carla was shaking with cold in a low-cut black sweater. I turned to Curtis, gestured toward Carla and asked if we could go.

His unreadable eyes swept over us. "You three think you can make it through the rest of the night without getting into trouble?"

We nodded and started edging toward Carla's Mercedes.

"Latrelle," said Davis. "Stay someplace different tonight."

Wells stepped closer, the revolving blue lights reflecting off the lenses of his glasses. "Tell whoever's in charge at Laurel to call me. We'll straighten this thing out. You're pretty much clear at our end."

"I am?"

"Yeah, we've been doing our homework. Know more than you think." He made me promise to come into the CID in the morning for a statement, then turned me loose.

We climbed into Carla's car and she drove onto the deserted road leading away from Sandy Bay Park, past the place where the SUV had hidden, and surprised me by swinging onto Route 50 in mere moments.

We headed west, passing the exit for Annapolis.

"Thought I was a million miles from anywhere," I said.

Lorna leaned forward from the back seat, sticking her head between Carla and me. "So you think those detective dudes believe you now?"

"They're starting to." I fingered my forehead.

"Leave that bandage alone." Carla's eyes flicked on me, sharp and tired. I figured my disappearance had been hard on her and put my hand in my lap.

"Where to?" Carla asked.

Silence filled the car. We all knew I had no place to go.

"I should check on Hellish, so I guess back to Dimsboro," I said.

"I don't *think* so." Carla stared at me like I was crazy.

"No way. Besides," said Lorna, "I went, like, everywhere, looking for you. Including Dimsboro. That Mello guy was feeding your horse, around 5. Said you were in trouble. I'm, like, duh." Lorna flopped back into the rear bucket seat. "Hellish was fine. Hay, water, clean stall, the works. I got an extra bed in my room. Mom won't mind. You heard that cop — you should stay with me for a while."

"Done," said Carla, speeding down the big highway. Though headlights and road lamps lit the wide pavement, the surrounding night encased the road like a soft black tunnel.

To tell the truth I was glad somebody else was making the decisions. I needed food, a good night's sleep, a safe place to lick my wounds.

Lorna's family didn't live far from the Silver Diner. Carla dropped us off in the restaurant's lot next to my car, making me promise to call her in the morning. Lorna found the extra Toyota key I kept in a magnetic case in the passenger wheel well and drove us to her house.

Lorna's mom, probably in her late 50s, greeted us at the door, her head a halo of gray, overcooked perm. She fussed over me and made grilled cheese sandwiches, which Lorna and I inhaled. Slippers sat next to a kitchen table leg, glaring at me. By the time I swallowed the last crumb and finished a glass of milk, I was almost asleep in the chair. We climbed the carpeted stairs to Lorna's room, where posters of heavy-metal rockers threw hard-ass stares from the wall. Pink flowered quilts covered twin beds.

I eased into one, and my cat hopped up, crouching near me, examining me like I was an unfamiliar creature. Just before I sank into sleep, Slippers relented into purr mode and Lorna asked, "Nikki, how'd that Mello dude know you were in trouble?"

*　　*　　*

During the night I remembered the voices. I drifted from a deep well of sleep, humming with anxiety, until I remembered I was at Lorna's. The gentle rhythm of her breathing as she slept in the nearby bed reassured me. I inhaled a measured breath, then exhaled, trying to capture the memory or dream that had evaporated upon waking. Quiet filled the Doone house. Only the occasional sound of a distant car passing broke the silence.

Three men talking. A Spanish accent. My mind shied from the sharpening recollection, but I pushed back into it. With the park only a 45-minute drive from Laurel, where had they kept me from midday til dusk?

Concentrate. My hands bound, my mouth sealed shut. Whatever drug Vipe had injected in my veins insulated the panic, but I could still feel it. The accented voice must have been Vipe's. The other, Clements'. The nasal tone filled me with revulsion. Who was the third man? I listened to the memory. The voice was disturbingly familiar, yet surprised me with its cruelty, as if a mask of goodwill had loosened and tumbled from its place. My mind chased the sound, but the speaker's identity danced out of reach. Vipe's high-pitched laugh echoed in my head. I sat upright in the twin bed, wrapping my arms around my sides, rocking back and forth.

37

Lorna's mom, Betty, made hazelnut coffee at 6:00 A.M. the next morning, and I waited at her kitchen table for the first cup out of the pot. Good kick-start with the plate of eggs Betty slid onto my place mat. Lorna was long gone for the Laurel track by the time I'd awakened again at 5:30.

"Sweetie, you should have that head injury checked out at the Laurel clinic." Betty knew how to fuss.

"They looked at it last night, said it didn't need to be stitched." I looked worse than I felt, my forehead swollen and purple. Thought I'd go to Dimsboro, then to the CID to see Detective Wells. By the time I drove through Pallboro and into the track, my earlier energy had gone south. I felt shaky and knew better than to climb on any horses.

Mello sat on his broken-legged stool in front of Hellish's stall, wearing a yellow bow tie and a tweed jacket one step up from shabby. "You wants to watch out, Miss Nikki. Felt footsteps on a grave."

I shuddered, stared at the man.

His hands were folded over his knees, a brown paper bag sat by his feet in the dirt. He saw my glance at the bag. "Rough times. This be medicinal."

"They've probably got Vipe and that Arthur Clements by now." I made my voice bright and confident. "Cops are on to them. Probably nothing left to be scared of."

Mello shook his head, swung a hand down and grabbed the bag. Long fingers crinkled back the paper, exposing an amber bottle. He took a swig of liquid and wiped his hand over his mouth. "I afraid for you. Somebody bad. He ain't finished yet."

"*He?* Mello, do you know who it is?"

"Wish I did. Indeed, I do." His hand trembled and reached again for the bottle. "Can't see him, just knows he's there, stepping on that grave."

His words spun me back to the dream. The third man. A shiver shook me from inside. I moved over to Hellish, stroked her neck, grateful for her body heat. Her stall smelled clean. Fresh hay filled her rack. "Thank you, Mello. You've been really good to us."

"I always good to Gallorette." His words slurred a bit.

I hated to see him drink, but after my misadventure I could understand his desire for the familiar comfort of booze.

Hellish shifted a few times, then spun in a tight circle, squealing. She needed to get out. I led her to a round pen and turned her loose. The enclosure was made of sixfoot-high, heavy wire mesh and filled with deep sand. Hellish bucked and leaped, spun and kicked until her muscles swelled and her veins popped. With her head and tail held high, her nostrils dilated, she looked a picture.

Chocolate hurried toward the pen from the direction of Raymond Marteen's barn, her eyes glowing, hands clutching some papers. "Looky here." She radiated enthusiasm, shoved the papers at me.

My hands held a certificate and a brochure from Prince George's Community College. "I just passed me a high school GED."

"Chocolate, that's so cool. You —"

"That ain't all. Talked to a man at Prince George's College, and he say I can enroll in marketing and sales. In January."

I could feel a grin stretching my mouth.

She tossed a look at the arena. "That blond woman we met when they had the food? She in sales, right?"

I nodded.

"How much money she make?"

"Enough to own a Mercedes Roadster."

"That's what I'm saying." Chocolate's black-and-blond braids shook as she nodded her head. "Sales be my speciality." She pronounced it, *spesh-eee-ality*. "No more Marteen, no more you-know-whatsies." She held up her palm, and I slapped it. She snatched her papers back, turned and sped off, filled with possibilities.

I put Hellish away, then looked for Mello, but he'd disappeared somewhere, and I didn't have a chance to say goodbye. I cranked up my Toyota and headed for Crownsville. I'd have felt almost as optimistic as Chocolate, if they'd caught Vipe and Clements. If I wasn't pursued by the disembodied voice of a nightmare man.

Detective Wells opened his desk drawer and pulled out my cell phone. I took the molded plastic, staring at it like it might hold answers, slipped it in my pocket and sat in the visitor's chair. His desk stood against the mint-green wall near the interrogation room they'd shut me in a few weeks earlier. The cool wall color and plush carpet did little to soothe my wariness.

"I don't suppose this is yours?" He slid his hand back in the drawer and withdrew the Phillips.

"Yeah, that's mine. It was . . ."

Wells held up a hand. "I don't want to know." His drab blue suit jacket hung on a nearby wall hook. Today's tie, a pale gray edition, featured miniature blue police cars, emblazoned with red roof lights.

"How'd you get the phone?" I asked.

"An officer found it in Clements truck after they pulled the gun out from underneath." Mention of the gun made him smile. A big smile. "It's the right caliber. Crime lab's running a ballistics test. Maybe it'll match the one used on O'Brien."

I hoped Vipe or Clements hadn't closed my fingers around the thing while I dozed in la-la-land. Sickening to think of them watching me, touching me, while I was out of it. And that other man.

"You all right, Miss Latrelle?" Wells' eyes rested on mine. Curious or concerned?

"You said you know more about this. Is there a third man?"

Wells' eyes shifted away from me a moment. "Why do you ask about another man? Is there something you want to tell me?"

He was worse than a psychiatrist. "Forget it," I said, feeling a spark of anger. "I just hope I don't get hurt because you like to keep stuff to yourself."

Wells picked up a pencil covered with teeth marks. He jabbed it at me. "You are not a police officer, okay? You don't need to know everything. Just stay out of trouble."

I sank back in my chair, the fight ebbing out of me. "So can I have the Laurel security chief call you?"

"Yeah, yeah. We'll talk to him."

Trent Davis burst into the room, saw me and stopped. Hesitated a moment, then moved toward us. "They found Clements."

"Is he here yet?" asked Wells.

Davis's eyes remained blank, but the muscles in his neck bulged, and I could see the pulse throb from where I sat. "He's not coming in. He's dead."

My fingers white-knuckled the wooden arms of my chair.

"Hell." Wells shoved his chair back, stood up. "Tell me," he said, sliding on his suit jacket.

"Somebody slit his throat. Patch of woods behind the Laurel Wal-Mart.

I thought I was going to be sick. "I need a bathroom."

"Over there." Wells pointed at a door near the interrogation room. "You going to be alright?"

I nodded, stood up. Took a step and held on to the back of the chair. "Vipe has a knife."

They stared at me.

"Come on Charlie," Davis said. "We gotta roll."

They moved toward the door, Wells turning back to me. "You watch it. Like I said, don't go anywhere alone, stay at the Doones'. We'll have a patrol car driving by the next few days."

In the bathroom I leaned over the sink, throwing cold water on my face. The nausea passed, and I headed for my car and Lorna's house.

"This is really scary," said Lorna. We stood just inside the Doones' front door. That's as far as we'd gotten since she'd let me in, seen my face, and asked what was going on. "That Vipe's a nasty dude. What are you gonna do?"

"I don't know." I moved to a brown wing chair and collapsed in it. Closed my eyes, saw Vipe's knife, and jerked my focus back to the Doones' living room. Beige carpet, taupe-and-gold patterned curtains. Framed prints of bucolic landscapes on the wall. I kept seeing the knife.

"I should call Offenbach." I dialed Laurel Park, reached the security chief and brought him up to date.

He was silent a moment. "I know the chief at Crownsville. I'll talk to him. If it's going like you say, I'll notify the stewards myself."

I thanked him and called Jim.

"Police were swarming all over Clements' barn this morning," he said. "He always was a hard case. Brought this on himself." He paused a beat. "Everybody misses you. Hurry up and come back in."

"As soon as they let me."

By 3 P. M. Lorna and I'd watched two movies, eaten ham and cheese sandwiches and were going stir-crazy.

"I can't stand this."

"Who could?" Lorna zapped the TV off with the remote.

"Listen," I said, "Mello was drunk at 8 o'clock this morning. He may forget to feed Hellish."

"You're not going alone." Lorna set her hands on her hips, gave me her fierce look.

"How 'bout we go right now, before it gets dark?"

We were out the door in two seconds, on the road in about five. We zipped down Route197, turned onto 301 and stopped. Dump trucks, school busses, 18-wheelers, endless cars inching along the choked highway. No choice but to join them.

*   *   *

"Well, that was the ride from Hell," I said, exiting the miserable highway at a crawl and accelerating into Pallboro. As we zoomed over the bridge and turned into Dimsboro, a bank of dark clouds rolled toward us from the west, blocking the sun.

"It's getting dark." An uneasy prickle stirred me.

"That damned traffic," Lorna said, glancing up at the heavy clouds flattening into a solid lid overhead. "And we're just off daylight-saving time. I forgot how early the sun goes down."

"Let's feed and get out." I grabbed my cell phone, hurried from the car, heading for Hellish. A stiffening breeze, sighing beneath the cloud bank, blew bits of trash and rolled a discarded beer can along the gravel lot near my feet.

Lorna, hustling alongside, suddenly stopped, her eyes scanning the grounds. "Where is everybody?"

Dimsboro looked like a western movie when the bad guys ride into town — everything silent, deserted. Did the locals hide behind locked doors and barred windows? A few cars lay parked down by Bubba's and Marteen's, but not a soul was in sight, no bustle, no boogie. We stood still a moment, listening. "Let's do it and get out of Dodge." I tugged the sleeve of Lorna's jacket. We ran the short distance to my barn. No sign of Mello. Hellish saw us coming and sounded a "feed me" nicker. We bustled around, throwing grain in her bucket, freshening her water, giving her stall a quick pick-and-clean, tossing fresh straw down and hay up into her rack. We were brushing stray chaff from our clothes when Lorna froze.

A ghost of movement flickered at Vipe's barn. The thin boy stared at us from the aisle way. He stepped out from under the dark overhanging roof into the gray light. His arms were rigid against his sides, his eyes wide and frightened.

38

"Maybe you should call the cops," said Lorna.

I slid my phone from my pocket. Before I flipped it open the thing started ringing and pulsing. We both jumped backward. I took a breath, looked at the caller ID. Old lady Garner . . .

"Martha?"

"Nikki?" Her raspy voice sounded tentative. "Jim just called me. I want to apologize, the way I treated you."

"Forget it, Martha. You didn't know." I could hear the click of a lighter, her mouth pulling smoke into her lungs.

"But I shouldn't have . . ."

"Martha, don't worry about it. Can I ask you a question?"

"Anything."

"Did Janet LeGrange have an insurance policy on that horse? The one that died?"

A long exhale. "Sure, honey. She's the one found me my policy."

"On Gildy?"

"Yeah. She put me in touch with that smoothie Reed. He handled both our policies."

"*Clay* Reed?"

Lorna fidgeted, left foot to right foot, her hands making urgent hurry-up signals. "That's the one," said Martha.

"But we talked about Clay. I asked about your policy. You never mentioned his name."

"You must not have asked."

I all but bit my tongue not to scream at her. Took a breath. "He's a scam artist, Martha. Please tell me you didn't buy that horse he was trying to sell you."

"No. Not after you warned me about him."

Martha started coughing in my ear. I held the phone away while she struggled to subdue it. Down the way, the thin boy suddenly spun and started running from Vipe's barn.

"We got to get out of here," Lorna hissed, flicking an urgent glance at my car.

"Nikki, there's something else you should know." Martha's voice, sounding tinny from the cell's earpiece.

I rushed the phone back in place. "What?"

"Clay. He's the agent bought the horse for Janet. The one that died."

Jesus Christ. A Dark Mountain bay. "Martha I can't talk now. I'll call you back." I pressed the end button, punched 911.

Lorna stared open-mouthed down the shedrow. "We're screwed."

A man had materialized around the barn's corner, moving rapidly toward us along the aisle, one hand holding a revolver, a pleasant smile on his lips.

That handsome smile, that pretty-boy face. Clay.

"Nikki, I've been looking for you."

I pressed the send button on my phone. Clay leaned in, whipping my hand with the pistol. A jolt of pain. The cell flew to the dirt, as adrenalin shot through me.

Lorna yelped as Farino rounded the same corner and jogged toward us.

"Jack, good," Clay said. "Could use your help here."

Farino nodded, never taking his eyes off us. "What do you need?"

Clay turned to answer. I grabbed Hellish's pitchfork and rammed the tongs into the small of his back. He staggered forward, dropping his gun, and Farino punched him in the jaw.

What the hell?

Tougher than his smooth cover, Clay refused to go down. He lunged at Farino. I grabbed Clay's gun from the dirt, while the two men grunted, punched, and kicked. Farino fell. Clay stood over him, hands on his knees, gasping for breath.

"Stop it," I screamed. I held the gun in both hands, trying to keep it steady. Lorna stood wooden with fear to my right.

Clay straightened, took a step toward me. "Nikki, I'd never hurt you." That velvet voice.

"Stop. I swear I'll shoot you."

Farino's predatory eyes fastened on me. "Don't let him sucker you in again, Nikki."

The gun wavered back and forth between them. As if from far away, I heard Lorna's shallow panting breath, the filly's restless hooves churning up straw. Memory flashed through my head — Farino's quiet hands on Hellish, her willing acceptance. Mello liking him. I turned the gun on Clay.

"You'd never shoot me," he said, then rushed me.

"Sure I would." My fingers squeezed the trigger. Loud noise, acrid smoke, sharp jolt in my hand. Clay kept coming, leapt on me, knocking me down. I heard Lorna screaming.

"You missed." Clay's words breathed in my ear. Not his usual sugary tones, an ugly whisper. The one from my nightmare. He grabbed for the gun, fingers closing around my wrist, twisting, loosening my hand's grip on the revolver.

Sirens wailed in the distance, the sound growing closer. Clay's head whipped toward it. I snatched the gun with my other hand, cracked it against Clay's head. Rolled from underneath him, and scooted backward. When my scrabbling hand felt the barn wall, I shoved my back against it, sitting in the dirt, supporting the gun on my knees.

A bunch of Prince George's County squad cars tore into Dimsboro. The first one came to a skidding halt, facing us. Two police officers flung the doors open, crouching behind them, weapons drawn.

One called to me, "Ma'am? Set the gun down. Move away from it."

No. I clutched the gun like a lifeline. Must not have hit Clay hard enough. He sat up, pressing fingers to his scalp where I'd cracked him. Farino stayed on the ground, raising his hands into the air. Lorna sat in the gravel, head down, arms wrapped around her knees. Her red hair hid her face. I could hear her crying.

An unmarked car flew into the lot spraying dirt and gravel from its wheels. The driver circled the police vehicles and pulled up next to the cop yelling at me to put the gun down. Detective Davis unfolded himself from one side and Wells stepped out the other. They hustled over to the agitated county officer, saying something I couldn't hear. Davis and the Prince George's cop hurried toward us. I recognized the policeman from the arena. Wells hustled over to Farino.

"Nikki," said Davis, "this is officer duCellier. Has a warrant for Mr. Reed. If you'll hand me that gun, he'd like to make an arrest." duCellier pulled a set of cuffs, locked them onto Clay's wrists.

"What about him?" I stared at Farino.

"Jack? Don't worry about him." A smile lit Davis's face, warmed those jaded eyes. His voice dropped. "He's not even homicide. Officer Farino's with vice. Undercover."

39

On a chilly morning late in October, about 6 A.M., I drove Mello into the Laurel Park backstretch. We breezed right past Fred Rockston at the stable gate. Nobody was going to tell me Mello couldn't watch Hellish's first speed work.

Lorna pulled up about the time we did, and the three of us walked into Jim's barn. The trainer sat behind his desk. The tabby cat lay curled asleep in the nearby chair. A dusty picture of Gallorette stared from the wall, and Mello stepped over to it, tracing the champion's face through the glass with long, gnarled fingers.

Jim set his coffee cup down. "You working her today?"

"You said it was time." I leaned over, stroking the cat's fur.

"She be ready," said Mello. "I get her groomed up." He mumbled something about brushes and moved away down the shedrow.

"They found Kenny Grimes," said Jim.

"Alive?" My shoulders tightened against the answer.

"He's exercising horses for a trainer in Florida. Gulfstream Park."

"That son-of-a-bitch! Bet it was him gave those syringes with my fingerprints all over them to Clements."

"Kenny had gambling problems," Lorna said. "They probably paid him to do it."

It fit. Kenny had always hustled for extra money. "Then I found O'Brien dead. Kenny must have panicked." I eased onto the edge of the cat's chair, organizing my thoughts. "Detective Wells called me yesterday. Said they think Vipe got out of the country. Cops spotted him at Del Mar Racetrack in southern California. Then he disappeared again."

"Del Mar's just north of Mexico," Jim said.

Lorna leaned against the wall. Sometime during the last week she'd changed her green streaks to a more flattering copper. Sun poured through the office window, lighting her hair to a burnished halo. "So there were four of them," she said. "O'Brien and Clements are dead, Reed's in jail, and Vipe got away."

I didn't want to think about Vipe anymore. "I'll see how Mello's getting on with Hellish."

Lorna followed me down the shedrow, and, nearing the stall, we could hear Mello humming "Camptown Races." Inside, the old man rubbed the filly's bright chestnut coat in time to the song, and Hellish bobbed her head with each brush stroke. A tang of liniment sharpened the air.

I heard a car door slam and stepped outside the stall, Lorna close behind. Carla breezed toward us wearing a mocha-colored suede jacket and boots. She'd been at some kind of meat convention for almost a week. After we did the hello thing, her eyes settled on Lorna's copper streaks.

"Didn't I tell you Bronze Babe had your name on it?"

Typical Carla. Should have seen her hand in Lorna's color change. "We found out stuff since you left, Carla."

"Tell me."

"Clay and his buddies had a betting scam, like we thought, switching back and forth between Whorly and Noble Treasure." I paused, thinking about the money. "Did you know in England it's legal to bet a horse to lose? They'd enter Whorly in a race he couldn't win, call him Noble Treasure. Then they'd use a British outlet and bet the horse to finish out of the money."

"With a tortoise like Whorly, they didn't have to bribe a jockey to hold the horse." Lorna threw Carla a loaded glance. "But we might need to pull the reins on that Jack Farino."

Carla's face sparked with interest. "Do you like him, Nikki?"

"He likes *her*," said Lorna, sidestepping the colt next door who nipped at her from over his stall gate.

"No way," I said.

"Oh, yeah." Lorna grinned. "Big way. He's been hanging around our Nikki."

"He just came over to explain stuff." My face felt flushed.

Carla let it slide. "So what about the insurance thing?"

"Clay found buyers like Janet and Martha, people who'd let him handle everything, including the insurance," I said. "He'd get them to sign a document saying he was their agent, could act on their behalf. Jack told me Clay'd take out two policies, one for the real owner and one for himself as agent."

"How could that work?" Carla looked dubious.

"Jack said as long as the insurance underwriters didn't notice Clay's name popping up too many times, he'd probably get away with it. Apparently, Clay used aliases to keep the underwriters in the dark. Clements' shuffled the horses around, O'Brien . . ." I had to slow down, breathe some. "O'Brien or Vipe would kill them. I don't know how Clay established the insurance value."

"I can fill in that part."

I swung around. Jack stood behind me. He knew how to sneak up on a woman. His gunslinger eyes didn't frighten me anymore. I understood their predatory look . . . cop eyes. Now that he wasn't undercover, he'd trimmed his dark hair short. He looked good either way. I could smell soap and some pleasant underlying scent.

He greeted Carla and gave me a wink. My body responded. How could a wink hold so much power?

Jack almost smiled, then turned cop. "Reed and his buddies formed partnerships. They'd use the partnerships to sell a horse back and forth."

"No doubt raising the value every time," I said.

"Exactly. They had Noble Treasure up to $400,000. Don't think his days weren't numbered."

"But why kill people?"

Jack shifted, took a breath. "We're not sure yet, Nikki. A lot will probably come out in the trial. I think Clay's gun will be a match for the one that took out O'Brien."

"My God," said Carla.

"We don't even know for sure it was Vipe that knifed Clements. I'm guessing Reed's operation was falling apart, he went over the edge and started killing his own people."

I closed my eyes, pushed away the images. "I got a horse to work."

Mello had Hellish looking like a stakes winner, her mane and tail combed to a silken finish, her hooves painted with oil. The old man and I tacked her up, and when I led her from the stall, Carla's eyes got big. "What a beautiful horse. She's so classy." Never one to restrain herself, Carla said, "Nikki, I want to buy into her. Can I?"

Startled, I thought a minute. Carla would make a great partner, as long as she didn't try to take the horse to Nordstrom's. "It'd be fun. But I'm not sure how to work it."

"Sell me 40 percent. That way you keep controlling interest and still make some money."

"Don't know how much to charge." I put a soothing hand on Hellish's shoulder. She knew it was time to do something, didn't want to stand around while we discussed percentages.

"Whatever you think is fair." She held out her hand. I shook it.

Lorna watched us seal the deal. Her gaze shifted away and she studied her feet.

"And Lorna," I said, catching her eye, "you get 10 percent because . . . you're Lorna."

She lit up like a candle, for once speechless.

Jim headed toward us, his lips pressed tight with impatience. "Better get her out of here, before she explodes in the barn." He stepped next to me, laced his fingers together, making his hands into a stirrup. I slid my knee in, and he tossed me into the saddle. "I'd go an easy half-mile," he said. "We'll watch from the gap."

I gathered the reins and headed out. I sent her around the wrong way to warm her up, then jogged to the starting gate. One of the gate crew, a guy named Buster, walked toward us. "What're you doing with her, Nikki?"

"Going a half, but I'm looking for company." Some other horses milled around the gate waiting for their turn. A gray mare, trained by a man named Murray Lawrence, stood alone and arrogant. She was a solid performer, a stakes winner.

Lawrence stared at me, nodding toward his horse and jockey. "We're working a half, and these two . . ." he spoke to the riders of the horses near him. "They'll go a half with us."

Buster stepped closer, his hand closing on Hellish's bridle.

"I don't know if I want to go with them." I gestured toward the stakes mare. "Might be asking too much."

"Might as well find out what you got, Nikki."

I paused a beat, then nodded, letting him lead Hellish into the gate. The other three loaded, and the starter scanned the track, waiting for a break in traffic. Two horses sped by. Behind them a long gap opened before the next group. I glanced at the gray mare in the gate beside me. Ahead the track stretched wide and long. We weren't going to the wire. The five-sixteenths pole, near the end of the turn, measured the half-mile from the gate.

The starter called, "Everybody ready?"

Hellish tensed beneath me. Nobody said anything. Then the bell shrilled, the doors slammed open, and I was out of there on a rocket.

Two horses fell behind us as Hellish and the gray mare ripped down the backstretch, head and head. I'd never gone this fast. I hadn't even asked her. We flew into the turn, Hellish on the outside, eating more ground. The five-sixteenths pole came at us, and the gray pushed her head in front. Hellish pinned her ears, dug in, and shoved her nose ahead of the mare's. The pole rushed by.

I stood up and thought my knees would buckle. When I got to the gap, Jim was staring at his stopwatch, clearly astonished. Everybody was talking at once, but all I heard was Mello, not humming, but singing, "Doodah, doodah. Runnin a race wid a shootin star . . . "

THE END

Aknowledgements

Some wonderful people helped me around every turn of this novel.

Support from the writing world was phenomenal — Sisters In Crime, the Guppies, my critique group members, especially Bonner Menking. I'm still astonished that best selling authors Barbara Parker and Dick Francis took the time to read some chapters and make comments early on. The brilliant publisher of Wildside Press, John Betancourt, grabbed me and the manuscript when we were about to go under for the third time.

From law enforcement, I received advice from Detective Stephen Luersen, Homicide Division, Anne Arundel County Police Department; Joe Poag, Chief Investigator for the Maryland State Racing Commission; and retired Prince Georges County Homicide Detective, Jerry DuCellier.

From the veterinarian world, I thank Doctor Forrest Peacock, the Maryland State Veterinarian and man who read and vetted the manuscript and wanted to read more!

For moral and emotional support I thank my husband Daniel Filippelli, my sister Lillian Clagett, my niece and nephew Alidia and Bartholt Clagett, and a tremendous thank you to friend and cohort Margie Hugel.

Because he is so bright and experienced in the world of horse racing, input from racehorse trainer and steeplechase rider Barry G. Wiseman enabled me to write this story. Barry vetted the manuscript for accuracy. Even more, he believed in my home-bred horses enough to train them and get me my first win at Pimlico, and nothing can beat that!

CPSIA information can be obtained at www.ICGtesting.com
Printed in the USA
LVOW082012240112

265382LV00007B/28/P